D0049555

CRAGBRIDGE HALL

# THE AVATAR BATTLE

CRAGBRIDGE HALL

# THE AVATAR
# BATTLE

## CHAD MORRIS

ILLUSTRATED BY
BRANDON DORMAN

SHADOW
MOUNTAIN

*To my brave daughter.*

*And to everyone who helped spread the word about*
*The Inventor's Secret when I couldn't.*

Text © 2014 Chad Morris
Illustrations © 2014 Brandon Dorman

Visit us at ShadowMountain.com

This is a work of fiction. Characters and events in this book are products of the author's imagination or are represented fictitiously.

**Library of Congress Cataloging-in-Publication Data**
Morris, Chad, author.
 The avatar battle / Chad Morris.
    pages cm. — (Cragbridge Hall ; book 2)
 Summary: The evil Muns tries to convert Abby into helping him change the history of the world while her and Derick's grandfather asks Derick to finish a challenge that a trusted teacher was never able to finish.
 ISBN 978-1-60907-809-6 (hardbound : alk. paper)
 [1. Space and time—Fiction. 2. Boarding schools—Fiction. 3. Schools—Fiction. 4. Twins—Fiction. 5. Brothers and sisters—Fiction. 6. Grandfathers—Fiction.] I. Title. II. Series: Morris, Chad. Cragbridge Hall ; book 2.
 PZ7.M827248Av 2014
 [Fic]—dc23                                              2013038732

Printed in the United States of America
Publishers Printing, Salt Lake City, UT

10  9  8  7  6  5  4  3  2  1

# CONTENTS

# CONTENTS

# GIFT

Derick pushed his bulky legs forward, running with his head slightly lowered and his two-foot horn leading the way. He barreled ahead, feeling the weight of his steps, the thickness of the skin at the top of his legs rubbing against his tough body. It wasn't really him, of course. Derick's real body was hooked up to sensors and straps suspending him from the ceiling in an avatar lab. The high-tech equipment allowed his movements to control the robot avatar. What he did, the rhino did. And what it felt, he felt. It was as though Derick really was a hulking beast.

"11 . . . 10 . . . 9," Dr. Mackleprank counted down. "You'd better hurry, Derick. You're doing better than ever, but I'm not sure it will be enough. A real white rhino can run up to thirty miles per hour and Rafa may be able to go that fast." As the teacher spoke, Derick could hear his classmates cheering him on from behind the viewing window. It was definitely one of the louder days in Zoology. Their yells fueled him to move faster. He knew they were all gathered in one of the large rooms outside the created animal habitat, watching intently. The habitat, complete with trees, boulders, and watering holes, was a place where they could practice being animals. If they studied hard, passed all their tests, and excelled enough with the avatars, they could one day interact and play with the real animals nearby in the school's zoo.

Derick leaned and rounded a boulder. He could see the tree with two monkeys sitting completely still at its base— the first switch point. He was almost there. But he wanted more than cheers. He wanted to win.

"Three. Two. One. Rafa, go!" Dr. Mackleprank shouted. Derick's head start was over.

He could hear another rhino bounding forward behind him. He didn't have time to look. Rafa was fast, extremely fast.

Derick's rhino skidded to a stop, nearly tumbling over onto the monkeys.

"Careful, Derick," Dr. Mackleprank's voice warned over the speaker. The avatars were made to help some of the best students in the world improve, fulfilling Cragbridge Hall's mission to prepare youth to change the future of the world for the better. And Dr. Mackleprank didn't want them broken.

Derick guided his mind away from the massive rhino robot and focused on his real human body in the avatar lab.

He pressed the button on the back of his neck. His virtual connection with the robot animal severed; the rhino in the practice field fell limp, a huge heavy mound on the dirt. For a moment, Derick looked out of his own human eyes at the simple white walls of one of the booths in the avatar lab. There were no windows. He didn't need them—the booth was designed for him to connect with an avatar and look out of robot animal eyes. He blinked hard and adjusted the suspension system from holding him horizontally—ideal for moving like a rhino—to holding him in a mostly upright position, compensating for a tail. It was time to be a squirrel monkey.

With the flick of a finger, Derick selected his monkey, Goggles. He had named it that because the white fur around the squirrel monkey's eyes made it look like it was wearing goggles.

Derick pressed the button on the back of his neck again. After a wave of dizziness, his point of view changed. He looked up at a massive tree towering above him. It was slightly disorienting to see the world from a lower perspective, but he had done it many times before—it was still awesome. He used his small furry hands to dig into the bark and nimbly climb the trunk. He loved the feeling of being so light and limber, a little trapeze artist.

Rafa. The thought nagged at him. Derick was the best at the avatars in his class and maybe his whole grade, but Rafa, the zoology teacher's assistant, was the best Derick had seen—maybe the best in the school. He was a total prodigy.

And he was gaining on him during the last zoology class of the semester—Derick's final chance to beat him.

Derick ran along a branch and leapt to another—four more trees to cross. He launched himself again. Squirrel monkeys can jump nearly six feet, and Derick could almost match that distance with his avatar.

"Rafa has his monkey," Dr. Mackleprank announced. "This is his best time yet, Derick. Hurry, but no jumping from the branches to the ground. I don't want to have to make any more repairs." Hollers from his classmates nearly drowned out their teacher. Derick found more energy. He could beat Rafa. This would be no different from when he finally beat Jax Carlson at one-on-one basketball, even though Jax was over a year older than him. Or when he conquered the virtual game Mitchell had designed pitting Vikings against a mutant sea monster before even Mitchell did. Derick usually won. At least he used to. He needed this.

Derick shimmied down the final tree. He could hear the soft sounds of branches moving and swaying with the light weight of a monkey behind him. Rafa wouldn't let up; that was for sure. Derick jumped the last few feet, willing to brave what Dr. Mackleprank might say. He landed next to a gorilla, pushing the button on the back of his neck only a second later. "C'mon, Kong. We can do this," he spoke to the avatar as he changed perspective once again. Then he was up and running the last leg of the race. Using his long arms and short legs to barrel forward, he heard the grunt of another gorilla behind him. He didn't have much of a lead after all.

He bounded up a thick metal ladder and swung across the overhead bars of the obstacle course, skipping handholds where he could. On one swing, he caught a glimpse of a black furry shadow close behind him. No. He wouldn't lose. No more failing. Derick grunted as he hit the ground and raced forward.

Ten feet to go. He used his arms and legs in a fast rhythm across the ground, the gorilla's raw power pushing him forward. He wouldn't look back. Five feet. Four. Rafa was nearly even with him. Three. Two. Derick let out a roar and lunged for the finish. One.

Less than a minute later, Derick and Rafa were unhooking their gear and putting it back in its place on the wall. Derick rubbed his hand through his short dark hair, scratching his scalp.

"*Muito bem, rapaz.*" Rafa slapped Derick on the shoulder. He stood a few inches taller than Derick, but he was two grades older as well. A smile crossed the Brazilian's bronze face.

"I'm not sure what you said, but it doesn't help me feel any better." Derick walked out from under Rafa's hand. "Unless you said that you were lucky, and I'm really much better at this avatar stuff than you."

Rafa's grin broadened, a long strand of black hair slipping from his ponytail and falling over his face. "I said, 'You did well.'"

"Nope. Didn't help." Of course no one had expected Derick to win. At least they shouldn't have. He was the underdog. But he had wanted it so badly.

The two started walking toward the door. Derick slowed his pace; the class was waiting outside.

"Seriously," Rafa said, "you're becoming pretty impressive." He paused. "A few of us get together to practice on the avatars a couple times a week. It's a small group—like a club, I guess. Since I have access to the lab, Dr. Mackleprank lets us get together. I can't make any promises, but I'll ask the others if you can join up if you are interested."

*Avatar club? That existed?* "Definitely." Just the idea of getting a chance to get more practice on the avatars made Derick's heart beat faster. He wondered what they did to practice and what they were capable of doing that he hadn't even thought of yet. His mind filled with images of monkeys having contests leaping from tree to tree, rhinos breaking through walls, and gorillas doing triple backflips and aerials.

"Plus, you came up with the idea for a relay race," Rafa said. "I hadn't done anything like that before. We could use your creativity." He grabbed the handle to the door. "I'll let you know." After a quick pull on the door, he motioned Derick through to greet the rest of his class.

The students who had been waiting congratulated Rafa and said things to Derick like "Nice try," "You were really close," and "Next time." It still bothered him, but with the possibility of joining the avatar club on his mind, it wasn't so bad.

Dr. Mackleprank was also waiting for them. "Good job, you two," the zoology teacher said, then turned to the rest of the class. "Good work today, everyone. I hope you did well on your final and enjoyed the end-of-semester challenge. It has been a pleasure to teach you this semester. Hopefully I'll see some of you in my classes next semester." As the students began to file out of the room, Dr. Mackleprank reached out and put a hand on Derick's shoulder. "Could you stick around for just a few minutes?"

Rafa waved at Derick and his teacher. "*Até a próxima vez.*"

"English!" Derick called out, as Rafa walked away. "I saw it on the homesite. English is the official language of this school."

Rafa didn't turn around.

Derick looked to his teacher. "I can't help but think he's either insulting me or cracking jokes."

"He is," Mackleprank said.

"You understand it?" Derick asked.

Mackleprank nodded. "*Claro que entendo.*"

Derick palmed his forehead.

"Sorry, I couldn't resist. I studied Portuguese for a while." The zoology teacher chuckled. "And I was kidding. He just said, 'Until next time.'"

"Oh," Derick said. "Good to know that someone understands him."

"Step into my office." Mackleprank gestured toward the doorway. Derick followed his teacher out of the viewing area and through the largest of the avatar labs, a room with several stations for students to control the robot animals. At the back of the lab, Mackleprank unlocked the thick door to his office. A desk and several tables covered in avatar parts lined the walls. Derick noticed a gorilla arm, a set of robot eyeballs, and a monkey with half of its inner robotics exposed. Various sets of machinery and tools lay beside the parts. Charts of animal skeletal structures and muscles were displayed on the wall screens. A large set of doors stood at the back of the room. Derick guessed it was some sort of storage.

Mackleprank sat on the edge of the desk, the same position he usually took while teaching zoology class. He looked around for a moment, scratching the nape of his neck just below his light hair, a mix of blond and white. "Let's wait just a moment."

Wait? Why step into his office just to wait?

There was a knock at the open office door. Derick turned to look into familiar eyes. His grandpa walked into the room, his cane tapping the ground every other step. As usual, he wore a simple collared shirt and blue blazer, the school crest featuring a watchtower embroidered over the breast pocket. "Hello, Derick," he said, a smile sweeping over his wrinkled face. He shuffled across the room rather quickly for a man of his age and gave Derick a hug. It probably would have made Derick feel uncomfortable when he had first started at Cragbridge Hall, but after having his grandpa kidnapped and almost losing his parents earlier in the year, he didn't mind.

"You didn't start without me, did you?" Grandpa asked Mackleprank.

"No," the zoology teacher answered.

"Good." Grandpa turned and motioned for Derick to sit down. Derick chose a tabletop. Grandpa brushed a robotic wing—only partially covered in feathers—off to one side and leaned against the desk next to Derick. "You know that I trust you, Derick. After what happened last semester, I would be a fool not to."

Derick hoped he wasn't turning red.

"Dr. Mackleprank has approached me with an interesting dilemma. After discussing it thoroughly, we decided that he should give something of his to you."

"Please say it's a woolly mammoth avatar," Derick said. "Or a centaur."

"No," Mackleprank laughed. "Those are both great ideas, though. It's actually more important." The teacher's smile disappeared. "And much more serious."

"It is something I first gave Dr. Mackleprank," Grandpa explained.

Dr. Mackleprank reached forward and opened his hand—a locket. Just looking at it flooded Derick's mind with memories and gave him chills.

"This locket led me to four challenges. I made it to the end of three, but the last is incomplete," Dr. Mackleprank said.

Derick immediately remembered having his own locket and following clues his grandfather left inside it to discover his secret. But Derick had failed. Just thinking about it made his heart beat heavy and slow. Thankfully, his sister had continued where he left off and finished the challenges. "I'm flattered. But why give it to me?" He looked at his zoology teacher. "Why not finish the last challenge yourself?"

Dr. Mackleprank and Grandpa shared a look.

"You'll have to trust me." Dr. Mackleprank explained. "I have my reasons." Why didn't Mackleprank finish the challenges? Did he not trust himself to find out Grandpa's secret? Had Muns blackmailed him? Did he simply not want to be involved? Or could he not pass the tests?

Grandpa tapped Derick's leg with his cane. "Of all the other possible candidates in this school," he said, "you deserve this locket the most. And that includes adults, teachers that are world-renowned. If it wasn't for you, we would not have protected the secret to which this locket leads."

Derick took a deep breath. He looked down at the locket, then back at Dr. Mackleprank. "You're sure?"

Dr. Mackleprank nodded and dropped the locket into Derick's open hand. Grandpa nodded too.

As soon as the metal touched Derick's skin, a shiver rushed through him. Could he do it this time?

# DETECTIVES AND PSYCHOPATHS

Abby focused her thoughts as she read aloud. She knew her whole English class could see what she imagined as she read. Every detail was portrayed on the screen behind her. It was all due to the chair she sat in, another fantastic gadget invented by her grandfather for Cragbridge Hall. The Chair was made of cedar wood lined in places with dark metal. Something in the metal along the tall back of the chair connected to the reader's thoughts and relayed images of them to the screen. Over the course of the semester she had imagined *Oliver Twist*, *Little Women*, and *The Call of the Wild*. But today was different. As Abby read, she imagined two men meeting for the first time.

"You have been in Afghanistan, I perceive," the taller of the men said. He had a pointed nose and square chin, his eyes dancing with self-confidence. He knew he was right.

Abby imagined the other man's surprise. It was easy. She just had to think of how she would feel if someone could deduce a lot of information about her after only knowing her for seconds.

"Can anyone guess who these two men are?" Abby asked, looking up from the words to her classmates. Class participation was a requirement for her end-of-semester presentation, and she needed to fulfill *every* requirement.

Several students raised their hands. She called on a girl with short black hair. "Sherlock Holmes and Dr. Watson," she answered.

"Very good," Abby said. She hoped she didn't look as stupid as she felt. All of the others were geniuses and had probably known everything she said since they were in fourth grade.

As she continued to read, Sherlock explained all the clues his sharp eyes had detected. He saw that Watson had a tan face and hands, but paler wrists. Sherlock deduced it was from wearing a long-sleeved uniform somewhere warm. From simple gestures and mannerisms he could tell Watson was a doctor and had served in the military. He also noticed that Watson held his hand stiffly. "Where in the tropics could an English army doctor have seen much hardship and got his arm wounded? Clearly in Afghanistan," Sherlock concluded.

Sherlock fascinated Abby. He noticed so much and was able to quickly access and use what he knew. She wished she were that way. If she were, perhaps her palms wouldn't have been sweating and she wouldn't be trying desperately to keep from imagining the grade she would get and display-ing it for all to see.

Abby stood up from the Chair and glanced at Ms. Entrese, her English teacher. Ms. Entrese was wearing black pants, black shoes, a black belt, and a black V-neck T-shirt trimmed in pink. It was the first shard of color other than black Abby had ever seen her English teacher wear. She was the one Abby had to impress. Abby hoped her presentation wouldn't lead to another C. At Cragbridge Hall a C was pathetic, and based on her midterms she was in danger of getting three. Not to mention two B minuses and two Bs.

"But my assignment is to show how literature has af-fected real lives, or was influenced by real life." Abby continued her presentation. She tried to act like her twin brother Derick would, confident and smart. Of course *he* was confident because he got the family genius genes.

"The author, Sir Arthur Conan Doyle, based Sherlock Holmes on a real person, one of his medical school profes-sors named Joseph Bell. Bell encouraged his students to ob-serve patients carefully and deduce information about them because it helped in diagnosing their problems and diseases. And he showed them how. I'll switch over to the Bridge to show you an example."

Abby stepped away from the Chair and used her rings, a small computer on each of her fingers, to sync to her class's copy of the most famous of her grandfather's inventions. The Bridge showed history three-dimensionally throughout the room. It was a faded image of the past, but an image just the same. Over the semester her teachers had stood in front of their classes and used the Bridge to show Abby and her classmates real soldiers fighting for freedom, presidents addressing their nations, and artists creating masterpieces. But now Abby stood with the controls. She selected the date she wanted and soon the faded image of a small lecture hall appeared. It was history, live and 3-D in her English class.

A few rows of students from the past sat ready to take notes. A teacher stood in front of the room, tall with a thin nose—much like Sherlock.

A patient entered the room gazing around from under a hat. As he met Dr. Bell for the first time, the man explained his medical symptom; it felt like his skin was hardening on the inside of his legs.

"Well, my man," Dr. Bell said in a Scottish accent that Abby loved, "You've served in the army."

The man looked surprised, but responded with an "Aye, sir." He was equally Scottish.

"Not long discharged?" the doctor asked.

"No, sir."

"A Highland regiment?"

"Aye, sir." The man's brow furrowed, obviously trying to figure out how the doctor knew so much about him.

"A non-commissioned officer?"

"Aye, sir."

"Stationed at Barbados?"

At this, the man's jaw fell limp for a moment. He looked completed dumbfounded. "Aye, sir."

The doctor turned to his class, some now with their mouths equally open, others shaking their heads in disbelief.

He explained that because the man hadn't removed his hat, Dr. Bell could tell that he had served in the military, as that was their custom. And the patient hadn't been home long enough to drop the habit. And from his complaint, he had elephantiasis, which was much more common in Barbados.

Ms. Entrese raised her hand to signal that Abby had thirty seconds to finish.

Abby stepped back into the middle of the room. She had to try to bring it home. "It completely changed my attitude toward Sherlock Holmes when I learned he was based on a real person," she said. "That meant it could really be done. You really can deduce a lot from observing. In fact, Joseph Bell actually helped in several real crime cases. So while literature can entertain us, it might inspire us to gain new skills and improve ourselves as well."

The class clapped as Abby walked back to her seat. She hoped they were sincere.

The hum that ended class vibrated through the room. Student after student filed out while Abby waited to talk to Ms. Entrese. Carol, Abby's best friend, was waiting too. Abby's heart was pounding. Had she raised her score at all?

"Great job, Abby," her teacher complimented. "That was well thought out, professionally presented, and very interesting."

With each accolade, Abby felt her cheeks redden. "Thanks."

"Yeah, I thought it was awesome!" Carol chimed in. She spoke as fast as most people could think. "Probably even better than my presentation, but just barely. I think I did a near-superb job. At first, I wanted to do a presentation on how Jane Austen books inspired the romance in my life, but somehow I didn't think that would get me a very good grade. Plus, I don't have a lot of romance in my life. But the coals are in the grill, if you know what I'm saying." Carol had been flirting with Abby's brother, Derick, for months now. Of course, she also flirted with about any boy with a pulse.

"Carol, that's enough," Ms. Entrese interrupted. "Abby, I think I can deduce your intentions for studying Sherlock Holmes and Joseph Bell."

"Why is that?" Abby hoped she didn't look as surprised as she felt.

Carol jumped in before Ms. Entrese could answer. "Maybe she wants to learn how to deduce a lot about boys just by looking at them." Her mouth dropped open. "Wait! That is a fantastic idea! I'll be starting in on Sherlock Holmes very *very* soon. Just imagine walking up to some boy and saying, 'I see that you worked out recently, probably in gym class because the edges of your hair are still wet from the shower. And that you've been writing poetry because you were silently mouthing well-composed lines that rhyme in Italian.' Okay, that last one would probably never happen, but a girl can dream."

Abby smiled. "Very cool in concept, Carol, but creepy if you actually told a boy that—scary stalker-girl creepy."

"I agree," Ms. Entrese said. "But back to the subject at hand. I think you studied Holmes hoping that somehow his example could help you when Muns strikes again."

Abby didn't answer for a moment. The English teacher's solemn expression reminded Abby that, of the many people with whom Muns would want to even the score, Minerva Entrese might top the list. She had worked for him before and betrayed him.

"That is *if* Muns strikes again," Abby corrected, knowing full well that she was most likely wrong.

"*If?*" Carol asked. "That man is an obsessed psychopath."

"I don't believe he's a psychopath," Ms. Entrese said, "but he's definitely determined, eccentric, and very dangerous."

"That is just a really nice way of saying obsessed psychopath," Carol replied.

"I think we all know that Muns will retaliate. He refuses to lose. Frankly, I'm surprised it's been so long. I thought he would strike before the semester ended."

"He must be planning something," Abby admitted. She had been nervous earlier about giving her presentation, but thinking about Muns brought fear in deep swells. She knew Muns would seek revenge, but he would also do it with a certain style, a sense of the punishment fitting the offense. He was well practiced at getting revenge. He had done it in his many businesses. One of his employees had used a secret bank account to steal money from him. Muns not only found a way to get all his money back, but he also arranged to transfer all of the money the man possessed into an account so secret he could not find it. Even the trouble Muns had caused earlier in the semester had the same pattern of fitting. He had placed Abby's parents on the sinking Titanic because of something Grandpa had said years earlier—that no one should mess with time travel even if they could save the Titanic.

Muns had to be planning his revenge. Clues to what he might do were probably in the details of how they had already stopped him. Abby wished she was like Sherlock Holmes or Joseph Bell—then maybe she could know what Muns planned next.

"I agree," Ms. Entrese said. "He will do something."

"That's what obsessed psychopaths do," Carol added.

# MESSAGE

Finally—lunch! Something about an entire semester of work gave Abby quite the appetite. But she still chose a salad.

She had stabbed her first bite and raised it to her mouth when her rings vibrated; she had a message. Maybe she had forgotten something in English class and Ms. Entrese was letting her know. Or maybe her mom and dad just wanted to check in. They lived on the grounds of Cragbridge Hall now and every now and then they would find a few minutes to meet. Or maybe it was Grandpa. But as she scanned the message icon, it wasn't from any of them. It was worse. Much worse. It was a personal video message from—the name itself brought a bad taste to her mouth and a hollow to her gut—Charles Muns.

Why would that terrorizer ever send *her* a message?

Should she even open it? It was probably some sort of terrible virus that would corrupt all her files, send him copies, and delete them. Or, knowing Muns, he had probably developed a way to make the virus seep into her contact lenses and blind her.

Abby ran a quick scan.

Clean.

She ran another.

Clean.

She switched to safe mode which would open the file on an online server. She had taken every precaution.

She clicked on the video.

In an instant, a man in his late fifties appeared on the screen in Abby's contact lenses. His gray hair was slicked back over his head, and he wore a finely tailored suit, a light green shirt, and an orange tie. With his money, he could afford to be the high fashion type, but the combo made Abby think he looked like an inverted pumpkin.

"Hello, Abigail," he said, his voice thin. "I probably should have tried sooner to communicate directly with you, but since you are a minor, I wondered about the appropriateness of such an action. I would like to congratulate you on your heroic feat several months ago." He smiled, showing teeth several shades whiter than should be humanly possible. "Going back in time to retrieve your parents took a diligence and grit that many do not have. I have watched the footage several times. I am quite impressed."

It was a compliment, but coming from Muns, it didn't feel like it.

He sneered. "Of course, you did stop an event that would have changed our entire world for the better. I can only believe that you didn't fully understand the situation. I was moments away from gaining the secrets to right all wrongs, to reverse all tragedies. Doesn't that sound like a worthwhile pursuit to you?"

Abby huffed in disgust. He was the one who didn't fully understand the situation. She had heard his arguments over and over. They sounded good at first, but changing events in the past could have huge ramifications. Changing time could destroy everything.

Muns raised a finger. "I will be bold here. You would probably expect no less. If you will help me gain two more keys so I can change time, I will guarantee your parents', your grandfather's, and your brother's safety." Abby felt sick. After following her grandpa's clues, various people at Cragbridge Hall, most of them adults, had earned a key that allowed them to enter the past. She was one of them. Her grandpa had designed the system so that three people had to use their keys together in one of the two Bridges in existence before it would work. Requiring three keys was a protection. Muns had stolen one Bridge, and thanks to Abby, he had one key. Now he needed two more. "In addition, I will let you choose the first tragedy we fix. You decide. Do you want the world to avoid World War II, to evacuate Pompeii, to save the dodo before it goes extinct? The choice is yours."

He was trying to convert her, to bring her over to his side—even after having threatened her parents and kidnapping her grandpa. Abby's insides swirled with hate and anger. She would never turn on her family—or their cause.

"All you need do is respond. Give me the word. Tell me what you would want changed. I may ask a few questions, but that is all. I will do the rest."

What information did he want and how did he plan on gaining the other keys?

He rubbed his temples. "Of course, there is a chance that you may be foolish enough to disagree with me and side with your grandfather. If that is the case, I counsel you to simply bow out. This is a dangerous game. I don't believe *children* should be players in it." That at least *sounded* responsible. Then again, Abby had helped to stop him the first time. Maybe he was trying to get rid of the competition. "I do not know how you ended up on the Titanic. I do not know if you have a key. I would find it strange to entrust such power to someone as young and naïve as you. I do not know how you and others managed to outwit Mr. Hendricks and my team. I will know eventually, of course. Again, I urge you to bow out."

He leaned back in his cushy leather chair. "Something is about to happen. It will not be safe. You are a young girl, and should be worried about your friends, grades, boys, the next dance—not this. I hold no ill will toward you. Please leave this alone. As Oscar Cragbridge's granddaughter, you have a bright future ahead of you. You don't need to take part in an old man's quarrel."

He leaned in closer. "Abby: Leave this alone."

Abby involuntarily shuddered as she closed the message. There was something about that man that gave her the creeps. It was probably how amazingly smooth he was. He sounded so logical and merciful, yet she knew he was willing to do terribly inhumane things to get his way— he was a wolf in sheep's clothing, a poisonous snake in the flowerbed.

She immediately sent a copy of the message to her parents and her grandfather. They would know what to do. Maybe it would give them a clue, tell them something.

Of course she wasn't going to help Muns. That was out of the question. She could only imagine what might happen to the world if he was successful. But she couldn't stay out of it either.

Could she? The thought of letting others—*adults*— worry about protecting time did have its appeal. Plus, she did have her share of worries just trying to survive in a school full of geniuses.

No. She couldn't.

Unless they already had it all under control. Muns could be right in that the adults would probably do a better job.

Abby stared at her salad. In one message, Muns had stolen her appetite. One phrase replayed in her mind: "Something is about to happen."

"Hey, Abby," Carol said, holding a tray with a hamburger, fries, and two side salads. "I'm *sooo* hungry. But that's pretty much every day. It might have something to do with geography; just looking at tundra makes me cold . . . and *hungry*." She put her food down and sat across the table from Abby. "Oh, and the fact that the Valentine's dance is coming up brings on the appetite too. I know it's still a couple of weeks away, but I need fuel for my moves." She began to shift, point, and swivel, dancing in her chair. She looked over her shoulder at a group of boys seated behind her. "That's right, gentlemen. That's just a little taste of what's going to be on the floor at the Valentine's Day dance. You're just going to have to wait until then, but know I'm going to bring my A game."

No one appeared to be listening. In fact, they seemed to be purposefully ignoring her.

Abby couldn't decide if she wanted Carol to be quiet or if she liked the distraction. She lifted a fork full of salad to her mouth, but then put it back on her plate again.

"I really think we need to have a ten A.M. emergency snack to keep the engine fully rebooted," Carol started up again. "You know . . ." her sentence trailed off as she tilted her head to look at Abby. "You okay?"

"Yeah," Abby said, twisting her hair into a temporary ponytail.

"No, you're not. You always do that when you're anxious. I've been your friend for forever, which in this case is like four months, but I know you, girl."

"Okay, something *is* bugging me," Abby admitted. "But I'm still thinking about it. I don't know if I want to talk about it yet. I'm not even sure what all of it is."

"I usually just say everything I'm thinking," Carol said.

"I've noticed," Abby said. She took a big bite of salad so she wouldn't have to talk. Carol shrugged and bit into her hamburger. Somehow she managed to chew off nearly a third of it. Not very ladylike, but impressive. With her mouth full, she might be quiet for a minute. Of course, there was no guarantee.

"Muns sent me a message," Abby finally mumbled.

Carol stopped chewing. "I *knew* it," she said, her mouth half-full. She quickly chomped and swallowed. "I was trying to let you say it first. My geography teacher told me that I need to be more discretionary with what I say. I think she thinks I talk too much, but I'm going to try it anyway. That was pretty good, right?"

"Yes, but how did you know?"

"He sent me one too. I was kind of flattered. It's the first time any president of multiple companies has ever sent me a personal message. Really, it's probably the first of many. He told me not to get involved and that things are about to get crazy. Well, I guess he didn't say *crazy*, but that's what he meant. That guy is so creepy—he gives me the creepy creep-a-loos. He really should look into a film career. He could be the bad guy in just about anything. *Oh!* He'd be a fantastic Iago or Dracula—or Satan!"

"If you reply to him, you ought to tell him that," Abby said.

"Thanks. I'm usually quite insightful and helpful. I'll send it with my suggestion that he take a flaming jump in a lake of gasoline."

Before Abby could ask her friend any more about her message, Derick sat down next to her. "Hey, you two."

"Hel-lo," Carol said, twisting to face Derick and wink. "Did you beat Rafa in your big end-of-semester race?"

26

"No," Derick answered, raising his overstuffed hamburger to his mouth. "Dumb prodigy."

"I understand your jealousy," Carol said. "He's pretty fantastic, plus his long hair is so shiny. I can never get my hair past the dull glow phase."

Derick held up a finger to signal that he needed a moment to chew. "You're not really helping, Carol. Let's not talk about it."

"Okay," Carol said. "We'll go back to what we were talking about before—how Muns sent us—" Carol cut herself off by slamming her hands over her mouth. "Not discretionary. I shouldn't have said that. Your hotness kind of confuses my thinker."

Derick set down his burger. "You too, huh? He didn't have anything on me other than the fact that Grandpa pulled me up in the assembly. Muns told me to leave this all alone." Several months before, Grandpa had brought all three of them, plus Rafa and the two gym coaches, on stage in an assembly to thank them for helping save him. It had been televised.

"That's all he had on me, too." Carol pointed to herself. "Which was kind of disappointing, because we both did *so* much more than that. We should get more credit for stopping Sir Evilbritches."

"I'd better send a message to Rafa," Derick said. "If the three of us got messages, chances are he got one too." Derick's fingers moved quickly.

"Good idea," Abby said.

"This is intense," Carol said. "Threatening messages

27

from an evil guy. Me across the table from a really attractive guy. Kids who know a huge secret that could destroy the world. Sitting across the table from a really attractive guy."

"You said that one twice," Abby pointed out.

"Maybe it was twice as exciting." Carol raised her eyebrows.

If Derick heard, he didn't acknowledge any of it.

"Rafa got one too," Derick said, apparently reading a message on his rings. "Muns knows about all four of us."

Abby knew Muns had the most on her. She was the only one he had seen go back in time and save her parents. For the rest, he was banking on the fact that Grandpa had presented them in the assembly. Grandpa had done it as a strategic move to bring attention to them, making it harder for anything to happen to them without the world finding out. Perhaps it had backfired.

"What do you think's about to happen?" Abby asked.

"I wish I knew," Derick said.

"All I know," Carol answered, "is that I really don't like this. It's like that moment in the movies when the evil mastermind is so confident in his plan that he actually tips his hand."

"It seems just like that," Abby said, a little surprised she was agreeing with one of Carol's random statements. "And I hate the fact that Muns is so confident."

# LITTLE ROUND TOP

Derick rubbed the locket in his hands. He checked over his shoulder before turning down the janitor's hallway. Classes were over for the day—for the semester. His history teacher had let them select whatever they wanted to watch using the Bridge. They saw the Wright Brothers' first flight, Walt Disney drawing his first cartoon, Evel Knievel crashing his motorcycle after jumping the fountains at Caesar's Palace—ouch!, Muhammad Ali boxing Joe Frazier, and Taylor Swift's final concert. They played "Name That Tune" in music class, but with a twist. After the music played for twenty seconds, the teacher would show the artist performing it using the Bridge. That helped a lot. Derick had done all right for his team, guessing Beethoven's "Für Elise," Duke Ellington's "Take the A Train," and John William's theme music to *Star Wars*. Of course the other classes had their final tests, presentations, and parties, but he hadn't thought about them much. He didn't even allow himself to daydream about what the avatar club might be like. He only thought about Muns's message and the locket.

As he moved down the empty hall, he surveyed the crown molding. Decorative squares hung evenly spaced along the ridged border. Most had the tower of the Cragbridge insignia carved into them, but Derick knew one was different. Perhaps only one. Last semester he and his sister Abby had discovered a square showing a ship stuck in the ice. There it was. No one would notice the difference if they didn't know what to look for. With a quick jump, he pressed the square. A slab of the brick wall pivoted as if on hinges, leaving enough room for Derick to slip into a secret hallway unnoticed by anyone in the school. The brick wall closed behind him.

Memories flooded his mind as he walked down the dimly lit corridor and began climbing down the chilly steel rungs of a ladder deep into the basement of Cragbridge Hall. The last time he was here, his parents' lives were on the line. He clenched his eyes shut for a moment, not wanting to remember. He had failed facing this challenge, the final challenge in a series to gain a key that could allow him to enter the past and save his parents. He wanted to spit . . . as if he could taste the lingering defeat. Thankfully, Abby had succeeded.

Derick remembered Muns's message. He was about to strike again, but this time Derick could have a key. And if Muns tried to alter history, Derick could use that key to fight against the man who had kidnapped his grandpa and endangered his parents. All he had to do was finish where Dr. Mackleprank left off. He had to face the same sort of challenge that stopped him last time.

He could do this. His grandfather trusted him to do it. Dr. Mackleprank believed he could. And most of all, using the final key was the only way to help prevent Muns from changing the past.

Derick shook his head. He didn't normally have to tell himself that he could do something. Then again, until the last time in the simulator, he couldn't really remember the last time he had failed. He got into Cragbridge Hall. He made the competition soccer team. He even made his own virtual samurai game. But he had failed when it was most important. And to top it off, he had lost the avatar race to Rafa. He hoped failing wasn't going to become a habit.

Derick had climbed down for what felt like more than three stories before he finally reached the floor. He had no sooner touched the ground when the image of Grandpa appeared, glowing in the darkness. He walked through the image as his grandfather explained that he had developed a simulator that would allow him to feel what a figure in history felt.

"If you are to proceed," Derick heard his grandfather's recorded voice behind him, "you must complete a challenge that someone through history has passed. The question is, will you? Doing so will take more than curiosity or knowledge. You must have a cause so important that, like these people in history, you absolutely refuse to give up. If not, you will not pass."

Give up. He hadn't meant to give up. It was only—he thought of his last time in the simulator—a bear attacking him like it had a famous mountain man in history. It had been too much. He could still feel every blow.

Derick exhaled and approached a large metal door with thick bars and gears that had locked it closed. Secure-looking lockers covered the wall beside it. Today he would not give up. He would survive whatever challenge he faced. He opened the locket that Dr. Mackleprank had given him and removed a small key. It was not the final key that would allow him to change time, but it would open a locker along the wall. Derick retrieved a visor and sensors. They were similar to those from the avatar lab. He knew his life wouldn't be in any real danger, but he would feel every pain until he came back out again. He had to have the same de-termination and will, the same character as a great person in history. He had to prove that he deserved the final key.

A lump formed in his gut. He closed his eyes and swal-lowed hard just thinking about it. "Failing once doesn't really mean anything," he whispered to himself. "How many people would last as long as I did against a grizzly?"

•  •  •

Abby and Carol walked back toward their dorm.

"I can't believe how free I feel—done with the last day of first semester!" Carol bounced up and down. "It feels so monumental. Like we just climbed Everest, or won the Super Bowl, or successfully made manicotti—that is not an easy pasta dish to throw together, at least for me. But boy is it worth it—heavenly cheesy epic awesomeness!"

"I'm not out of the woods yet," Abby said. "Plus I still can't quit thinking about Muns's message."

"Sure. Just squash all the fun because the creepy guy threatens us," Carol said.

"Sorry," Abby said. "I *am* glad classes are over."

"Me too," Carol agreed. "So what should we do to celebrate?"

"I'll try not to worry about Muns, but I should still pray that my teachers have mercy on me and that my grades aren't as bad as they could be."

"I'm sure you're fine," Carol said, waving her off. "Let's get some of that double chocolate brownie ice cream and log on the Bridge and watch the history of boy bands or basketball back when they wore those short shorts. Or even better, we could start a dance party on our floor. Check out my moves." Carol started jumping and whirling, twisting and swaying. "I'm feeling the groove. That settles it. Let's dance, dance, boogie, boogie, dance-a-boogie!"

At one time Abby would probably be embarrassed to be walking with a crazy dancing girl, but not now. Carol had been a friend when no one else would. Abby could endure some pretty crazy stuff for that. She even started to dance a little herself.

Until her rings vibrated.

Not again.

With a touch of her thumb, she turned on her rings. Immediately a small screen lit up in her contact lens. The message scrolled across the screen. This time, it was from her grandpa, not Muns.

> Come to the basement immediately. You will need to bring your key to the Bridge, so take every precaution.

Not exactly the way Abby would have liked to celebrate.

• • •

Derick looked at the message and groaned. Why couldn't Muns leave it all alone? But Grandpa would need help. Derick's first reaction was to wait for Abby. She had the key to bypass this challenge and lead him further on into the basement where they could stop Muns.

He stopped himself. Why? Why did he need to be there? Abby had one of the final keys. He didn't. They would do just fine without him. The thought made Derick feel hollow. For most of his life he had been the go-to guy on the team or the smartest one in the class. Not now, apparently.

Then he smiled. All that would change when he earned his own key. Then he would deserve to be there. In fact, if he hurried, maybe he could complete his challenge and meet them there.

He heard footsteps coming down the hall. He had to enter the simulator now before anyone tried to persuade him otherwise.

Derick took the key from the locket, put it into the lock, twisted it, and the thick metal door swung open with a groan. He closed his eyes and stepped in. When he had entered before, his simulation began with a peaceful scene in the mountains. This time there was no peace about it.

He stared at a gun barrel, part of the musket he was apparently holding. He glanced to either side and saw men in blue uniforms with their guns aimed downhill. They formed a line a few soldiers deep along the slope of the mountain. He could sense the tension in their deliberate breaths.

"Look!" It sounded like fifty men said it at once. Down the hill, lines of enemy soldiers moved toward them. A shot fired, then another, and another. The hill filled with sparks and smoke spouting from gun barrels. A musket ball slammed into the rock wall in front of Derick, spraying fragments of lead and rock into the air.

He ducked, still trying to process what was happening. He was obviously in some sort of battle with men in gray uniforms shooting at him. *Wait. Blue and Gray. Oh, no.* He had to survive a battle in the Civil War.

"Fire!" he heard someone command. "Hold this flank." Flank? He searched his memory. He knew what that was— the far side of the army. It was important because it kept those attacking from getting behind the rest of the army. If the flank fell, it was likely that the army would lose. Derick was in the middle of an essential position.

He lifted his long musket. He pointed into the mob of gray coming up the mountain, but he hesitated to pull the trigger. It felt different than the war video games he had played. He could hear the men's cries, see their breath. He didn't want to shoot anyone even though he knew it was just a simulation.

Derick looked down the barrel of his gun. These men had been real; they had to be willing to fire on another person for their cause. If he was going to complete this task, he had to show the same character, the same determination as the people in history. They were fighting to keep their nation together. Derick bit his lip and pulled the trigger. The musket rammed back against his shoulder. It felt like someone had just hit him with a rock. With his musket kicking back as it had, Derick was sure he had shot well above his enemies' heads. He hoped none of the other men had noticed what a terrible shot he was. He quickly aimed again and pulled the trigger. Nothing.

Oh. These were old-time muskets that had to be reloaded after every shot. He ducked further behind the rocks and felt them shake as bullets collided into the other side of the wall. What a nightmare.

Derick watched the soldier next to him as he loaded gunpowder, a metal ball, and rammed it down the barrel before shooting again. He found he was carrying the same tools and mimicked as best he could.

He raised up and readied himself to fire again, looking down to see hundreds of men charging up the hill at him and his regiment. Hundreds. It looked as though his enemies had twice as many men. Not fair.

"C'mon," he heard a soldier next to him say. "I don't want to die. Not today. Not at Gettysburg. Not anywhere."

Gettysburg? He was in one of the most important battles of the Civil War. The North needed this victory. It was one of the events that kept the United States of America to-gether, united as a nation. Derick fired, this time holding the gun tighter against his shoulder. It still hurt, but not nearly as much. He didn't hit anyone.

The smoke and smell of gunshots became stronger and stronger. A scream tore through the air off to his left. Derick wanted out of there.

# THE BASEMENT, BULLETS, AND BAYONETS

Abby walked down the hall as fast as she could without drawing any attention to herself.

Carol wasn't helping by talking the whole way. "Not only is Muns up to something, but he killed our dance party before it could even get started. Preemptive dance party murderer!" Carol shuddered. "Oh, that man is evil."

Abby was too nervous to respond. She knew what Muns was capable of and she wasn't sure if she was ready to find out what he had done this time.

"Do you think he kidnapped someone else and put them in the past to die?" Carol asked.

"I hope not." Abby knew her parents were safe. Cragbridge Hall was one of the safest places in the world. No one got in or out without passing by guards and through several stations through a thick, guarded wall. Still, her stomach felt like it had turned to stone. She was back in the basement, the place where it had all happened months ago.

The two girls entered the basement and approached two doors. One was to the simulator, which Abby thankfully didn't have to go through again. One tribe of Native American braves chasing her down with spears was enough for her. She moved toward the other door. It would bypass the simulator, but only with the key she had gained from going through it.

She reached down and gave a distinct pull on the upper rim of her belt buckle. The buckle shifted, revealing a small metal compartment underneath. Abby touched the metal, knowing that it would read her fingerprint and open. Her grandpa had designed it. She could always keep her key with her but keep it secret and protected as well.

As Abby took another step toward the door, something moved out of the shadows. Carol gasped. Abby wanted to shriek but her fear stole the sound. A hulking gorilla stood in front of her, its thick hairy body only feet away.

"All right, I know you're an avatar," Carol said, trying to regain her breath. "I'm guessing a real gorilla wouldn't live down here. At least I'm really hoping. Really *really* hoping."

Abby looked at the gorilla. It had to be an avatar. It could be her own brother and she would have no idea. "Can we please pass?" There was no time to talk; they had to move on. Grandpa needed them.

The gorilla moved aside, his fingers . . . typing? Whoever controlled it must have just used their rings—though it looked very strange. A message came in on Abby's rings. She saw that it also had been sent to Carol.

It's me, Rafa.

"Thanks, Rafa," Abby said over her shoulder as she continued toward the door. She felt better. If Muns somehow could get his men back into Cragbridge Hall and they tried to ambush their meeting, they would have to tangle with quite the opponent. A robot gorilla can do some damage.

"Rafa," Carol said, following Abby. "Remind me that I owe *you* something scary. Unless you teach me how to samba, or you tell me the secret to that healthy shine to your hair, then I'll call it even. Really, a boy shouldn't have prettier hair than most of the girls in this school. It isn't fair. I'm referring to your human hair, of course, and not your gorilla hair. No offense."

Abby slid her key into the door and twisted it, sending the gears and levers into motion. Soon the massive door whirred open.

"Since I technically wasn't invited, I probably shouldn't go in any further," Carol said, staring at the giant door. The message had only come to Abby. Abby had a key. Carol did not. "I'll just wait in the creepy dark hall with the gorilla."

"Though that sounds strange, it's probably best," Abby admitted. "Once I find out what this is all about, I'll tell you . . . if I can." She waved, twisted her hair into a ponytail, and descended down another ladder into another dark, twisting corridor. She wondered if Derick had also been invited. He didn't have a key, but he had been instrumental in her efforts to get one. She hoped he would be there. She eventually heard Grandpa's voice in the distance.

Abby stepped into a giant room. In the middle was what looked like a massive metal tree, its limbs sprawling up into the ceiling: the original Bridge. The branches contained connections that wove through the floor of the school to hundreds of Bridge stations. Every student knew that the Bridge could portray logged and charted moments of history from any angle they chose. But they couldn't go back further than four thousand years and no more recently than fifty years ago. And, of course, they could not interact with history. It was simply a faded image of what had happened. What most students didn't know was that if three people with keys placed them in the original Bridge, they could enter history itself.

Four people already stood in the room. No Derick. Abby wasn't surprised by three of them—Grandpa and coaches Adonavich and Horne, her gym coaches from the last semester. She knew she could trust them. It was the fourth person Abby hadn't expected: a tall, thin man with blondish white hair—Dr. Mackleprank. He had been her zoology teacher, but unlike Derick, she had no natural talent in the avatars. She had fallen down so many times as a squirrel monkey she was convinced she had real bruises.

"Abby," Grandpa greeted her. "Quickly." He motioned for her to enter. "Muns has used another energy burst."

"Where . . . ," Abby began to ask, but shook her head, "I mean *when* did he go in? Where is he in time?"

• • •

"Hold the line!" Derick heard an officer behind him call out. Derick bit the end off the package of gunpowder and poured it down the barrel. He noticed his hands were black and sooty. He was sure his face and arms were too—the signs of a black powder war.

Another musket ball whizzed by him. In a simulator or not, he would never get used to it. He tried to steady his heart and his hands as he dropped the metal ball in the barrel and used the rod to push it down. After readying the spot on the gun where the spark would hit the powder, he lifted his gun to aim. The other soldiers could shoot nearly three times in a minute. Derick was grateful to get off a shot and be halfway into loading the second in the same amount of time.

A man to his left cursed and fell to the ground clutching his arm. Someone to his right seemed to be mumbling a prayer. Derick was surprised he noticed it, surprised his brain even worked under the circumstances. How long would he have to endure this?

Derick thought of the others meeting in the basement right now. They could have to go into the past and keep Muns from altering it. Muns might even be trying to change something like the Civil War, and that would have ramifications to billions of people. He needed a key. He needed to be able to help.

A musket ball thudded as it pierced a tree several feet away. It sounded so flat and powerful, haunting and

42

threatening. Derick ducked behind the small rock wall and fished another packet of gunpowder out of his satchel. He rose and shot again, but most of the soldiers had retreated and the rest were quickly following.

Did they do it? Had they won? Derick waited for celebration. Nothing. "They'll be back," another soldier said.

Derick's heart sank. He couldn't take much more. The shooting. The death. Being in a war was brutal, so much more difficult than just reading about it. He wanted to back out, to be done, but he knew he couldn't. He couldn't fail.

Resolving to be ready, he searched for more powder. Nothing. He must have fired nearly sixty times and apparently that was all that he had. As he surveyed the other soldiers, he noticed many of them in the same predicament.

Some of the leaders were gathered behind him. One man had a long bushy mustache, long overdue for a trim, and Derick thought he overheard someone call him Chamberlain. Derick couldn't make out most of it, but when he casually wandered back a few feet, he heard phrases like "no more ammunition," "tired," "wounded," and "pull back."

Then Chamberlain spoke. "No. We hold," he commanded. "We are the extreme left flank." If they retreated, the other army could creep around the rest of the North's army and attack it from behind. The results would be disastrous.

Derick heard commotion down the hill. He saw glimpses of gray. They were coming. Then he heard a word that sent shivers down his back, a word from Chamberlain commanding his men to action. "Bayonets!" Derick had noticed a bayonet blade hooked at the gun's side. In war vids, when fights got to close quarters, soldiers would hook the blade onto the front of the gun and use it like a combination of a spear and a sword.

A soldier came to their front. "Fasten bayonets, men. We're going to charge."

What? Charge down the hill when they didn't have ammo? Sure, they'd have their bayonets on their guns, but the grays had bullets. Hadn't they ever heard that you're not supposed to bring a knife to a gunfight? Just because the knives are bigger doesn't make much difference. And the other army outnumbered them. This was crazy—this was suicide!

He watched closely as the solider next to him placed his bayonet at the front of his gun and fastened it down. Was he shaking? Derick couldn't blame him.

He attached his own bayonet the best he could, copying the other man. They had to do this. They had to defend the line and protect the far left flank to keep the enemy from getting behind them. But did all these men die? Was Derick about to? He knew he wouldn't really die, but he would still feel it. Was he willing to do that? He watched as soldier after soldier stood at the ready. They faced death for real. There was no simulator. There would be no waking up safe for them. Could he face death with them?

A coronet blasted, loud and brassy. It was time.

# THE CHARGE

We need to use the keys in the Bridge," Grandpa said, his face stern. As usual, he wore his blazer with the Cragbridge Hall crest.

"How do we know he used another burst?" Abby asked. The thought sent chills through her. Though she didn't know exactly how an energy burst worked, last semester Abby learned what Muns could do with one. He had figured out that a burst of highly focused energy could, for a few short seconds, make a hole in the shield Grandpa had invented between the present and the past. It was the same shield the keys allowed them to bypass. With the burst, Muns had a quick window of opportunity to travel into history—or send someone else.

"Because of the substantial amount of energy it takes, he must store enough to power the burst," Grandpa explained.

"That's probably why he has taken so long to act. Some friends and I have devised some equipment to register such a large amount of energy. There was another burst nearly ten minutes ago."

Amazing. Abby knew her grandpa had been busy while she was studying, writing papers, and preparing for tests, but she hadn't known that he had been working on equipment to detect energy bursts.

Grandpa's old but agile hands worked the Bridge. "We must be quick," he said. In the far half of the room a faded image began to form. Two men walked down a sidewalk between a tall brick building and a road. The building was several stories tall, with rounded windows on top and pillars supporting decorative eaves. The men both wore suits, one dark with a matching hat, the other a nearly white coat and dark pants. One of the men carried a dark brown leather suitcase.

"This is Germany in early May, 1937," Grandpa explained. Then he sped up the image. The two men walked down the street and turned. Then they disappeared. "This is the moment Muns's men are in time." Grandpa rewound the image and they appeared again. "They have not changed anything yet. Coming in through a burst is disorienting, so it buys us some time."

Grandpa cleared his throat. "The men just spent what would be thousands of dollars today to book passage on the *Hindenburg*. Now, like all the other passengers, they are probably going into town to buy dinner before the flight, and it is our chance to stop them."

"What's the *Hindenburg?*" Abby asked.

Grandpa worked the controls at the console of the Bridge. In a moment, the scene before them faded and another appeared. What looked like a magnificent blimp floated in the air across the room. It was massive, several football fields in length, like an ocean liner in the sky. It glided over a large city with crowded streets of people gazing up at the amazing flying spectacle, taking pictures.

A question formed in Abby's mind, but she sensed now was not the time to ask.

"This blimp, or dirigible, is the *Hindenburg,*" Grandpa said. The wind shifted, and the large vessel slewed closer to what appeared to be a giant tower. Another giant gust hit and the blimp began to try to turn around. Abby marveled at the dirigible. "As our history now stands, the end of this flight of the *Hindenburg* destroyed dirigible travel forever," Grandpa said.

In a flash, the massive blimp burst into flames.

Abby couldn't tell what started the fire, but it spread in a hurry. The back half of the dirigible exploded in flame and smoke. Gasps turned into screams. The massive craft sunk as the blazes engulfed it.

"It was a terrible tragedy," Grandpa said. "The *Titanic* of the sky."

Abby swallowed hard. That was fitting—the kind of detail Muns would use in his revenge. Abby, Derick, and the others had foiled Muns's last attempt on the *Titanic,* so now he was going to alter the fate of the *Titanic* of the sky.

"I believe these intruders in the past are going to try

and stop it." Grandpa raised his hand. "Though that may be appealing on the surface, it could have disastrous consequences. He may prevent one terror, but that act could cause many more. It may change everything from then until now. Some people would survive that did not survive in our current history. Those people would interact with others, changing what is now our past. They could marry, which would change the families we now have. They could cause new accidents; their children could do the same. People who exist now might disappear because their parents never married or died in the alternate history. This could change entire countries. Leaders may never be born. It could change even the course of our reality." He waved his cane emphatically. "We must stop Muns before he changes the past and sends us all on a path to destruction."

• • •

Could he do this? Could he charge an enemy when he didn't have any ammunition? Derick looked around at the men and boys with him. Would they? Could they face almost certain death?

Someone yelled, intense and shrill. Soon more battle cries from his regiment blended into one cacophonous roar. They held their guns firmly and began to charge down the hill. Soldier after soldier passed Derick. They were risking it all. Was it this important that the United States stay together? If they didn't stay together, would the slaves be freed in all the states? Would all the states progress as they had?

Would they then be able to stand against others in world wars? Derick wasn't sure of all the answers, but he knew this moment was important. But was it important enough to die for? He wasn't sure what reasons each of these men had, but they acted. They bravely rushed their enemy.

Derick looked at his legs, willing them to move. He knew this was a simulation, yet he didn't want to feel the bullets, the pain. It was not his life on the line, but he still wavered.

Something caught his attention ahead—a sword flashing. A man in a uniform much like Derick's was charging down the hillside. He was some sort of leader, but Derick didn't know his name. Doubt and wonder swirled through Derick's mind as the man raced a good ten paces ahead of all his men. He would be the first to meet the enemy. He would be the prime target. Yet he charged on.

Derick had to have the same character, the same heart as these men if he was going to pass the test. He had to truly be willing to die.

Derick searched himself. He had to fight against a different enemy, one who would change history, maybe even destroy it all. He had to gain his key, his weapon, but first he would have to be willing to charge down a hill almost without one.

Derick groaned, letting the deep sound grow into a yell. He leaned forward and began to speed down the hill. He gained momentum, rushing down the mountainside with his musket extended in front of him, a dirty bayonet on its tip.

He leapt over a tree root and shifted to avoid a patch of uneven ground. He pushed himself harder, trying to catch up to the men who bravely charged in front of him. He tried not to imagine himself—and the whole line of men with him—gunned down as they tried to do something brave. Adrenaline pulsed through him. He felt courageous. Until he saw the enemy with their guns raised.

• • •

Abby imagined what life might be like if the *Hindenburg* hadn't caught on fire. Would they have modern dirigibles? She couldn't help but wish to ride in one. But as for Grandpa's arguments, she had heard them before—and so had the coaches. It was hard to swallow at first, but she understood. Grandpa must have been giving the speech for Mackleprank.

"Plus," Grandpa continued, "we need tragedies. They teach us. We learn from them. Without tragedies, our hearts do not commit to avoid future ones. Without tragedies, many of our hearts would not turn to others, open up to them. And without tragedies, we do not have heroes, for they are not formed without great conflicts. For example," Grandpa fast-forwarded the image, "I believe there are some heroes in this very event." The flaming blimp approached a spot to land and anchor. In the middle of all the chaos, a boy ran from his safety on the ground into the flames, trying to save the others.

Abby wondered if she could run into a fire to help.

"I do not know his name. I haven't had time to study this episode in history, but I remember his courage."

"Harry J. King," Coach Horne said, his fingers moving, looking up the information on his rings. "He was a baggage handler."

"Thank you," Grandpa said to the coach. "He deserves to be remembered." He turned back to everyone. "This is what I propose, though it will require your trust. Abby, Coach Adonavich, and I will turn our keys. Then we will send Dr. Mackleprank in to retrieve the two men and bring them back out through the Bridge."

Send in Dr. Mackleprank? That wasn't what Abby was expecting.

"No disrespect to Mackleprank," Coach Horne said, "but shouldn't Coach Adonavich and I go in as well? That way we guarantee we get it done." That made sense. Especially since Coach Horne was a former world champion weight lifter and Coach Adonavich had been an Olympic gymnast.

"You are still recovering from the last Bridge incident," Coach Adonavich said, motioning toward Coach Horne's chest and leg, where he had taken two bullets at the beginning of the school year. "I'll join Dr. Mackleprank."

"I hoped both of you would be willing to stand by if we needed your physical prowess," Grandpa said to the two coaches. "However, I am going to ask you to wait and only cross into the past if necessary. The fewer people we send means the smaller chance of doing irreparable harm. I think we'll find that Dr. Mackleprank is aptly suited for the task.

Though he does not have a key, I trust him completely and have invited him here precisely for this chore." He nodded in the doctor's direction.

Dr. Mackleprank looked at Grandpa, his eyes wide. Abby thought he looked nervous. "I'm more than willing, but are you sure?"

"Yes," said Grandpa. "If anything goes wrong we will send the two coaches in after you." He looked over at the coaches for confirmation. They nodded.

"If I can get in okay, we should be fine," Dr. Mackleprank said.

Abby wasn't sure what that meant. Did he doubt that he could actually go back in time? She didn't blame him; this was all new to him. She might wonder too if she hadn't already seen—and done—it. She remembered crossing over, the heat and then the chill. She remembered the terror she faced. She knew firsthand that it worked.

"I ask you to please trust me," Grandpa said. "That includes Dr. Mackleprank."

"But if I am manning the keys," Coach Adonavich said, "I will be several steps away from entering the past if Dr. Mackleprank needs me."

"True," Grandpa admitted. "I would feel much better if you didn't have to worry about the keys and could simply stand ready to enter the past if necessary. It would be ideal if we had one more person here with a key."

• • •

Derick's voice joined the shrill yell. More gunfire from the enemy.

He could see them clearer now, but he saw something new in their faces—surprise. There was no way they would have expected this. The distance shortened. They would meet in thirty feet.

More shots. More echoing yells.

Several men fell.

Twenty feet.

Some of the enemy started to turn and run.

Fifteen.

Their shooting was more accurate now, the men so close. Still more of the opposing army pivoted and looked downhill.

Ten.

The charge with bayonets was sweeping the enemy back down from where they had climbed.

Ugh!

Derick fell back, reeling to the right. He hit the ground hard, scratching dirt deep into his forehead. He clutched at his chest and rolled over.

He had been shot.

Derick slowly stood, wincing and gritting his teeth. A ball of metal was somewhere between his ribs. He glanced down at his hand and then his chest. Blood. Dark red every-where.

He tried to raise his gun, but fell forward. He plunged the bayonet into the dirt and used the musket for a brace. He couldn't give up now.

# STAND BACK

Grandpa put his key in the console. Abby reached down and once again pulled on the upper rim of her belt buckle. The buckle shifted and she pressed her finger against the metal compartment underneath. It quickly verified the tiny ridges in her fingerprint and opened to reveal her key.

She placed the metal key in the slot next to her grandfather.

Coach Adonavich ran her thumb along the side of her shoe. A slot in the heel opened and she pulled out her key. Grandpa had obviously been very busy helping all those with keys to keep them secret and safe. Abby wondered if he had set up the same system in several different styles of shoes so Coach Adonavich could always have the key with her. He had made Abby several belts for that reason. The coach stepped forward with her key.

• • •

Derick fought to keep the pain from taking over his mind, his whole body. He had to keep going. He had to have the heart of the men around him. It was not whether he was shot or not. It was whether he kept trying.

Derick gritted his teeth and lifted his bayonet in front of him. His mind felt slow and hazy. Maybe it would be better to lay down and rest, hoping someone could give him some medical attention. Pain pulsed through him again. It gripped his mind.

No. His fellow soldiers were still running down the mountain with only bayonets as weapons. They needed him.

He screamed, the sound drowning out the pain. He moved his body down the mountain, each step uneven, but he began to gain momentum.

Then he saw an enemy soldier, his gun pointed at Derick.

This was it.

He could move on with one musket ball to the ribs, but he knew he couldn't take another.

The only thing Derick knew to do was barrel onward. He took in another breath and screamed again.

The enemy looked up from his gun and looked around. Then he raised his barrel to the sky.

Derick slowed, stumbling.

The soldier was surrendering.

Derick held his bayonet at the man's chest and looked

around to see what he should do next. Surrounding him, men in his matching uniform guarded the captured enemy. They marched them into groups.

They had won.

Derick felt lightheaded. The ground tilted one way and then the other. He was going to collapse.

No! He was too close. He had made it this far—he would not fail again.

He closed his eyes for a moment and tried to right himself, stand tall. His chest felt like mush—mush on fire. His vision started to tunnel.

He breathed deep.

A little more. A little longer.

Derick opened his eyes. His pain was gone.

Where was he? The hill, the soldiers, the muskets were all gone. Now he was in a dimly lit room.

His grandpa stood in front of him. Not his real grandpa but a recorded image of him. "Congratulations on passing such an arduous test," he said. "You have earned the right to know, and perhaps even use, my secret."

He made it! Just barely, but he made it. He wouldn't have to share the "just barely" part with anyone else. He stood and instinctively wiped his forehead, his hand wet with sweat as it glided over his skin. He walked slowly, but his steps felt solid. He had faced a war and made it. Successful Derick was back.

Grandpa continued to explain his secret, though Derick already knew it. He spoke about becoming obsessed with finding the secret to time travel and eventually succeeding.

But he also spoke of meeting Muns and learning of the businessman's dangerous ambitions to change the past. That was why Grandpa had created the shield and the keys to protect history.

After passing through a giant door, Derick climbed down a chilling ladder, noticing other ladders on other sides of the basement. He knew there were other paths to the Bridge; the basement was a very large place.

He walked through another dark, twisting corridor, hearing echoes of people talking. The hall finally opened into a giant room and Derick's senses ignited. He immediately took in the great metal tree—the original Bridge. Its thick trunk held the main console; its branches split into hundreds of channels and disappeared into the ceiling. People surrounded the trunk—Abby, Grandpa, and Coach Adonavich; Coach Horne and Dr. Mackleprank stood beside them watching something happening in an old town.

Grandpa counted to three and he, Abby, and Coach Adonavich all twisted their keys. To work, they had to all twist at the same time. That way even if someone managed to steal the keys, he couldn't twist them by himself—no one person could twist three keys at once.

Immediately the view of an old town changed from a faded image of the past to a vivid reality. The dust and wind from the past blew into the basement. The other half of the room in the basement of Cragbridge Hall was now a part of the other side of the world and a century and a half in the past.

Grandpa found the scene of two men walking down

a back street. "Let's bring you in behind them," he said. Derick's pulse quickened. Was Dr. Mackleprank going in? Did those two people not belong in the past? Derick began to understand the situation. But there were two of them and only one Dr. Mackleprank. Maybe Derick could help. He slowly stepped forward toward the past.

Grandpa continued, "Unlike other situations, let's leave the connection to the past open." Usually, after someone crossed into history, it would be safest to turn the keys and close the Bridge through time. That way no one from the past could accidentally step into the future. "Dr. Mackleprank may need to send these trespassers back through at any moment."

Derick's heart beat faster as he watched Dr. Mackleprank approach the line between the present and the past. He was about to see his teacher in action. Sure, it wasn't in an avatar, but this was better. One-on-two, live and in high-definition color.

Dr. Mackleprank looked one more time at Grandpa and then stepped into history. Once on the other side, he paused, lifted his arm, and looked at it. It was like he was surprised he could still move and breathe. Derick couldn't blame him; it must be weird to go back in time.

And then he was to the task. It was like watching an action movie. Dr. Mackleprank walked up behind the two men, grabbed one from behind, twisted him around, and pushed him straight through the divide of time. It was that fast. The man's eyes grew larger as he passed through. The briefcase he carried crashed against the basement floor.

Luckily, Coach Horne quickly punched the man and he crumpled to the ground. Ow! There is no way Derick ever wanted to be on the receiving end of a blow from a former weightlifting champion. It must feel like a small car had hit your face.

"Make sure he doesn't go anywhere," Grandpa commanded. Derick rushed forward. "Derick, stand back," Grandpa called out.

"I just want to help," Derick said.

"Not now," Grandpa replied.

Coach Horne had already taken it upon himself to stand over the man.

Derick ran to the back of the room and retrieved the briefcase.

"And don't open that briefcase, just to be careful," Grandpa added, barking orders like the general of an army.

After the man fell, Coach Horne held him down with a foot on his back. The coach couldn't be light. Derick was glad he wasn't that man.

On the other side of the room, Dr. Mackleprank fought with the second man. The time intruder whirled around, throwing a punch. Dr. Mackleprank nimbly dodged the strike. The man lunged again; not only did Mackleprank block the blow, but struck the man quickly afterward. The battle continued, each man attacking the other. Yet Mackleprank was far superior. Beyond superior. He was amazing. With that kind of body control there was no way Derick could beat him in an avatar race. His moves were powerful, yet graceful, like a dance. He noticed there was almost a rhythm to the doctor's movements.

Mackleprank spun into a kick, throttling the man across the backstreet. The teacher picked his opponent up by the collar, threw him through the divide, and then walked back into the basement.

Awesome.

"Close it," Grandpa commanded.

Immediately, Grandpa, Abby, and Coach Adonavich twisted the keys, closing the gap into the past, just in time for a passerby to appear and look into the empty alleyway. Thank goodness he hadn't seen one man throw another into the future. That could definitely lead to a trip to the psychiatrist.

They had done it.

Derick exhaled in relief. And then he realized they hadn't needed him—or his key—at all.

# LIKE A NINJA

Dr. Mackleprank hauled one of the time intruders over his shoulder, Derick carrying his feet. At least Derick was doing something.

"Where did you ever learn to fight like that?" Derick asked, half impressed and half jealous. "I stumbled in and you were like a ninja flying around everywhere. You've definitely gained 3,000 awesome points in the last few minutes. Not bad for a teacher."

"I'm glad you were impressed," Dr. Mackleprank said with a quick glance over his shoulder, "but it isn't much really. Remember how I told you that I lived in Brazil?"

"Yeah."

"Well, I picked up something called *capoeira*. It's a Brazilian martial art, but it has a little flair, ties to dance and music."

"I don't get it," Derick admitted.

"Well, it is a little difficult to explain. It is a martial art, but the way you practice it is more like playing a game to a beat. One person plays a big stringed instrument that produces a twangy sound and rhythm. You move to the beat. You try to stay in complete control, complete rhythm, and you kick, fling fists, everything, but without actually touching each other."

"It's like a dance fight," Derick said. "Sorry . . . that sounded really wimpy coming out of my mouth."

"Did it look wimpy?"

"No, no, no, no, no." Derick tried to cover up. "It was amazing! And it was definitely more than a dance. "

Dr. Mackleprank looked over at Derick again. "For me, it is a great way to practice body control, which is an essential trait in my line of work."

That made sense—amazing body control for the avatar teacher. They walked on through the dark corridor, following Grandpa. The legs Derick was carrying were starting to get pretty heavy.

"And speaking of body control, you're getting better all the time with the avatars. The fact that Rafa wants to ask his club if you can join is a huge compliment."

"I hope it works out," Derick said.

"I hope so too. You have a lot of potential, Derick. But you ought to know that they are pretty intense. Racing Rafa is just the beginning."

"Oh," Derick said, looking down. "I hadn't thought that it might just be one more way I can lose to that guy."

Dr. Mackleprank stopped, which forced Derick to stop as well. "Rafa is quite the prodigy when it comes to avatars. But you realize that learning is not a race against anyone."

Derick nodded.

"And that if someone is better than you at something, that doesn't actually decrease what you learned or your abilities at all."

Derick nodded again. Easy for him to say—the amazing ninja fight-dancing avatar teacher.

"Good," Dr. Mackleprank said. "Be careful. A little healthy competition is good for just about everyone, but when it becomes only about winning or beating someone else, people tend to make some pretty rash and foolish decisions." The avatar teacher gestured toward the men they carried. "Like Muns, for instance. I don't think he's playing anymore. And this is definitely not a healthy competition."

•  •  •

Abby followed Dr. Mackleprank and Derick as they carried a time trespasser through the large metal door. Carol and a gorilla were waiting for them.

"Wow, it isn't every day you see this, huh?" Carol said, watching them pass. Coaches Horne and Adonavich carried the other man who had entered into the past. "You'd better fill me in here, Abby."

Abby just smiled. They did it! Despite all of Muns's threats, they had stopped his efforts to change the past.

Abby felt silly for ever having been so worried. Grandpa had been perfectly prepared.

The gorilla rushed over and took the unconscious man from the coaches.

"I can still carry him," Coach Horne protested.

"We all know that," Dr. Mackleprank said over his shoulder, panting. The way he struggled for air, Abby thought he might be faking a little. He might be stronger than he let on. Maybe he was trying to ease up on Coach Horne's pride. Plus, the coach was still recovering from his injury. "But let the avatar take him. Robots are quite useful for carrying large loads."

"We all know you could carry him," Abby agreed. "You could carry all of us put together."

"Yeah," Carol added. "You're the buffest old guy I know."

"*Old guy?*" Coach Horne said, raising his eyebrow.

"Oh . . . that was probably one of those moments I shouldn't have just said whatever came into my head, right?" Carol said.

"Right," Coach Horne agreed.

Grandpa carried the intruder's briefcase in one hand, his own cane in the other. He led them down another corridor, one Abby had never been in before.

After a minute or so, Grandpa approached another large metal door with the same crossbars and gears of all the other doors in the basement. He hooked his cane over his wrist while he inserted a key and twisted. He nodded and Dr. Mackleprank, Derick, and Rafa dropped the two trespassers on the cold hard ground. In a few moments, both stirred back to consciousness.

"I designed a few rooms as a secure place to store essential equipment. Now they will have to serve as cells," Grandpa explained.

"You will be treated humanely," Grandpa said to the trespassers. "Which is perhaps better than you deserve, considering what you intended to do." He looked down at the men with a look that surprised Abby. She had never seen him that furious. She had seen him stern, but the way his eyebrow bent inward and his lip slightly curled up into a snarl was so much more than stern. "Will Muns never stop?"

He glared at the two prisoners. They didn't answer.

"Tell me what Muns has planned next before he ruins our entire existence."

Again, silence.

"Do you have any idea how much trouble you could have caused? Do you think about your own actions, or do you merely follow Muns blindly?" Grandpa shook his cane in the air.

Abby grinned as Grandpa lectured the men on the dangers of meddling with time for the next several minutes. Grandpa never shied away from a chance to teach, but this was more than that. Abby thought perhaps Grandpa was trying to help them understand, even scare them into telling him anything about Muns. "I must know what he plans to do, or everything is at risk," he said.

No answer.

"I don't know if he promised you that he would go back

in time to bring your relatives back from the dead, or give you a chance you never had, or help you rid yourself of some regret," Grandpa continued, "but it is *not worth it*. And it wouldn't solve anything anyway." Sweat glistened from Grandpa's bald head in the dim light. "We can't waste all our energy wishing the past were different—we must learn from it and move forward."

The prisoners acted like they had heard it all before. Their faces were blank, looking throughout their new cell, looking anywhere but at Oscar Cragbridge.

Grandpa lifted up the briefcase he had been holding. "I don't suppose you'll tell me what's in here."

The two men looked at each other, but did not reply.

"No matter what it is, it is horrendously dangerous to bring anything from the future to the past." He handed the case to Coach Horne. "Would you give this to the Trinhouses? Tell them we don't trust it and want to make sure it's safe before we open it. Have them keep me informed."

The coach took the case and nodded. Abby wondered who or what the Trinhouses were.

Grandpa turned to leave, then shifted back. "Did it even occur to you that Muns's energy bursts can only send you into the past, but cannot bring you back? There is no way he could create one in the right place to stay open long enough to retrieve you. He sent you on a kamikaze mission into the past, and you went!" He pointed at one with his cane and then the other.

Abby hadn't thought of that before, but it was true.

Muns would have left them there whether they succeeded or failed.

"Fine, then," Grandpa said. "I will have to decide what to do with you." He stepped back and motioned for Rafa to close the door.

"Naïve cretins!" Grandpa burst out, clanking his cane on the ground as he walked. "Ignorant moldwarps! Do they understand nothing?"

"Wow," Carol whispered to Abby. "I think his genius undies are in a bunch. He's angrier than a wolverine with stickers in its paws, pine cones up its nose, and its tail on fire."

"This time travel stuff is serious," Derick said.

Grandpa waved the group toward him. "We have much to think about and to decide. I'll be contacting most of you soon."

*Most* of you? Abby wondered if he would contact her. The group gradually spread out as they made the journey back up toward the school.

Abby inched up closer to her grandpa. There was still something she couldn't figure out. Maybe it was the right time to ask. Derick and Carol followed. "Grandpa," Abby said quietly, "I have a question."

"Go ahead," Grandpa said, his red face slowly fading back to its normal hue.

"I understand that you must have some sort of device that told you *when* Muns used an energy burst, but how did you know where in history Muns had sent his men?"

Grandpa looked over his shoulder, then spoke softly. "Derick and Carol, did you both hear that question?"

They nodded.

"I don't believe anyone else did," Grandpa said. "Do not share that question with them. I have been preparing for quite some time to answer it, but would like to address it my way. But it is a very good question." He cleared his throat. "The kind that needs an answer."

Abby walked alongside her Grandpa. She waited for him to tell her more.

"There is something I have become increasingly worried about," Grandpa said. "There is more to understand than even those with keys know. Now that Muns has acted again, the urgency has increased." He took a few more steps. "Yet some answers shouldn't just be given."

"What does that mean?" Derick asked.

"Just as with the secrets you learned from inside your lockets," Grandpa said, "some answers you need to earn. The answer to your question is just as serious as the answer you learned about our ability to go into the past."

A rush went through Abby. Really? Something that serious?

"It is not a trifling matter," Grandpa explained. "Monday morning, check the safety deposit room." Abby had seen that room before. It was on the main floor of the Hall, a place where students could store valuables they didn't feel comfortable keeping in their dorms. Abby had never used it; she hadn't had the need. "I will send you a retrieval code. Please keep secret what you find there. Derick and Abby, because you have keys, you will find special information there. Carol, you do not have a key, but you know the secrets of the Bridge already. If you desire, I will let you assist Abby and Derick. No one but you three should discover what you find. I urge you to treat this seriously. After tonight's events," he paused for a moment, choosing his words carefully, "it has become very important for someone else to know the answer to that question. It could be essential in the future if Muns continues to strike."

# THE BLACK BOX

The three students approached the safety deposit room. Carol yawned. It was still early. The cafeteria hadn't even started serving breakfast. Most of the school was still sleeping. The room was long and thin, a row of twelve doors down one side, each with a scanner beside it. Derick approached a door and raised his hand so the machine could match his fingerprints and verify his identity. He waited for a moment.

"Nothing here for me," he said. "I bet Grandpa sent it to you, Abby. You were the one who asked the question."

Abby raised her hand. She couldn't feel the scan, but knew it was happening. Almost immediately a message came through her rings.

Your belongings are being authenticated and delivered.

A light turned green beside the door. Abby opened it and stepped inside. There was barely enough room for one person. A framed metal door the size of a cereal box hung on the wall at eye level. Abby was scanned again. They really protected people's stuff. Of course, a lot of kids at Cragbridge Hall came from wealthy families—or had already gained some decent wealth themselves. They would have some things they'd want to keep safe. Abby could hear the muffled sounds of metal on tracks, movement behind the wall. She had heard how the rooms work. Behind the wall, a delivery system would retrieve a unit with her belongings from the vault in which it was kept and then place it behind the door. Scans of both her and the unit ensured that the right items were delivered to the right person—and only the right person.

A light on the smaller door glowed green. Abby opened the door, discovering it was several inches thick—not nearly as heavy or thick as the huge doors protecting the Bridge but still impressive. Inside was a small package wrapped in brown paper. It was about the length of two candy bars and a couple of inches wide.

Abby retrieved the package and stepped out to see Derick and Carol waiting. "Oh, it's like Christmas, or my birthday, or Easter, or graduation, or just Fridays when my mom has had a stressful week and she feels like doing some shopping therapy. Present time!" Carol clapped her hands.

Derick leaned over and read the tag tied to the top. "To those who ask the right questions." He looked at Abby.

"Can I open it?" Carol asked.

"Sure," Abby said, "but let's go to a study room first. I know it's probably too early for anyone else to be around, but we should probably be careful. Grandpa said to keep this private."

Moments later, they were in a secluded study room along the commons. Carol ripped at the paper. She was impressively quick at opening a gift. From the remaining wrapping, Carol pulled a rectangular black box made from dark metal or extremely reinforced plastic. On the front was a silver metal lock shaped like a question mark, a keyhole in the body of it.

"It needs a key," Carol said and looked over at Abby and Derick. Whatever was inside was intended for those who had already faced the challenges and could be trusted with the power to go back in time.

"Here," Derick said, pulling a key from his pocket. Grandpa hadn't yet made a cool way for him to save and protect it. "I really want to use this." Derick had told Abby last night about enduring a Civil War battle to get a key. He hadn't said too much, but after surviving her own simulation, she had an idea how hard it had been. Boys never gave enough detail in their stories.

The key fit perfectly. With a twist and a click, the black box opened. A small, three-dimensional image of Grandpa appeared. He was only four inches tall.

"Hello," Grandpa said. "Whoever you may be, you have

been asking questions. I admire that. Questions are to be valued . . . treasured. They are the beginning steps of some of the best journeys. I have probably spoken to you about the importance of this particular journey. I need others besides me to know more information, though you must be prepared to receive it. In fact, I hope I am not too late in extending it to you." Grandpa exhaled and rubbed his eyes. "But you must ask yourself how much you want the answers. Because answers—real answers—cannot simply be given; they must be earned. The answers to the question or questions you have asked especially must be earned. Those answers come with power and consequences." He motioned toward the open box below him. Inside it, Abby found what must be a small compartment. Covering it was a touch panel that, when she moved her fingers near it, showed a grid of random letters and numbers. It must take some sort of code to open. On top of the panel lay a small rolled-up piece of paper. Abby picked it up and unrolled it.

"Another Bridge code," Carol said out loud, reading the piece of paper over Abby's shoulder.

The image of Grandpa spoke again. "So . . . how badly do you want to know?"

• • •

Derick, Abby, and Carol all entered the Bridge booth. Such booths lined history classes and labs in the school and in the dorms. Each booth had enough space for several students, who could study without anyone else seeing what they saw. Abby entered in the code, ready to see an event from the past. Soon all three students were looking at the faded image of a bald man with a long beard who was dressed in robes. In some ways he reminded Derick of Grandpa, though this man was much more muscular.

A young man approached, standing tall with a wide smirk on his face. He began to speak a language Derick didn't recognize or understand.

"Turn on the translate feature on your rings," Derick said, switching his own rings on and searching for the right setting.

"Or we could just talk for them—like voiceovers—and say what we think they should say," Carol said. "Like," she began to speak for the young man. "Oh, great bald one! I have come from afar to see the great shine of your scalp. You have a legendary noggin of great gleaming wonder."

Abby snickered. "Very funny, but I don't think it's going to lead to the answer to my question."

In a moment, all three of them had turned on their translators. Derick's showed that it had detected ancient Greek and began translating it into English so he could hear it in his earpiece—the same earpiece that allowed him to hear messages he received on his rings.

"Socrates," the young man addressed the older one. Socrates? The bald man with a beard was the great philosopher? Interesting.

"Sorry, Socrates," Carol mumbled. "I was just playing, but you *do* have an amazingly bald head."

There was something about the young man that Derick

didn't like—he had annoyingly good posture and he seemed to keep his chin too high. "I have come 1,500 miles to gain wisdom and learning," the young man said, definitely proud of himself. Wow. If Derick lived at the time of Socrates he thought he might search him out too, ask him some questions. But he probably wouldn't have traveled that far. Well, he might now on a speed train or plane, but definitely not on foot. "I want learning, so I came to you."

Derick watched as Socrates motioned with his strong arm and invited, "Follow me."

Derick couldn't help but wonder how watching Socrates would help them with Abby's question. What did any of this have to do with how Grandpa knew where to go back in time when Muns attacked?

The philosopher led the young man down to the shoreline, the water a blue-green. Socrates gestured again for the young man to follow him as he waded into the water. Not what Derick expected.

"This is weird," Carol whispered. "He asked for knowledge, not swimming lessons." Abby shushed her.

The young man was apparently willing to humor Socrates because he followed him in. Soon the water was up to both of their waists. Then the strong philosopher grabbed the young man by the back of the neck and plunged him in under the water.

"Weirder," Carol said. "This is just getting weirder."

The young man struggled under the water and tried to stand up, but Socrates wouldn't let him surface.

"And I thought I had some mean teachers," Carol said.

"He must be teaching him something," Derick replied.

"Pay attention," Abby said.

"Well, he would be a horrible swim teacher," Carol mumbled. "And he'd get terrible scores on a rate-your-teacher site."

Derick waved Carol off. Socrates let the young man up for air. "What do you want?" he asked.

"Knowledge," the young man replied.

Socrates pushed him back under the water longer than he had before, then pulled him up again. "What do you want, young man?" he repeated. Derick didn't think Socrates was trying to be mean. He didn't seem like he was angry or bitter, just determined.

This time, it took the young man longer to answer. He breathed in heavily before responding, "Wisdom, great Socrates."

Again Socrates plunged the young man under the water. This time, he held him longer. Finally, he pulled the young man back up from the sea. "What do you want?" he asked again.

The young man sputtered, gulping in air as deep and as fast as he could. "Air! I want air!"

"If I were him," Carol said. "I would say 'air' and 'to punch you in the face.'"

Both Abby and Derick suppressed their laughter.

Socrates pulled the young man back up onto the shore. He crouched down and looked at him closely. "When you want knowledge and understanding as badly as you wanted air, you won't have to ask anyone to give it to you."

The image faded out. Derick had to think about that for a minute: if the young man wanted knowledge, he could find it. He didn't have to ask someone else for it—he just had to really want it. In fact, if he wanted it badly enough, that might be the best way to learn.

Abby looked down at the black box. "So what now? I really want to know the answer, but all we have is a keypad."

"We obviously have to type in some sort of password," Carol said. "I think with your grandpa, it would have something to do with what we just saw." Carol pointed where the image of Socrates had been moments before. "Maybe type in Socrates."

Abby started to type in S-O- . . . "Um, there's no C on this keypad."

Dead end.

"There are tons of words we could type in. There has to be more of a clue." Abby looked down at the keypad. "The letters are all out of order. I mean, they're not in alphabetical order or the order they're in on our rings' virtual keyboard. And there are numbers in there too. Let's see . . . there are . . . twenty characters . . . four are numbers, so only sixteen letters we can pick from."

"Wait." Derick raised his hands. "The last thing Grandpa said in his message was a question: 'How badly do you want to know?'"

Derick thought for a moment as he looked down at the keypad. How badly did they want to know? He stared at the random assortment of letters, letting his mind rearrange them, trying to make sense of them. In a flash, he had an idea. He looked closely, searching the keypad for an A and then an I. There. And an R. Yep. He let his eyes backtrack to see if the letters before a-i-r were there. He moved the remaining letters around in his mind. Yep. They were all there. "Look," Derick said. He began to punch in the letters:

### a s b a d l y a s y o u w a n t e d a i r

"That's what Socrates said," Abby said, then felt weird for having said something so obvious aloud.

The panel slid to the side, opening the compartment in the black box. Grandpa appeared again, blocking Derick's view of what was inside. "Very good," he said. "It is an interesting story, isn't it? If we are determined enough, we can always learn. I believe this is what Socrates was trying to teach. It wasn't that he was unwilling to teach the young man, but that he wanted his pupil to be an active learner, not one who expects others to simply give them answers. Though I am happy to help you find your answers, the question is, really, *How determined are you?* I require determination. Do you want the answers as badly as you want air?"

Derick looked over at Abby, who raised her thumb. Carol smiled big. He wasn't sure if that was because she wanted to know or if she was flirting again.

Grandpa continued, "Learning to think in new ways, to ponder consequences, and to contemplate possibilities is a noble endeavor. Learning to learn is worth the journey." The image of Grandpa disappeared. Inside the compartment were three small white spheres, each about the size of a grape.

"So, cool little marbles are going to help us figure out how your grandpa knows where in time Muns has attacked," Carol said. "I'm not sure I see the connection."

"I'm not sure I even know what these are," Abby admitted.

"Let's figure it out," Derick said, reaching in and scooping up the spheres. Once in his hand, one of the three glowed. It was a dim glow, but it glowed just the same.

"Whoa, trippy," Carol said. "Maybe it's just a really cool flashlight for when we go in the basement."

"It's not that bright," Derick said. "Besides, what about the other two that aren't glowing?"

"Maybe they're out of batteries," Carol suggested.

"Can I hold them?" Abby stretched out her hand. Derick agreed and passed them to his sister. Once they changed hands, the glowing sphere went out, but a different one began to glow. "Huh. Why did that happen?"

"My turn, my turn," Carol squealed. Abby passed the orbs. The same thing happened again, but this time, the third sphere illuminated. "There's one for each of us."

"Awesome," Derick said, taking the sphere that glowed with his touch.

Abby picked hers up, holding it close for a better look. "Now all we have to do is figure out what to do with them."

# A VIRTUAL BRIDGE

Abby tried not to think about flaming dirigibles and Brazilian dance-fighting teachers. She tried not to think about Muns. She tried not to think about the sphere in her pocket that lit up when she touched it. Now it was the first day of a new semester. Abby had a new start. She had to focus.

"Welcome to your second semester at Cragbridge Hall." A tall, thin woman with dark brown skin and short cropped hair stood at the front of the room. "I hope that you enjoyed your first semester, but because my class wasn't part of it, this semester will go down in your personal histories as the best so far." She winked. "But I have a question first, 'Who is ready for some *MATH?*'" She asked it like she was introducing a rock star or beginning a prize fight.

She didn't get much of a response.

"What?" she said. "I said, 'WHO is READY for some MATH?'" She put her hand to her ear like she was waiting for the class to go wild with cheers and applause. It didn't happen. "How about some ENGINEERING?" A couple of people clapped.

She stood up straight. "I can see I have some work to do. My name is Mrs. Trinhouse, and I will be your Math and Engineering teacher. And before you leave my class, you will be so much more excited than this." She smiled big, her white teeth standing out against her full dark lips.

Trinhouse. Abby had heard that name before.

"You have already completed your first semester of math and that will be absolutely vital to what we do here. But now it is time to amp up the learning and your experience. You'll notice that, like many classrooms at Cragbridge Hall, this one has several booths along the walls. Each booth is designed for a more interactive experience. I will invite you to enter a booth, and then put on the suit and sensors that you find there. The booths and their equipment are very similar to the avatar equipment you've used. Oscar Cragbridge has found methods of using much of the same technology in many different ways. In this case, your suit will not connect to a robot avatar or even to any place that is actually real. These virtuality booths will allow you to experience a world that doesn't exist. You will see what has been programmed, what has been built. You will feel what someone in this virtual world would feel. The experience is completely immersive."

Mrs. Trinhouse opened a flat case and displayed what

was inside to her class. Abby gasped. It was a series of small white spheres about the size of grapes. Each rested in a soft encasing. "These are the worlds I have built," she said. "Because creating each world requires massive amounts of data, we have to use physical spheres to hold it all." She plucked one marble from the case and held it up for the class. "Building each one of these worlds took months—some took years—but it was well worth the work. We will all use this one today." She pressed a button on a console in the front of the room. A small arm emerged, and Mrs. Trinhouse placed the orb within its three mechanical fingers. It then retracted into the machine.

Abby couldn't believe it. Was *that* what her sphere contained? A virtual world? Her mind filled with possibilities and questions. What information was in that sphere? How would it answer her question? And how might it help stop Muns in the future?

"It's your turn," Mrs. Trinhouse said. "Go ahead and hook up."

Abby left her desk, entered an open booth, and put on the equipment. She hoped she was better at this than she was at the avatars. Once she had her sensors and visor on, she hooked up to a suspension system.

"Are you all ready?" Mrs. Trinhouse asked.

A few mumbles of "yes" were her reply. That was not enough for Mrs. Trinhouse.

"I *said*, are you *READY?*"

This time the class began to respond.

"We're getting there," Mrs. Trinhouse said. "As you

know, you can use math for all sorts of things: measurements, equations, planning, and so forth. But it is essential in *creation*. I'm going to show you one of my worlds and as you watch, think about how measurements and math equations may be necessary to put it together. What calculations would you have to make? What designing? What engineering? Here you go." As she started the program, a whole new world blossomed before Abby—buildings, mountains, a deep green sky, a large ocean, a red and an orange moon at different points in the sky. It had all the depth and detail of somewhere real.

"I am going to give you a few minutes to explore before I give you your first assignment. Oh, by the way, brace yourselves." All of a sudden, Abby was in the air high above the buildings. Somehow she was hovering. "The pads that cover your virtual suit take in air and push it back out at such a rate that you can float," Mrs. Trinhouse said. "Or fly. Though right now these suits only exist in a computer program, in theory they would work in real life if anyone would spend the money to build them. Just tilt your arms and legs to move. The pads on your underarms and along the sides and back of your legs will guide you."

Abby practiced. She could move from one side to another. And if she tilted her whole body forward, she could dive down and come closer to the city.

"Can you imagine the math and engineering necessary to make these suits?" Mrs. Trinhouse asked. "That is extremely advanced. In this class, we will start out simpler . . . but first, go and explore."

Abby moved over the ocean, gradually going faster as she became more comfortable. Drawing closer to the city below, she saw a variety of buildings and parks. The closer she came, the more perspective she gained. The skyscrapers looked taller than any she had ever seen and some of the buildings were completely unique. One looked like a giant spiral, another like a woman balancing on one leg—some sort of dancing pose. Another looked like a lion's head. Absolutely incredible.

Abby glided through the city. The park had lakes contained in giant saucers stacked on one another. Each had a drain and children could travel from one to the next. A giant slide wrapped around trees and shrubs. One tree had an entire house in its branches, a net dangling beneath it for safety. As she flew between buildings, Abby noticed the streets below were thin, leaving no room for cars. Strange. But the place seemed so clean. Perhaps that was why.

"Be sure to see the system underground as well," Mrs. Trinhouse instructed. Abby saw an entryway with stairs leading downward. She glided over, careful not to hit a wall. That would still be painful, even in a virtual world. Line after line of subway cars waited on tracks. Each was a single car large enough to fit one family. Using the controls visible through her visor, Abby turned off her suit so she could walk. She entered one of the cars and selected a location. She shot through the underground, making turns at frightening speeds, yet it was more comfortable than Abby would have expected. It was the fastest and most personal transportation she had ever experienced. No wonder there were no cars above.

"Remember math and engineering," Mrs. Trinhouse's voice echoed through the booths. "These things do not get built without math and engineering."

Abby came up above ground in what looked like some sort of amusement park. She saw huge rides—coasters, sky lifts, and massive carousels. But one particular attraction stood out. A giant robot dragon thumped and roared in the middle of a group of squealing children. They each had guns and were shooting lasers at the beast. Different spots were marked with different amounts of points. "I totally nailed him," one virtual child cried out. "Give me the princess back, you horrible beast," another screamed.

"As I explained before," Mrs. Trinhouse said. "I built this world. I invented it. I built it out of the virtual pieces I will give to you. The large difference between this program and a video game you might play is that my world here follows the laws of our world. You cannot build something just from sheer imagination; it must be something that can actually work based on the laws we know. All of this would work in reality. Of course, it would be extremely expensive, but according to the program, it would work."

Awesome. What did the sphere her grandfather gave her have in it? Was it another world like this? How would it prepare them to learn the answer? She wanted to see as soon as possible.

"I'll admit," Mrs. Trinhouse said, "for those of you who have seen the mechanical dragon in the amusement park, he would take quite a bit of maintenance if he were real. But I think Bubbles would be worth it."

Bubbles? Weird name for a mechanical dragon.

"This world can be a great place for you to practice your building and math skills. So, let's hear it for *math* and *engineering!*" Abby couldn't see her teacher, but imagined the same enthusiasm on her face. This time she got what she was looking for. The students howled and whooped. Abby joined in.

"Very good," Mrs. Trinhouse said. "That's what I like to hear. And it brings me to your assignment for today." There were no cheers for the word *assignment*. Abby's perspective through the visor automatically zoomed through the city to a place where there was a large river. It looked spectacularly blue, and too wide for Abby to want to swim across it. "Your assignment is to build a bridge. Any spot will do. I've included several possible designs with their weaknesses and strengths on the class site. You can see the list in the corner of your vision. Let me give you a moment to select your location. Be sure to leave a good amount of space, perhaps a quarter-mile or so between you and the next student."

Abby used her specialized suit to survey the river. With other students selecting spots, she didn't have as much time to decide as she would have liked. She found a location where the land jutted out slightly toward the water. It looked to be a solid enough place to build. She landed to stake her claim.

"It looks as though you've all decided," Mrs. Trinhouse said. "Very good. You will have to choose which design you want and how to build it. Just select any of the materials here in your stockpile." Immediately a fenced yard of cement blocks, metal beams and cables, piles of dirt and asphalt, and thick plastic supports appeared on the ground to Abby's left. They seemed just as heavy as their real-life counterparts. She remembered building Lego sets growing up. This was Legos on steroids.

"I have also programmed a work force to put your bridge together as you instruct them, so you don't have to worry about the labor, just the design." A small army of people wearing hardhats, some piloting large equipment like cranes and bulldozers, appeared by the supplies. "I have also cheated and made it so they work extremely fast—almost as if I put them on time lapse. They can do in a half hour what would normally take months. Notice in the assignment info that your bridge should be able to carry a certain amount of weight. You might want to test it before the end of the period. And . . . GO!" Mrs. Trinhouse said. "If you have any questions, please just ask."

Abby wanted to try to see if she could leave this world, the world her whole class was working in together, and put in the sphere her grandfather had given her. Could she? Did her booth have its own mechanical arm that would take her sphere and override Mrs. Trinhouse's? It had to, right? But if she put it in, would her teacher notice? Would everyone notice? And would they discover that she already had a sphere? Would someone check it? It felt too risky, especially when she was supposed to keep it a secret. Besides, this assignment was due at the end of the period. No. She would have to wait.

Abby immediately got to work looking at the model bridges. She started by selecting the archway. A three-dimensional view of an old Roman aqueduct built of stone appeared in her vision. Abby read the accompanying information. The archway was one of the oldest types of bridges and naturally strongest. The Romans built them from shaped stones, but there were many more modern arched bridges, like the steel arch and concrete arch.

Suspension bridges like the Golden Gate used long cables attached to towers, the cables bearing the weight. Abby clicked on the image of the Golden Gate Bridge, its long towers shooting out of the billowy fog in San Francisco. The caption said it spanned over four thousand feet.

Abby had no idea bridges were so interesting. When she saw the Sunshine Skyway in Florida, she knew that was the kind she wanted to build. It was majestic and had a nice style to it—like art met architecture. Like the suspension bridge, it had tall towers, but the cables hooked to the towers differently—all in one spot near the top. The caption said that those cables put all the weight on the strong towers.

Abby used a measuring tool she found in her materials. It sent a virtual laser beam over the river and hit the land on the other side—the distance was less than 2,500 feet. According to the information Abby read, a cable-bearing bridge could work there. It was better for shorter distances.

Soon she selected her material, solved several equations to estimate where to put the supports, and sketched out plans. As Abby worked, hints and pointers popped up through her rings to give her advice. Mrs. Trinhouse had obviously prepared her program to give some help. When Abby felt she was ready, she set her crew to the task. As promised, they were very fast. She watched them use their large machines to move the various materials into place. Every few seconds felt like a day's worth of work. The program also kept a tally of her expenses. In the instructions, it said that she had an unlimited budget, but that future projects would be graded with financial planning in mind. Once she had over a thousand feet built, the array of cement and metal began to sway back and forth. Abby sent her crew to try and better anchor what they had built, but a large portion snapped from its cables and ripped from the tower, crashing with a monstrous splash into the deep virtual river below. The water rushed over it as it sank into the river bottom.

Abby saw a few other students stop working on their bridges and look over. How embarrassing. Abby sighed. At least one tower still stood. Time to get back to it.

She felt a tap on her shoulder. Abby turned to see a smiling face with shiny straight dark hair flawlessly framing it—Jacqueline, her former roommate. Though they were both in separate booths, they could see and speak to each other in the virtual world. "Hey, Abby. Congratulations on making it through one semester." She sounded cheery enough. Jacqueline had kicked Abby out of their room at the beginning of last semester, refusing to let her back in because Abby's grandpa had admitted her to Cragbridge Hall without all the achievements or grades the other students had. Jacqueline was incensed that Abby was in the school instead of one of her friends. "It surprised me," she whispered. "I didn't think Miss Average could ride her grandpa's reputation that long."

"Thanks Jacqueline, it's great to see you too," Abby responded dryly.

"Of course it is," she smiled and flipped her hair. "But now you've been evaluated and graded for your first semester," Jacqueline's voice raised. "We'll see how you did. We'll see how we both did."

"Thanks for the heads-up," Abby said. She had learned not to care too much about Jacqueline's opinions.

"Did you know," Jacqueline asked, "that if you don't meet a minimum grade performance in this school that you get kicked out?"

"Really?" Abby said, actually surprised. She had never heard that before. "That sounds a bit harsh."

"Not really," Jacqueline said, looking down at Abby's bridge. "Some people are like that bridge of yours—broken. There's not much use for something like that. Just let it go down the river."

Abby wished she could come up with a quick comeback. She would probably think of one later. No one got on Abby's nerves like the girl who never gave her a chance.

Abby couldn't think about Jacqueline, she had to finish a bridge.

"Oh," Mrs. Trinhouse interrupted. "I should also tell you that at the end of the class period, each of your bridges will have to survive a weight test." Her voice raised and grew more guttural. "Just to give you a challenge."

Abby hoped her virtual working crew could follow her adjustments and have it finished. She had to make quick decisions when they came to ask questions. She also had to double-check that she had enough supports for the distance the bridge had to cross and the right amount of cables. She thought she had it right.

She had barely finished when Mrs. Trinhouse said, "Time's up. But don't worry too much about this round. This is sort of a pretest. Now let's see how well you did. I thought we should do so with a little flair."

Flair?

"As you saw earlier, most of the personal transportation in this world happens on rapid light-rail trains. The train cars will need to cross the river on your bridge. Our test, however, isn't train cars . . . too boring. This, though, will represent about the average number of train cars your bridge would encounter during rush hour."

A deafening roar rang through Abby's ears.

Oh no. Bubbles.

The large robot dragon approached Abby's bridge.

• • •

Derick stood in a virtual booth just like Abby but in a different class. He looked down at his hand. He held a virtual word—*futebol*—just like it was a ball. Surrounding him were four different three-dimensional pictures: a man's foot, a girl playing soccer, a pottery bowl, and two teams playing football. He threw the word across his virtual room until it collided with the girl playing soccer. It exploded into fireworks and points lit up in the corner of Derick's vision. *Futebol* was Portuguese for *soccer*. He was hooked up to sensors in a virtual booth and had just gotten another review question right.

Another word appeared in his hand—*forte*. He looked at his choices and threw it at the man flexing his muscles. More fireworks and more points.

"Round one complete," a voice said. Derick glanced at his score. Not bad for reviewing his first Portuguese vocab list. "Round two!" the voice said.

The world changed. Derick stood in front of an array of sleek racing motorcycles, designed for the air to streak over them and their riders. He picked a dark red one with silver flames painted on the side. As he mounted it, he noticed that his virtual self was dressed in a racing suit and helmet. He started it up and could hear the quiet purr of the engine. He could get used to this.

An announcer said something Derick couldn't understand in Portuguese. Maybe he could understand later after he had studied more. A man with a checkered flag waved. Derick twisted the throttle and jolted forward.

The same narrating voice spoke another Portuguese word, this time slowly and deliberately: "*rápido*." It then gave the definition: "fast." Derick was living that definition. As he looked ahead on the track, he saw a series of words floating over the race course. He found *rápido* and drove through it.

More points.

Derick continued for another five minutes, driving through all twenty of his vocab words of the day. Then after the race was complete, his motorcycle and its world faded. "It's almost time to go," his teacher said. "Please exit your booths and gather any belongings." Derick obeyed. On his way out, he checked the console again; he'd found where he could insert the sphere his grandfather had given him. He hoped *that* world was at least a fraction as awesome as his Portuguese review had been.

"Thanks for your work today," the teacher said. "It's a good start to learning a beautiful language." It was kind of pretty, but Derick hadn't switched his schedule just to learn a beautiful language; he was tired of not understanding Rafa.

"We may use other game tools to review in the future, but the booths are mainly used to put you in scenarios where you have to speak Portuguese with people who speak like real natives." Interesting. "Before you go," his teacher continued, "I believe your student body officers have an announcement."

A group of five students wearing matching jackets appeared in the virtual room. "Good morning, Cragbridge Hall!" a blond girl said. "And welcome to your second semester." She had a little too much pep in her—or maybe hanging around Carol had just made Derick hypersensitive. "There are going to be a lot of great activities coming up soon, like the virtual games for those in ninth through twelfth grades." A long groan echoed through the room. Their class were all in seventh grade. Derick could just imagine how fantastic it would be to use the virtual booths for contests. "But the big news is, of course, the dance." The room suddenly filled with images of royal balls, castles, parties at the White House, dance halls from the early 1920s. "We need suggestions and some decorations for this year's theme—so submit them to dance committee through your rings." A boy chimed in: "And remember that boys in grades nine and up should ask a girl out for the occasion, while those in seven and eight should not. For you, it's a large group event."

Derick wouldn't have to ask anyone for a few years. Good. No pressure from Carol. Wait. Scratch that. *Less* pressure.

A different girl, this one with a streak of green in her hair, continued, "I get the best—or perhaps the worst—of the announcements for driven students like us. You'll all be distracted for the next several minutes. Here it is: Your first semester grades have just been posted. Simply sync up to your Cragbridge Hall account."

Immediately all the students in the class began typing with their rings. Derick thought he might be one of the quickest. He was usually the winner in a search battle. And there were his grades—an impressive array of As. He did feel his heart sink a little as looked at an A minus. Who would give him an A minus? *Music?* Of all his classes he got an A minus in *music*? He wasn't even playing an instrument—it was music appreciation. Did his teacher not feel that he appreciated music enough? Derick could tell this was going to bother him for a very long time.

• • •

Abby moved slower than her classmates as she guided her rings. Not only had Bubbles destroyed her bridge, but now she had to look at her last semester's grades. She wasn't sure she wanted to know.

Before punching in the last few letters of her password, she paused. She was going to have to see them sometime. Might as well get it over with.

She looked at the list:

English: B minus. Good. Ms. Entrese had liked her Sherlock Holmes report. At least her grade was higher than it had been at midterms.

History: C. She wished she could blame that one on putting her last history teacher in jail, but he didn't have any control over her grades; he'd been rightfully fired. The C came from his replacement.

Gym: B plus. Thankfully she was a good runner. That had kept her grade up.

Zoology: D. Ugh. That was the worst grade she had ever received in her life! Any time she spent in the avatars felt like a new lesson in being awkward. Awkward she excelled at. Unfortunately, no one gave her points for that.

Three more classes and they were all Cs. Abby closed her eyes and blinked hard. She wouldn't cry, not after the announcement that they could finally check their grades. Besides, Jacqueline might be watching.

There was a number underneath her grades.

Class rank: 500

500? That couldn't be good. She quickly opened a new window with her rings and searched the Cragbridge database for the number of students in her year.

500.

She was the very bottom of her class.

Abby felt like she was going to be sick. One D, a few Cs, and she was at the bottom of her class. It would have been different at any other school in the world—she would have been an average student—but at Cragbridge Hall, she was apparently the worst.

Two lines popped up under her grades. What kind of message goes underneath your grades? If Grandpa had anything to do with it, it was pep talk about how grades didn't really measure a person's intelligence and that she should just keep trying her best. Unfortunately, Grandpa apparently didn't have anything to do with it. Abby's heart sank as she read the words:

> Due to your performance, you have been placed on academic probation. If we do not see significant improvement, you may be dismissed from Cragbridge Hall.

Jacqueline was right.

# THE IMMORTAL GAME

Abby swallowed hard. Probation? Dismissed from the school? Jacqueline said they could do this, but had anyone ever been dismissed? Or would Abby be the first if she didn't get her grades up? The worst in Cragbridge history?

And if she was dismissed, where would she go? Her brother, her parents, and her grandpa all lived on campus. They wouldn't make her leave, would they? No. She'd probably just have to do online classes through another school. Ugh. Compared to three-dimensional history, seeing people's imaginations, and building her own virtual bridges, that would seem intolerable. She had to get better grades.

"That's enough time on grades." Mrs. Trinhouse said. "Be careful what you think about them. Even if your grades are high, it doesn't mean that you've mastered a subject—or that you are any better than anyone else. Your grades only measure your performance on tests, quizzes, and assignments. That is all. I have seen many a student not live up to their potential because a good grade was their only goal. The goal should be learning, becoming better. That is what you should care about most." Abby liked what Mrs. Trinhouse was saying, but she couldn't help but think she was directing her comments to Abby more than the other students. Did she know? "I have heard that when Oscar Cragbridge began this school, he wanted to do away with grades entirely, but because of the powers that be, he finally gave in. Just remember that grades are important . . . but they are not the final destination."

The hum began, signaling the end of class. The students all got up to leave.

"So, Abby." Jacqueline walked up Abby's row. "Your bridge was cute until it crumbled. A pile of rubble isn't as attractive."

"I'll get better," Abby said, shutting down her rings. "It was just my first shot."

"If you think so," Jacqueline said, twisting some of her hair from behind her shoulder to in front. Of course it looked great either place. A few of Jacqueline's friends stood behind her and giggled. "And how were your grades?" Jacqueline asked. "Mine were in the top sixth percentile of our year."

Of course they were. Jacqueline must have ignored Mrs. Trinhouse's speech. No surprise. "I'd guess they were in exactly the sixth percentile," Abby responded. "Otherwise you wouldn't have said it that way. You wouldn't include any people that got grades slightly worse than you in your group."

"Got me," Jacqueline said, followed by a giggle. Jacqueline's friends weren't smiling anymore. Perhaps their grades weren't quite in the sixth percentile. "So you're not completely brain dead, but by the way you reacted when I asked, I would guess that your grades weren't in the top anything."

Most of the students had filed out of class now.

"Well, thanks for talking to me," Abby said, her words soaked in sarcasm. "It's always good to have you come build me up." She stood up to leave.

"Some things aren't worth building up if they are just going to come crumbling down," Jacqueline said, mimicking something falling apart with her fingers. "Maybe now we can get someone who deserves to be here instead." Jacqueline turned and left, still as fashionable and venomous as ever.

Abby slowly walked up the row, reminding herself not to react when Jacqueline provoked her. She knew she had something to offer, knew she belonged here. Well, she had known it until she'd learned she was on probation.

"Mrs. Trinhouse, I have a question," Abby said, approaching her teacher. Mrs. Trinhouse gestured for her to wait as she flicked her fingers a few more times. She was probably checking messages. With any luck, she hadn't seen or heard any of Abby's conversation with Jacqueline.

"Yes?" Mrs. Trinhouse answered.

"Is there a way I can use one of the booths to practice?" she asked.

"Of course," Mrs. Trinhouse said. "These are open during the same hours as the Bridge labs. Unlike the Bridge, there aren't virtual booths in the dorms, but here we have several worlds available for you to practice with. Over time, you can create your own."

"Thanks," Abby said, and started out the door.

"Oh, and Abby," Mrs. Trinhouse said, "I wanted to make sure that everything was clear about your grades and your probation."

Abby glanced toward the door, making sure Jacqueline was out of earshot. "Yeah. I mean, I think so. If I don't bring up my grades then I'm out." She hated saying the words and hoped her face wasn't reddening quite as much as she thought it was.

"Essentially, yes. But that doesn't mean that you can't have help. Keep tabs on your grades throughout the semester. If your grade in my class starts to slide, come see me. We'll see what you can do to bring it back up. Of course, if you study and spend some time practicing like you just asked about, you should be fine."

"Thanks," Abby managed. At least someone was on her side.

She stepped out into the hall to see shiny black hair and an evil smile. "Problems?" Jacqueline asked.

If there was any one person in the whole school, in the whole world, from whom Abby would love to keep her probation a secret, it was Jacqueline. And if Abby had to guess,

Jacqueline had heard the whole thing. Abby walked away and tried to steel herself for whatever would come next. Jacqueline didn't follow her, but she was not one to let something like this go. She would do something.

As Abby walked down the hall, her rings vibrated. *Here we go. Here comes the taunting.* But as she scanned the message icon, it wasn't from Jacqueline.

Muns.

Abby stepped to the side of the hall to get out of the flow of students walking to their next classes. Why was he sending her another message? To congratulate her and all those who sided with her grandpa for stopping him on the *Hindenburg?* No way. But if he did, it might be enough to cheer her up after a slew of bad grades.

She ran the same security checks on the message as she had before. Once again, it was clean, and once again, she clicked on the video to see Muns in a suit with his slicked-back hair.

"Hello again, Abigail," he said. He sat in the same cushy chair in the same exuberant office. "I thought perhaps that I owed you a follow-up chat. Sadly, I have not heard from you or from your friends . . . at least nothing worth mentioning." Abby smiled remembering that Carol said she was going to tell him to take a flaming leap into a lake of gasoline. She also said she was going to recommend he play Dracula or Satan in a movie. Perhaps she had really sent the message. "I'm left to assume you are siding with your grandfather, or still deciding. I hope to be more persuasive today."

Persuasive? Muns just lost. What could he say?

102

He shook his index finger, a large ring at its base. "I'm not sure if you were involved at all in a certain . . . *incident* a few nights ago. I was hoping it would have ended with the safe landing of a magnificent dirigible, saving more than thirty lives as well as a fascinating transportation industry. But sadly, someone—or someones—let the tragedy happen all over again. We had the chance to stop it, and they stole it from me. Those who do not share my vision prevented a great intervention prematurely."

Abby's heart beat faster hearing Muns himself admit they had beat him. It felt great to think that the man who had been so confident was now at least set back in his plans.

Muns leaned forward in his chair. "Of course, I could only see anyone who entered into the past. This time it was not you. It was a new face, someone I hadn't seen before. I am hoping that you heeded my warning and stayed clear of this. If you did not, you cannot keep such things secret from me for long."

Yep. Still really creepy.

He leaned back again. "Abby, perhaps you enjoy a good game of chess." He moved his arm to show a checkered board on his desk with pieces intricately carved to look like soldiers, castles, and royalty. The base of each piece appeared to be solid gold. Abby noticed both the king and queen pieces had what looked like real jewels in their crowns. The pieces did not stand in their starting positions, but as though a game were in progress.

Chess was not where Abby would have guessed Muns was heading with his message.

"I am quite the chess fan; I am known to be rather good at it. I think that for today's message, a history lesson might prove helpful. I will use your grandfather's Bridge to show you."

Abby's temperature rose. Muns had broken into her grandfather's house and stolen that Bridge.

The image cut away from Muns. Abby saw the faded image of two men sitting across from each other at a restaurant with a chessboard between them. At least it was a faded image. Muns could not mess with this past without storing up for another energy burst or gaining two more keys.

The men wore old-fashioned suits and one had a beard that only grew underneath his jaw. She was glad *that* fashion hadn't returned. "The first real international chess tournament," Muns narrated, "was in London in 1851, and the man with the beard won. He was a German named Adolf Anderssen." Abby watched as the two men exchanged moves, stroking their chins and evidently thinking very intensely about each move. "But this game is very famous. It was called 'The Immortal Game,' and it happened at a local restaurant between rounds of an official tournament."

Why did she care about the history of chess? Was Muns trying to bore her into submission? "Watch closely," Muns continued, "and see if you can determine why this game earned such renown." Abby didn't really play chess. She knew the rules, but she didn't have the patience for it. She doubted she would notice anything. But as she watched, the man with the strange beard lost piece after important piece. His opponent captured his pawn, his bishop, then the two that looked like castles, and then he lost the piece Abby knew was the most important—his queen. All this time, his opponent had lost only three pawns, the least effective pieces on the board. The Bridge simulation paused.

"It is interesting," Muns said, "that to the untrained eye, this may not seem like an 'immortal' game at all. In fact, it may seem like a fairly pathetic showing. A casual observer might think Anderssen was doomed, that with each move his opponent grew closer to victory. But Anderssen was the master of the gambit. He would sacrifice pieces, letting his opponent build confidence, letting him think he had the advantage, but all the losses were deliberate and were calculated to set up the victory." The game started again, and in a matter of a few short moves, Anderssen—the man who had lost all his important pieces—won. Checkmate. Game over. Each move, including the losses, had lured his opponent into a trap.

The scene faded from Anderssen smiling at his victory to Muns at his desk. "Your grandfather and all those who side with him have a very important question to ask themselves: Did they just win a victory, or did they fall for a gambit? If what we are playing is an Immortal Game, one that will be more famous than any other before—and I am also a master of the gambit—your grandfather and his followers may have just fallen into a trap."

Half of his mouth curled up into a smile. "I must warn you, Abby. This battle is about to . . . ," he searched for the right word, "*escalate*." His smile broadened. "Those who oppose me"—his smile disappeared—"will first tremble in fear,

and then they will lose. Checkmate." Muns moved a chess piece on the board in front of him, then toppled over the opposing king. "Leave this alone. If not"—his eyes didn't blink—"I will treat you like the rest."

Abby quickly sent another message to her grandfather.

# THE SENTINELS

Derick hadn't given his grades another thought.

He sat in a class where he recognized almost no one. It was another change from his original schedule. He could feel his heart thumping.

The hum for class to start sounded, but there was still no teacher. Derick struck up a conversation with the brunette sitting next to him. She was two years older than him and absolutely loved squirrel monkeys; apparently a squirrel monkey named Miss Baker was one of the first two creatures to be sent into space and return alive.

"Good morning," Dr. Mackleprank said, walking slowly into the room. "I apologize for being late. It shouldn't happen again." Perhaps he didn't teach a first period and had slept in after all the excitement over the weekend. Or perhaps he was sore. Chances were he hadn't had to flying kick anyone in a while.

He sat on the desk at the front of the room, letting his legs dangle as usual. Something about it seemed slightly different, less natural. Again, probably sore. "Because this is an advanced avatar class and you were all invited to be a part of it," Mackleprank said, "you have shown a certain degree of competency with the avatars, as well as knowledge about the animals you have studied so far. However, because this is an advanced avatar class, I will also expect advanced performance." Derick couldn't help but remember the teacher spinning through the air. He would love to see what he could do in an avatar. It would definitely be advanced. Mackleprank was completely qualified for his job.

"Most of you are in your third year and have mastered the squirrel monkey, as well as having worked on the rhino and the gorilla." In their third year? So most were the same age as the brunette he had spoken to. Derick was still in his first year. No wonder he didn't recognize most of the other students in this class. He sat up a little taller in his seat.

"But today, we're going to challenge you," Dr. Mackleprank said. "Follow me." The class followed their teacher down a hall that was something like a path in a zoo. Off to either side were various habitats with live beasts inside. Derick had seen it many times, but still loved looking at the rhinos and gorillas. Both species were usually not very active—though the trees full of squirrel monkeys were always filled with chaos and movement.

*Fish. Please say fish.* The idea of darting through the

water with fins and gills sounded fantastic. Derick had seen lines of fish avatars on the shelves in the lab. He had seen the massive aquariums. In fact, they were approaching them now.

But they didn't slow down.

Okay, so maybe not. As they passed the aquariums, Derick watched all sorts of vibrantly colored fish swimming effortlessly through the water. One day, hopefully soon, he would be in there with them . . . *as* them.

Maybe they were going to the bird habitats. That would be even better. He could only imagine what it might feel like to glide across air currents and shift with the wind. But were the birds in this direction?

"Giraffes," Dr. Mackleprank said, as they approached a large glass wall with a safari-like scene behind it. The tall, lanky animals reached their long necks up into the trees and pulled off leaves with impossibly long twisty tongues and chewed, their jaws moving in a bizarre circular fashion.

Giraffes? Derick's stomach sank. Who would want to be a *giraffe*? So they had long necks—that might be thrilling for a minute or two, but after he got used to having a head higher than a basketball hoop, what else would possibly be interesting? He could get the same experience climbing a ladder. He didn't need to waste avatar time for that. Plus, this was an advanced avatar class—weren't they supposed to be doing something advanced?

"I can tell this isn't what some of you had in mind," Dr. Mackleprank said, still moving slower than normal, "but we've found it is rather helpful in the development of your skills."

He continued. "Some things you should know about this lanky wonder: Its Latin name is *Giraffa camelopardalis*; it is the tallest animal that walks on land. You may have heard the word *camel* in the root of its Latin name. If you will look at our giraffes," Dr. Mackleprank gestured toward the room filled with the towering beasts, "you will notice the hump to support the neck." He pointed at a giraffe slowly swinging its head from one branch to another for more food. Derick noticed the hump. He also noticed how lurpy the creature seemed to be . . . or, rather, how lurpy it seemed it *should* be. The giraffe seemed like it should move awkwardly, almost stumbling over itself, but it didn't. In a way it was graceful. "It also has ossicones on its head. That's the technical term for its stubby horns." They looked like the bottom ends of two black canes poking out of the giraffe's scalp. "But of course, the giraffe is best known for its neck. Anyone want to guess their height?"

A few students gave it their best shot.

"They usually range from sixteen to twenty feet, or from just under five to just over six meters. Not only are they tall, they are heavyweights. The average female weighs a little less than a ton, and the average male about 3,500 pounds. These guys are not light."

Dr. Mackleprank motioned again for the students to follow him, and walked them back to the classroom. Passing the other animals seemed like torture. Derick didn't have to try the fish or bird avatars; couldn't they just swing from some more branches as squirrel monkeys? Or spend some more time perfecting the big powerful movements of a rhino?

Dr. Mackleprank just kept teaching. "Other animal herds, such as zebras, like to stay close to giraffes. Any idea why?"

"Because they're tall and can see predators coming," Derick mumbled. The giraffe's one talent.

"Correct," Dr. Mackleprank said, pointing at him. "They can serve as sentinels. But if predators get too close, a giraffe isn't helpless." The class, now back in their desks, watched as Dr. Mackleprank flicked his rings and footage of giraffes in the wild played on the classroom's wall screen.

Derick watched a giraffe turning, almost spinning in its half-awkward, half-graceful way. It looked confused. Maybe they were lanky *and* dumb. Then Derick saw the lions.

Derick moved up in his seat.

The lions crouched low to the ground, creeping up on their prey. One sprang out from hiding, its paws raised, claws out, ready to grab onto the giraffe's hind leg.

It didn't make it. The giraffe kicked back and caught the lion midair, knocking it back like a rag doll.

"Ooohh," the class called out.

"Rejected!" Derick added.

The giraffe lurched forward, flinging its front legs stiff and straight. The lions backed up quickly to avoid the attack. "A giraffe," Dr. Mackleprank explained, "will do its best to defend itself and its kick can injure—or kill." The image faded.

"Giraffes can also battle among themselves for dominance." New footage started. Two giraffes stood hip to hip. It looked like the two were just good buds who liked to stand close to each other—really close. Bizarre.

And then it happened.

One of them swung its neck and crashed its head into the other's body. It was like the neck was a giant chain and its head a wrecking ball. The other quickly responded by slamming its head into its opponent. Crunching sounds rang out through the class. They were *definitely* not acting like friends.

"Ooohh!" the kids in the class cried out again.

Derick's heart beat faster. He had no idea giraffes could do that.

"The giraffe's neck is built to be able to take the pressure," Dr. Mackleprank commented.

Out of the corner of his eye, Derick saw many girls who couldn't watch, but he couldn't look away. The two beasts stepped forward, then backed up again, each trying to keep the other on their hip. As soon as one attacked with its head, the other responded. Crunch. Crack. One blow knocked the other up off its feet for a moment before it came back down.

"That's enough power to move a nearly two-ton opponent. There is a lot of force behind a giraffe's attack." Giraffes were so much cooler than they had been a few minutes ago.

After a few more blows, one of the giraffes surrendered, disappearing into the trees.

"That's it for instruction today," Dr. Mackleprank said. "So feel free to move into your lab spaces, hook up, and begin to practice. Begin with simple movements. Then try to pick something up from the ground. You'll have to stick at least one leg out to the side. It will be tough to keep your balance. If you would like to try to kick or hit with your head as you've seen here today, you can, but be sure to hit one of the hanging pads in each of your labs. However, I should warn you that being a giraffe will take practice. We simply aren't used to having our head so far away from our legs. Also, whipping that head around can be quite dizzying."

Before stepping into his lab and hooking up his sensors, Derick let the other members of the class filter out into their assigned spots. He approached Dr. Mackleprank. "Thanks for letting me into this class."

"Oh," Dr. Mackleprank looked at him. "You deserve it."

"Thanks. I'm not sure that's true, but I appreciate it." Derick lowered his voice. "And after having seen you fight, I'm not so sure I want to race you anymore."

Dr. Mackleprank's eyes opened wider for a second. He probably didn't expect Derick to bring it up here. Dr. Mackleprank looked around and then let out a tired laugh. "Well, you'd have to expect that the teacher of a certain subject would have the ability; otherwise why would they teach?"

"And thanks for the locket," Derick whispered. "I finished the challenge and got a final key."

Dr. Mackleprank smiled and whispered back. "Well

then, another set of congratulations are in order. Not many people can do that."

That last phrase rang in Derick's ears. It was a true statement. Not many people could do what he had done. He had and would do great things. No more failing. No more losing—and no more worrying about it.

Derick stepped into his own booth, his own lab space. He hooked up his sensors and his suspension system. He pulled down the large visor and selected his giraffe avatar. Almost immediately, he became disoriented. It was like he was looking down from the roof of a house. He had never been this tall. He looked to his left and saw a tree. Not the trunk, but three-fourths of the way up the tree was at eye level. It was like they were equals. He glanced down. His feet . . . his hooves . . . were so far away. This was better than he thought.

He took a step. Whoa. He stumbled a little, which led to a little more. He could only stop himself when he leaned up against the wall. He must have stepped on something. Most of the avatars came pretty naturally to him.

He took a deep breath and took another step. He nearly toppled forward. He felt completely off-balance. What was going on here?

What if he wasn't going to be any good at this? No. He would get it.

"Here we go," he whispered to himself. After a little practice, he could walk. He didn't feel sturdy, more like a little baby—every step was unsure. He slowly felt more secure.

Finally, with only five minutes left in class, Derick felt confident enough to try to swing his head at one of the pads. He reeled back and let his head sweep through the air. He felt it hit the pad with a snap, the pressure pushing against his cheek. It hurt, but it wasn't anything he couldn't take. He made a mental note to try to hit more with the stubby horns and less with his face.

Awesome. That was a lot of power. But he couldn't stop his momentum. One moment Derick was relishing the force of the hit, the next he was flat on his side, his straight legs wriggling around.

He tried to maneuver himself up, but his legs stuck straight out, giving him no leverage. He shifted to one side, hoping to roll back up somehow. He only succeeded in toppling more. He pushed his head against the ground, hoping to prop up the rest of his body. Just when he thought it was about to work, he fell back to the ground.

He hoped Dr. Mackleprank wasn't watching. He hoped no one was. Maybe he shouldn't be in the advanced class. Maybe he wasn't gifted with the avatars at all. He sighed and pushed the button on the back of his neck.

He had just hung up his equipment and was walking out of the thick doors that kept the avatar lab locked up and safe when his rings vibrated. A message from Muns.

# THE COUNCIL
# OF THE KEYS

O nce his visor was on, it was as though Derick sat in a completely different room—not the virtual booth he was actually in, but a conference room with a large mahogany table and black leather seats surrounding it. Derick sat in one chair and, as he surveyed the rest of the room, saw faces he recognized—Abby, Coach Horne, Coach Adonavich, and Grandpa. Each sat around the same virtual table. But there were two unfamiliar faces—a black couple. The man had broad shoulders and a beard. The woman was thin with short cropped hair.

Grandpa stood at the head of the table, wearing his usual blazer with the Cragbridge crest. His brow was furrowed, his beard and what white hair he had left looked more haggard than usual. "Thank you all for coming. I usu-ally prefer to meet in person, but this may prove to be more suitable under the circumstances." Derick didn't know what that meant. "I don't think we can be too careful when Muns may be involved."

"This meeting has been called as a precaution, but it is quite historic." Grandpa gazed at each person in the room. "Throughout your lives, every one of you has gained my trust." Derick looked from face to face imagining what the situations might have been that led to Grandpa's trust. "All of you know my secret, and carry a key to the Bridge, and have the power to manipulate time if accompanied by two others with keys." He introduced everyone. The black man and woman were a married couple, Mr. and Mrs. Trinhouse. He thought he had heard Abby mention that Mrs. Trinhouse was one of her teachers.

Wait. Mom and Dad. They had keys. Why weren't they here?

Mr. Trinhouse raised his hand and interrupted. "I thought there would be more of us, and I definitely didn't expect your grandchildren."

"I admit," Grandpa said. "There are more who know my secret and have keys, but I have decided to let you know only some of the others. It at least partially protects the identities of those with keys, and therefore protects them from our enemies." Derick thought he saw the wisdom in that. Grandpa explained how Muns had tried to gain the keys last semester, but had only succeeded in gaining one.

"I'm fine with not knowing everyone with keys," Mrs. Trinhouse said. "But have we given much thought to removing the need for protection? I know it may sound drastic, but perhaps we should destroy all the keys. Wouldn't that stop Muns and eliminate this danger?"

Derick liked Mrs. Trinhouse's style. She was quite animated as she spoke, but not overbearing, pretending to know it all. She was simply presenting a possibility.

"That is an interesting hypothesis," Grandpa said. "And if we could do it thoroughly, it would be a good solution. The danger lies in the fact that if just one person asked to return their key presents a counterfeit, or if one or two others refuse or depart without returning their keys, then we potentially leave Muns with all of the power. I'm not willing to risk that. I purposefully left keys to those I trust and there, I believe, lies our best safety."

"But Muns has a key," Coach Horne said. "Isn't there a chance that he can copy the key he has?"

"No," Grandpa said. "I won't bore you with the details, but each is unique, like a snowflake. The keys rearrange their internal codes continually. There is no way the code can be cracked or copied. If someone tries to open a key to see how it is configured inside, the key will self-destruct. There's not an explosion, but the key will no longer work."

Derick appreciated that the key he always carried in a secret compartment in the bottom of his pocket was not explosive.

Grandpa paused for a moment. When no other questions immediately surfaced, he continued. "For lack of a better name, I think I will call you the Council of the Keys. I must stress that you must keep each other's identities a secret. If Muns has any other traitors working at Cragbridge

Hall somehow, he would desperately want that information. He needs the keys we hold. This was why we did not meet in person. If a mole suspected any of you, it would have been easier for them to tail you and discover the others."

Grandpa had thought of everything.

"Muns already knows some of us that oppose him from the incident at the beginning of the year. In a bold move, he has contacted Abby and Derick as well as Carol Reese and Rafa Da Silva, four students instrumental in saving me and keeping my secret safe several months ago." Grandpa played part of Muns's message warning that something was going to happen and urging the kids to not get involved.

"Then, as some of you know, we recently had quite an incident." Derick listened as his grandfather described sending Dr. Mackleprank back into time to remove those who had intruded to try to change it. Every member of the Council had been there except for the Trinhouses. He must be bringing them up to date.

"But why would Muns tip us off by contacting the four students?" Coach Adonavich asked.

"We don't know," Grandpa admitted.

"I motion that we should actually do as Muns said," Mrs. Trinhouse proposed, "and not have students involved. Based on what little I know, it is too dangerous."

The two coaches both agreed.

No way. After all they had done? Besides, Derick wasn't too young to help. He hated it when adults thought he was too young. They underestimated him just because of his age. Unfair. He should at least get a shot.

"Though I agree that we should take care to protect them, they have proven themselves. Without them, my secret would be lost and Muns would already have the Bridge and the keys." Grandpa leaned forward across the table. "This school is founded on the idea of giving young people the very best—the Bridge, the Chair, avatars, you as teachers; the list could go on. We do it because we trust them to rise to the occasion. There are no four students I trust to rise more than Abby, Derick, Rafa, and Carol."

Mr. Trinhouse spoke, "I still agree with my wife that it may be in their best interest to—"

"No!" Grandpa banged his cane on the ground. Even in the virtual world it was loud enough to quiet everyone. "I am certain I want them and their talents as part of this council."

Derick's mouth curled up at the edge. *You tell 'em, Grandpa.* He saw Abby blink away a tear.

"We need all of us, including the students among us, to be ready at any hour," Grandpa said. "And we may just need all of us to defeat Muns." Though there wasn't open acceptance of the idea, no one opposed Grandpa.

"In fact, after this last incident, Muns contacted the four students again." Derick thought back on the message. Could it all have been a gambit?

"That message was one of the driving reasons for this meeting."

Grandpa showed part of that last message, showing Muns confidently teaching about chess and proposing that his last move had simply been a sacrifice for him to gain the upper hand. Derick knew that he, Abby, Carol, and Rafa had all alerted Grandpa about the messages they'd received.

"But how could that have given Muns the upper hand?" Coach Horne asked. "Those men didn't change the past and Dr. Mackleprank kicked their trash. Now they're locked up downstairs and bored to death."

"I'm not sure," Grandpa said. "But I want us to consider all the angles. It is possible that the briefcase is a piece to this puzzle." Grandpa gestured toward the Trinhouses.

Mrs. Trinhouse popped out of her seat. She used her rings to access something. "Oscar asked me and my husband to inspect the case." After moving her forefinger, an image of the brown leather briefcase appeared on the screen behind her. "We used Shandler imaging to see inside." The image on the screen changed to show the case, slightly transparent, criscrossed with overlapping lines—the outlines of what was inside. The colors of the various objects also overlapped. "Oscar was right to be cautious. There was a failsafe linked to the lock. You see there are a group of sensors on the case underneath the handle here. If we had tried to open it without putting in the right code, something in that container would release. It could be gas. It could be an acid that would destroy what was inside."

Derick squinted, trying to better make sense of all the lines. He thought he could make out the sensors under the handle and some sort of container attached to it, but he still couldn't tell what was inside the main body of the case.

Mr. Trinhouse took over. "Inside the case is a simple handheld device, about the size of your hand. From our imaging, I can't be certain what it does. Even if we could open the case and inspect it, I'm not sure I'd be able to deduce more. But I *am* sure that it is heavily password protected and coded."

He pointed to the bottom of the briefcase. "There is also another container here with some sort of solution inside, a series of small darts, and a long pipe or straw."

"Like blowdarts?" Derick asked, remembering them from movies where natives tranquilized explorers or other trespassers.

"Could be," Mr. Trinhouse said. "Perhaps they were going to tranquilize members of the *Hindenburg* crew."

"And then do something with the handheld device?" Coach Adonavich asked.

"That's our best guess," Mrs. Trinhouse admitted. "It's quite the mystery, but I'm glad we stopped them. We will continue to study the case. Perhaps with more concentrated image analysis, we could work out what the handheld device does."

"Thank you," Grandpa said. "Please let us know if you discover anything else." He turned to the entire group. "And, everyone, please ponder how Muns could use the position he is in now to strike against us."

# SPHERES

The Council of the Keys—Abby liked the sound of it. Even more, she liked the feel of it. Important. Historic. Also, she wasn't alone. She was one of them. Maybe sometime in the future, if all of this turned out well, someone would write a story about the Council of the Keys, and she would be in it. And she was the youngest member . . . by five minutes, but the youngest still the same.

As she walked down the hall with Derick and Carol, she was still trying to process everything she had just heard— the need to keep the Council's identity safe, the strange briefcase, and of course, Muns's message. If she was going to have a chance at making a contribution to something historic, she would have to do her best thinking.

Thinking. She wasn't as good at that as most everyone else here. In fact, she was number five hundred. Everyone was better at it than her. "I still don't know how Muns could use what he's done against us."

"Me neither," Derick admitted. "And I've thought it through a million times. He sent men in to change the past and we stopped them. They're in a cell in the basement."

Abby wanted to mention how she thought the briefcase had something to do with it, but she didn't know what Carol knew about that. She couldn't share too much information. And the Trinhouses seemed to be qualified to take care of it.

"All I know is that Rafa isn't that fun to talk to when he's a gorilla," Carol said. "It's mostly because gorillas can't speak. I do think we made an emotional connection, though. When I was telling him my theory about what causes a boy to break the threshold between being merely attractive to becoming the full package of hotness, he grunted a few times. Now those could have been I'm-bored-and-I-want-you-to-be-quiet grunts, but *I* think they were this-is-a-very-insightful-conversation-and-I-want-to-understand-you-better grunts. I'm pretty sure I can tell the difference."

"I don't know how to respond to that," Derick said, looking at Abby.

"Me neither," she responded. "But I still can't figure out how Grandpa knew where in time they were. Do you think that gizmo he made that senses an energy burst tells him?"

"I wouldn't think so," Carol said. "Those seem like two very different things."

"Agreed," Derick said.

"Couldn't he just use the Bridge?" Carol asked.

"How?" Abby asked. "How would he know where to look?"

"That's a good question," Derick said. "Maybe he has a spy in Muns's shop."

"That would be cool, but so dangerous," Carol said.

Abby pulled out her sphere from her pocket. "Grandpa prepared a way for us to find out. We've got to try these out."

· · ·

Derick rubbed his sphere, admiring its dim light one more time before placing it in the virtual booth's mechanical arm. He had no idea what he was about to see. He wondered if Abby would see the same thing in her booth. Probably not. Since each of the spheres only lit when they touched a certain person, that meant the spheres were meant only for them and whatever he was about to see was individualized.

At first, all he saw was the wrinkled face, bald head, and whispy white beard of his grandpa. "Hello, Derick," he said. "As you know, I have personalized this sphere for you. It glows with your touch. I'm glad you are searching for an answer, and I need you to find it. But when you find that answer, I need you to be prepared to know how to use it. And for that purpose, I designed this place for you."

Grandpa faded and a bustling city crowd appeared. Beneath skyscrapers, towers, and apartment buildings, swarms of people walked in every direction. A fountain stood at the center of many walkways, a park surrounding it. "As you probably know," Grandpa's voice entered, "when someone makes a world they can decide what rules to follow. At Cragbridge Hall this technology is typically used to study a variety of subjects using the rules that exist in our world. But what if I changed one of the rules? In this world, I have. Derick, what if you could turn invisible? What would you do?"

Invisible? Was that how Grandpa knew? Could he turn invisible and spy on Muns? No. That didn't make sense. That was something out of a fantasy or comic book. Grandpa was a man of science.

Derick looked at the crowd of people, each moving toward their next destination. He could see them, but could they see him? Was he invisible? He waved at a girl as she walked by. She smiled and waved back. Nope, not invisible.

"Hey. Were you flirting with my girlfriend?" A very large boy that Derick hadn't noticed next to the girl confronted him. Definitely not invisible.

"No." Derick said quickly. "Just waving." He waved again. "See. I'm waving at you right now. It's called being friendly."

The virtual boy didn't laugh or smile. "Just don't be friendly around me—or her. Get it?"

"Got it," Derick said as the virtual boy walked away. Grandpa's virtual world wasn't exactly inviting; apparently even virtual worlds had jerks.

An icon appeared at the top of Derick's vision, like a message he might see in his contact lenses, a simple outline of a person. Was that the symbol for invisibility? Using his rings, Derick pressed on the outline. Then he looked down—his shoes were gone. And his legs. And . . . everything else. Derick had completely disappeared. He lifted his hand, flipping it over, ready to see either his palm or the veins in the back of his hand, but there was nothing. It was as though he didn't exist.

He heard a woman gasp. Oh, no. He probably should have looked around before just disappearing. He moved behind a rebooting car. He pressed the outline again and reappeared. He waved at the woman, who blinked, shook her head, and continued walking. Hopefully, she wouldn't think too much about what she had seen. Then again, she was just a woman in this virtual world. It probably didn't matter too much.

This could be fun. He could spy on anyone he wanted. He could go to any concert or movie he wanted to for free. He could hang out unseen with groups of girls and listen to what they say when guys aren't around. He could do all sorts of stuff. As he wondered what to do first, it occurred to him that everything he'd thought of was wrong. It felt wrong. His grandpa and his parents wouldn't be proud of him invading people's privacy or cheating. But then, what good would it be to be invisible?

In the crowd, Derick saw someone grab a woman and begin to pull her rings from her fingers. In one swoop he got them all from one hand and began working on the next. He was definitely an experienced thief. If he could hack into her rings, he could drain her bank account, access her credit file—everything.

"Help," she screamed. "He's stealing my rings!"

Though it took the man another moment to finish the task, he was soon running through the crowd. A few tried to block his path unsuccessfully, but many either didn't hear or didn't know what to do. Or worse, they didn't care.

Derick moved behind a larger man and pressed the invisibility icon. He soon disappeared. He ran through the crowd, trying to dodge people as best he could. Occasionally he still bumped shoulders or tripped on legs. He hoped there were enough people around that a collision with an invisible boy wouldn't cause too much panic.

Derick began to catch up to the criminal. He burst through the crowd, the thief just ahead of him, an open shot through the park. Derick slammed into the criminal, sending him sprawling across the grass.

The man looked around, confused, and scrambled up again, trying to regain his speedy getaway.

Derick pushed him back down onto his backside.

"What?" the criminal cried out, his eyes darting around. "Who did that?" He tried to get up again.

Derick pushed the man a third time. This was fun. "You steal from women? What kind of heartless lowlife are you?" Derick said, using a line from a movie he'd seen.

"I . . . I . . . I'm desperate. I . . ."

Another shove.

"Why can't I see you?" The criminal screeched out, panicked. He scrambled to his feet again.

Derick thought quickly. "Because I'm a guardian angel." He rounded behind the man and pushed him from another direction. The criminal started swinging wildly in all directions.

"Leave me alone!" he screamed.

"You didn't leave that lady alone," Derick answered. He moved quickly to avoid being hit; his voice had given away where he had been. He snuck behind the man and tripped him. "Set the rings down and run away."

The man, terrified, quickly put the rings in a small stack on the grass. He got up to leave, but Derick knocked him down one more time. "If you ever steal again, I'll be watching."

The man mumbled something about never stealing again and then sprinted through the park.

Derick laughed to himself. This was fantastic. And he had done something good. He scooped up the rings, ducked behind a tree, and once again selected the invisibility icon, turning it off. He walked through the crowd, searching face after face. It took him much longer than he'd hoped to find the lady. "Excuse me ma'am," Derick said. "I got your rings back for you." He handed them to the woman, who hugged him.

"Thank you so much," she said. She tried to pay him several times, but Derick wouldn't take it. What good would virtual money do him anyway?

He turned and began walking again. What should he do next? There—the boy that told him not to look at his girlfriend. He could use a little lesson. Derick became invisible again and snuck up behind him. He was just about to trip the boy when he had second thoughts. This wasn't the same as stopping someone from stealing. This was just a guy who was being a jerk. Should he really terrify him? Was it right to do it because he'd made Derick feel bad?

Derick paused and watched as the boy walked farther with his girlfriend.

No. It didn't feel right. Derick stood there for at least half a minute. Still invisible, he was startled when a hand touched his shoulder. He turned to see his grandfather. Strike that—his *virtual* grandfather, who had draped his arm across Derick's shoulders. "Very good. You noticed that with unusual power comes some very difficult decisions. When do you use it? When do you not? When is it a case that warrants your gifts, and when is it not? Of course, I cannot make you invisible in reality as you are in this virtual world. That is no *direct* answer to your question. Though, in a way, there may be some similarities. If you truly seek your answer, you will need to wrestle with these decisions. You will need to be wise."

What could be similar to invisibility?

Grandpa continued, "If you feel that you have learned your lesson, then put your sphere back in the box and make the most of what happens to it."

• • •

"I was in this incredible world," Abby said from inside one of the booths. They had all crammed in for some privacy. "And I could see through walls. But the weirdest part was that Grandpa said that the answer was similar to my ability."

"I could turn invisible. And Grandpa said the answer was similar to that too."

"I knew tons of information," Carol said. "It was just instantly available to me—I would see someone, and their entire history would begin scrolling across my vision. I'd know so much about them. But I had to figure out what was important, when to use it, and I had to keep it a secret. I had to be more discretionary than I usually am. I think your grandpa has been conferring with my geography teacher."

Derick laughed. "So the question was how does Grandpa know *when* in time Muns attacked, and the answer is something similar to being able to turn invisible, see through everything, and know everything about everyone?"

"That seems a little over the top." Carol mimicked going over something with her hand.

"How could he do that?" Abby asked. "I mean, he has keys to see the past, but this is like stuff out of a comic book."

"Let's put the spheres back in the box and see what happens," Derick suggested.

Abby agreed and pulled the black box from her bag. Once again, she pressed the sensor on her belt, removed her key, and unlocked the box. The three of them placed their spheres in the open compartment, each within its indentation. At first nothing happened, but then each sphere began to glow, a bit brighter than before. Then one by one they dimmed to lightlessness.

"What just happened?" Abby asked.

"A little light show," Carol added.

"Whatever it was, let's make the most of it." Derick retrieved his sphere. Still synced up to the booth, he triggered its mechanical arm. He placed the sphere in its place and it slid back into the machine. "All right, ladies. If you'll excuse me, I've got to go into another virtual world."

Abby and Carol stepped out of the booth while Derick put his sensors and visor back on.

"I guess we should give it a shot too," Carol said. "What do you think the chances are that mine's turned into a world made of jelly beans and frosting?"

"Not good. That doesn't seem like Grandpa's style."

Just as they were about to enter their booths, Derick emerged from his.

"It's blank," he said. "It's been completely erased."

"*What?*" Abby gasped.

"Are you sure you didn't like drop it?" Carol stepped closer to look at the sphere Derick held in his hand.

"No. There's just nothing there."

Abby and Carol each stepped into their booths and discovered their spheres were blank as well.

"So what do we do when the spheres that are supposed to teach us have nothing on them?" Derick asked.

"I have no idea," Abby replied.

• • •

Abby thought she could feel bags under her eyes. The first classes of a new semester, bad grades from the previous one, a threat from Muns, the Council of the Keys, and trying to find out the answer to her question in a virtual world—it had been a very long day. With Carol by her side, she walked slowly toward their room.

"Decorations!" Carol squealed and ran down the hall to their door.

Sure enough, as Abby approached, she saw an array of paper and colors. "What's all this?"

Carol looked back, her eyebrows dipped toward her nose. "You know, I was absolutely sure that it was one of those cute ninth-grade boys breaking the rules to ask me to the dance . . . but it's Jacqueline. That girl must have swallowed some expired cottage cheese or some really sour lemonade . . . the kind that someone forgot the sugar—the lemon had no aid. She's made up another nasty rumor. It's not even that creative. I mean, she could have said that you still wet the bed, or you snore, or you have like a third arm you hide in the back of your shirt, or a tail. I guess that last one would be really hard to cover up, but you'd have to give her creative points if she made *that* up. But she didn't. So, no creative points for her. This was just mean." Carol motioned to the posters on the door.

Abby read bright glittery letters on posterboard: *It's been nice knowing you, Abby.* It wasn't the only one. The posters covered her entire door and some of the wall around it.

A poster just left of the door showed a girl with Abby's face wearing sunglasses and viewing a tourism guide screen with the caption: *Hope you enjoyed your short tour of where the smart kids learn.*

Another: *Bad Grades = Good-bye.*

Another showed a girl with Abby's head running from a pair of scissors: *Couldn't make the cut.*

Another was a calendar with pages you could rip off. *Days until Abby Cragbridge is kicked out of school for bad grades.*

"These could have been here most of the day." Abby realized how many people might have seen them.

"Yeah," Carol agreed. "But don't worry—people aren't going to just believe anything they read on a poster."

Abby bowed her head. "But it's true."

# FIRST STRIKE

Abby walked quickly down the hall. Carol was fast asleep and Abby didn't want to wake her. She didn't want to talk about her grades anymore. She didn't want to hear Carol say that she would totally get them back up where they belong. In fact, right then she didn't even want to worry about her homework. She wanted to figure out the mystery, to be like Sherlock. She wanted to try her virtual sphere again and see if she had missed something. There had to be another clue.

She slowed as she passed through the English hall. She spotted Ms. Entrese's classroom. The last time, it was Ms. Entrese who had played a huge role in helping her unravel the mystery. Abby realized that Ms. Entrese wasn't a member of the Council of the Keys and didn't know about Muns's threat. And that Muns would want revenge against her. Maybe Abby should step in and warn her if she was there. The light was on—maybe she was.

Abby opened the door to the English class. "Morning."

No one answered. Ms. Entrese probably just left the light on. She could still be in her apartment getting ready for the day.

Out of the corner of her eye, Abby saw something black on the floor behind the desk. She circled around to get a better look.

Her heart stopped.

She raced to Ms. Entrese, who was sprawled on the ground, motionless. "Ms. Entrese, are you okay? Can you hear me?" Abby grabbed her teacher's face, pulling it toward her. Her eyes were closed, her body limp. She shook her. No response.

No. Please no.

"Help!" Abby screamed over her shoulder, hoping someone was in the hall to hear. "*Somebody help me!*"

Abby lay her head against Ms. Entrese's chest and listened. Thump. It was faint. Thump.

Oh, thank you. She was still alive.

"Help me! Ms. Entrese is hurt!" she yelled again, then flicked on her rings. The Cragbridge Hall emergency line answered her call. "Help. I'm in Ms. Entrese's room and she isn't responding to anything I say."

The woman on the other end urged her to be calm and said that a team was on their way.

"Just hurry." Abby disconnected her rings.

Only when the medical team burst through the door

and began to care for Ms. Entrese did Abby break down into surging sobs. She cried and cried. What had happened? What had gone wrong?

The medical team placed Ms. Entrese's body on a wheeled stretcher and began to guide it out the door. One of them invited Abby to come with them. As she stood up, she noticed a small object on Ms. Entrese's desk. It was a wooden castle tower—a chess piece.

Muns.

. . .

Derick woke up to his rings vibrating.

Whoever it was could wait.

He rolled over, his thumb searching for the place on the ring to ignore the message. He tried twice. Something in the movement woke him up enough to remember the day before—Muns's message, the Council. One eye opened. He'd better check just to be safe.

It was a message from Cragbridge Hall administration:

**STAY WHERE YOU ARE.**

Derick opened the message:

> Good morning. We ask all students to stay where they are as the administration performs a routine safety check. Again, please stay where you are until notified otherwise.

Strange. If it was so routine, then why . . . Derick didn't finish his thought. He knew why—Muns.

He sat up in his bed, and sent messages to Abby, Carol, Rafa, and Grandpa. Rafa and Carol hadn't heard a thing, though Carol added a line that made Derick cringe:

> . . . but I haven't seen Abby all morning. We talked about waking up early to try out our spheres, but when I woke up she was gone.

Where was his sister?

Derick clenched his eyes shut. Muns wouldn't go after Abby, would he? There was no way for him to know if she had obeyed his message or not. Unless he knew about the Council of the Keys. But there was no way. Was there?

Derick didn't bother changing out of his pajamas. He didn't care that the school had mandated him to stay where he was. He burst out of his door. He would check the virtual booths, then Abby's dorm. He'd have to get permission to get in there, but he'd find a way. Halfway down the hall, his rings vibrated.

Please be Abby.

It was from Grandpa and entitled EMERGENCY.

> Something has happened. We need to meet.

It had to be another Council of the Keys meeting, but Derick wasn't changing his plan to look for his sister. He continued toward the school, but messaged his grandfather as he walked. *I can't find Abby.*

He made it halfway across the grounds before a reply came back.

She's fine. I will explain in a few moments.

Derick stopped.

You're sure?

Yes.

Derick took a deep breath. At least she was okay. He rushed down to a virtual booth where he could join the meeting. He didn't care that he was still in his PJs.

Grandpa stood again at the head of a virtual table. "Something has happened. Muns struck last night. Please pay attention as we discuss the attack; we will need all our intellects to figure this out. I recorded the first victim's testimony and would like you to hear it."

Victim?

Dr. Mackleprank appeared. He looked the same as he always did, though his blondish/whitish hair appeared far more tousled than normal. "This morning," he began, "I woke up to . . . this." The recording moved from the teacher's face to his room. It was a mess. Screens were detached from the wall, their connecting wires strung in every direction. An avatar rhino head lay upside down, a squirrel monkey on top, other unfinished avatars carelessly thrown across the floor.

Derick heard gasps from other members of the Council.

Dr. Mackleprank continued, "I would like to think that I would have been able to stop the intruder, but I never saw him. Whoever it was . . . well, you'll see. Oscar Cragbridge has authorized you to see the security footage."

Dr. Mackleprank disappeared and a view of a hallway took his place. One simple lamp partially illuminated a corridor. It was probably how all the halls looked in the middle of the night. A shadow moved down the hallway and gradually made its way to the door. The person wore a hood, and as a hand reached forward, Derick could see he was wearing gloves as well. The shadow attached a small device to the lock, then, after removing something else from a pocket and playing with the door handle, the figure slid the door open, making very little sound.

None of the Council said a thing as they watched the man slip quietly through the doorway. The shadow put something long and straight up to its mouth. Strange. It looked sort of like a straw. Derick heard a brief whir and a *thock*. A blowdart? Was it the same as the ones in the briefcase? "He hit me with some sort of tranquilizer," Dr. Mackleprank said, pointing to a small bandage on his neck. "I don't remember a thing."

Dr. Mackleprank rubbed at the bandage. "As you know, for our privacy, security cameras are not posted inside our quarters so you cannot see any more of what happened. All I can guess is that he was looking for a key—a key I didn't have. This must have some correlation to Muns. He must have attacked me because of my work with the *Hindenburg* incident. And if Muns was watching his goons trying to change the past, I would be the only one he would have been able to see."

"Oh," Dr. Mackleprank said, "and one more thing. Whoever it was left this." He held up a small horse head with his fingers—a chess piece. "I have no idea why. It isn't mine." The image of Dr. Mackleprank faded and those in the virtual room began to murmur.

"It had to be one of the men we took captive. But how did they get out of the basement?" Coach Adonavich asked.

"They didn't," Grandpa answered. He moved his fingers and showed security footage of the men's cell and then the prisoners themselves. "They were there all night. Absolutely no sign of anyone escaping."

"But no one could sneak into the school, could they?" Coach Horne asked.

"Doubtful," Grandpa answered. "Our security outside the school is as good as it gets. It is more likely that it was someone from the inside."

Derick noticed that the Trinhouses sat very quietly. Perhaps he knew why. "What about the straw and tranquilizer?" Derick asked. "I mean . . . are those the same ones that were in the briefcase, or were they just the same shape and size?"

Mrs. Trinhouse stood, her face somber. "It's the same straw and darts. I kept the case in my lab space at our apartment. I locked it in the room at night and it was there in the morning. I didn't suspect a thing until Oscar messaged me. I rescanned the case and . . ." she paused for a moment to rub her temples, "now it's empty."

"Was it the same guy who tranqed Mackleprank?" Coach Adonavich asked.

"We don't know," Grandpa said. A new clip of security

footage showed on the screen. "This is from the camera outside the Trinhouse's room."

The light flickered out and the scene went dark. Derick and the others watched an empty, dark hallway for a few seconds. "I don't see anything," Derick said.

"Precisely," Grandpa said. "There is no footage of anyone even approaching their door. Because the case was inside personal quarters, there is no security footage of the thief from inside."

"That's not all," Mr. Trinhouse said. "The device the man used to get into Dr. Mackleprank's room looks to be about the same size as the device we saw in the case. It's probably a lock-hacking computer to allow him into the room. To get in through our locks, though, it must be the best of its kind."

"So," Coach Horne started, "somehow someone breached our school's outer perimeter, then stole the tools out of a suitcase in a locked apartment so that he could break into a separate apartment? That doesn't make sense."

"No. No, it doesn't," Mr. Trinhouse said.

"It also seems strange that he would break into your room and not tear it up looking for a key," Coach Adonavich pointed out. "And he didn't tranquilize you."

"Very strange," Mrs. Trinhouse agreed.

"Wait," Coach Horne said. "He couldn't have used the handheld device to crack the lock of your apartment because it was locked inside the case inside your room. How did he get in?"

"We don't know," Mr. Trinhouse said.

"And you two were some of the very few who knew about Dr. Mackleprank's role in the *Hindenburg* incident," Coach Horne said.

Mrs. Trinhouse stood up. "Are you accusing us of something?"

"It does seem suspicious," Coach Horne said, his deep voice growing an edge.

"We didn't have *anything* to do with this," Mr. Trinhouse's voice rose with every word.

"Then where's the security footage? Why didn't he need to break in? Why isn't there any sign that he was there?" Coach Horne's voice escalated into a shout.

"Please!" Grandpa yelled, waving his arms, his cane in one hand. "We don't need to accuse one another. What little we have of the intruder's facial and body measurements, we ran through our security programs and found that whoever it is is not either of the Trinhouses."

"But who *does* it match?" Coach Horne asked.

"No one on record," Grandpa said.

Silence fell as everyone thought for a moment.

"Wait." Derick raised his hand. "He used the device from the briefcase. There is no reason the two intruders would have needed that on the *Hindenburg* hundreds of years ago. This was a setup. The *Hindenburg* was a gambit. It was all part of Muns's plan."

# DOESN'T FIT

M uns played us." Coach Horne pounded a fist into his other open hand. "And now he has someone with tranquilizer darts and some device that can let him through any locked door running around the school. What do we do?"

"And when will he strike again?" Mrs. Trinhouse added.

Derick shivered. She hadn't said "if." She said "when." He immediately thought of Muns's message. Muns wanted him to stay out of it. Was Derick on the list if he didn't? Could someone break into his dorm room in the middle of the night and tranq him? . . . and Abby, Carol, and Rafa? The thought sent chills pinging through him. If they ignored Muns's warning and got involved, Derick was sure that was what it meant. Muns did not cut corners when it came to revenge.

With more and more questions, the meeting began to spiral into chaos. Grandpa pounded his cane again to get everyone's attention. "I know you have questions, but I need to finish giving you the facts we know, though they are unpleasant."

There was more?

Grandpa swept the security footage away with his fingers. Derick saw a new image, a woman in a bed in the health center—Ms. Entrese! Abby sat next to her, holding her hand.

Grandpa flicked his fingers and showed another hallway—the whole scene shockingly similar. The same hood, same straw in the man's mouth, same gloved hands. But this time it was in a classroom.

"The security camera in the room malfunctioned, which is suspicious, so we did not see what happened." Grandpa scratched the side of his head. "But this was how Abby found Ms. Entrese this morning." Grandpa then told about Ms. Entrese's pivotal role in saving him from Muns several months ago.

"The dose in her tranquilizer dart was much higher," Grandpa explained. "Dr. Mackleprank's dart was designed to keep him out for the night. From the levels the doctors have detected, Ms. Entrese could be in a coma-like state for weeks . . . maybe months."

Mrs. Trinhouse gasped.

*Months?* Muns had not killed her, but he'd incapacitated her for a long time. He was not one to show mercy. He had risked Abby's parents' lives. He probably thought that he could finish this, that he could take over time travel by the time she woke up—and she would wake up to Muns's reality. That would be some heavy revenge.

"That eliminates one player," Mr. Trinhouse said. "I don't like this guy."

"Our security team is finishing a sweep of all the grounds now. We have also programmed our security cameras to recognize his silhouette and alert security immediately. If he comes anywhere near a classroom or apartment again, he will be met with a most unwelcoming party. I was tempted to close the school down until we find the intruder, but I believe that may be playing further into Muns's hands. He wants us to be afraid. He wants the students to be afraid. From what we can tell, whoever this intruder is, he poses no threat to the students—only to us, only to those who oppose Muns. School will continue as it has until this theory is proven otherwise. Keep this a complete secret."

Everyone agreed.

"However," Grandpa raised a hand in the air, "we cannot count on security to protect us. All of us must take great care."

"But if I had to guess, some of us have to take more care than others," Coach Horne said.

"Yes," Coach Adonavich said. "He is most likely targeting those he knows have taken an active role in stopping him. Coach Horne and I—and all the Cragbridge family—are probably next on the list."

•  •  •

It felt like ice had seeped into Abby's chest. She was probably on the list.

Grandpa had sent her the file of the Council meeting. He encoded it several times of course, and she had to answer several security questions before she was able to watch it. But she knew Coach Adonavich was right. Abby probably was on the list. Whoever it was that had attacked Dr. Mackleprank and Ms. Entrese would likely come after her if she got involved. The thought was terrifying—having someone coming after her in the night. Abby didn't know if she was going to be able to sleep ever again.

She continued to watch the video file. "With that said," Coach Horne added, "he would likely only put us out for the night and steal our keys. Putting someone out for months was probably a special revenge just for Ms. Entrese for having worked for him and then betraying him." Abby noticed the coach looked at Derick while he spoke. He was probably trying to soften the situation, soothe any fears.

"Yes," Grandpa agreed. "And it is most likely that he will target myself and the two coaches. He does not know whether or not my son, his wife, or their children have keys."

"That's possible," Mrs. Trinhouse said, "but the fact remains that if any of us have a key, he will want it. He only needs two more, so I wouldn't say the rest of us are in the clear. If anyone knows we have a key, they may come for it. Which is all the more reason to keep each other's identities secret."

Grandpa looked around the room. "Hall security has

been given every bit of what little information we could gather about the intruder and they are looking for him. They will also double their rounds, making special efforts in our halls. I did not give them your specific apartments to guard in order to keep our identities safe from anyone watching how we react to this intrusion. I have also scrambled all of the entrance codes to your rooms. I will add another layer of encryption after this meeting and you will need to devise a password which only you know and no one could ever guess. No cracking device like the one the burglar had—no matter how state-of-the-art—will be able to enter. We should all be safe now that we understand the threat. But I would suggest that 'safe' isn't good enough."

Grandpa flicked his fingers. A picture of a man with an old hairstyle, parted and bushy on the sides, with a ponytail in the back, appeared. He wore a waistcoat and a fluffy cravat. "This is Sir Edmund Burke, a member of the British Parliament in the mid-1700s. He is famous for a saying, a saying that I want you to remember very well from this moment on. I have stated over and over again that we should learn from history and not try to change it. Well, learn this lesson well. Burke taught, 'The only thing necessary for the triumph of evil is for good men to do nothing.'" Grandpa paused. "I propose that we do more than nothing. I propose that we do everything we can to tie up any loose ends to this puzzle and find the person who attacked Mackleprank and Entrese."

"But we don't have any leads," Coach Adonavich pointed out.

"True," Grandpa admitted. "And so far, the only people I'm sure I don't trust are the two in the cell. I'll question them and send you all a video of the interview. It is the only place I know to start."

Coach Horne raised his large arm. "May I suggest you use the Chair? We may get images for clues even if they won't talk."

"That is a fantastic idea," Grandpa said.

"And I mean no disrespect," Coach Horne looked at Mr. Trinhouse, "But to calm my suspicions, would the Trinhouses mind also sitting in the Chair and answering questions about that briefcase?"

"Not at all," Mr. Trinhouse said. "It is wise to check every avenue for clues and we are happy to help."

Mrs. Trinhouse nodded too, but slowly.

That sounded good. Though Abby liked Mrs. Trinhouse as a teacher, she had to admit something didn't feel right about the situation. There were too many unanswered questions. But if either or both of the Trinhouses had helped the criminal, or somehow one of them was the criminal, they would not likely agree to sit in the Chair.

The Sherlock inside of Abby thought it all sounded like a good way to move ahead. But something bothered her. It was Ms. Entrese. Not just that she had been attacked, but the way that it had happened. Muns always went through so much trouble to make his revenge fitting. Either he had abandoned his habits or this didn't seem to fit. Abby reviewed in her mind the details of Ms. Entrese's involvement in their last adventure to double-check if there was anything

Muns might have used in his revenge. Ms. Entrese had told Derick about Muns. She'd even brought Derick and Rafa's avatars to the place Muns had been holding Grandpa hostage. They had used gorilla and rhino avatars to free him from watching his own children die on the *Titanic*. How did getting shot with a tranquilizer fit as revenge for that? The *Hindenburg* was like a *Titanic* in the sky. That fit, but the only thing it had to do with Ms. Entrese being tranquilized was that the intruders from the *Hindenburg* brought the briefcase into Cragbridge Hall. It just didn't seem like Muns's style. There was a clue there somewhere. Abby wasn't sure what it was, but she was pretty sure it was there. If only she were more like Sherlock.

Then again, to figure out these clues, she might have to make it clear that she was involved, that she had ignored Muns's warning. Abby remembered what Grandpa had quoted about evil winning when good people do nothing. He was right, but when Muns had threatened and then shown what he could plan and succeed in doing, it was hard to volunteer.

# TRYOUT

Abby held her mom. She and her dad had met Abby in Ms. Entrese's recovery room in the med center. Though they weren't part of the Council, it seemed like they were up on most of the details. Maybe they had their own separate Council of the Keys.

Mom squeezed Abby. "I'm sorry you were the one who discovered Ms. Entrese. That must have been terrifying."

Abby agreed, trying not to relive it in her mind.

Dad paced the tile floor of the room. "This is insane. I'm still trying to figure it out—and figure out what to do next."

The door slid open and Derick and Grandpa stepped into the room. It had been announced that the school was finished with its routine safety check and would continue in another half an hour, all classes on a shortened schedule. Security had finished their rounds, but they found no one. The man must have fled to some unknown corner of campus. He couldn't possibly have escaped from the entire school. But for now they had determined the school was safe.

"I must admit," Grandpa said, walking with his cane in hand, "I'm full of both regrets and confidence. Part of me regrets getting you and Derick involved in this at all, Abby. As you have heard—and seen the evidence—we are in the middle of a very dangerous game. Perhaps Muns is right and you should no longer be involved." His face was stern, his wrinkles deep. "But the other part of me realizes that you are very capable of making very important contributions. In fact, just as last semester, you may prove to be entirely invaluable. You two have surprised even me with how resourceful and fearless you can be."

Surprised him? They had exceeded the expectations of a genius? That felt good. Yet Abby also felt the danger. A mix of pride and horror rolled through her insides.

"Should they sleep in our apartment?" Mom asked. "Or should we all move away from the school?"

"No," Grandpa said. "The school is the safest place for us, even with this incident. Outside these walls, Muns would do nothing but attack—and attack quickly. I'm not sure you would be any safer outside. I believe we are safe where we are. Do you trust me on that?"

Dad nodded. Mom looked grave.

Grandpa turned to Abby and Derick. "If you still choose to help, I need you to keep your eyes open; watch out for anything suspicious or unusual. You never know what may be the clue that leads to a resolution of this mess. Let me or Hall security know as soon as you can. The security is already on the lookout and there aren't that many places to hide. Chances are that we will have caught our person of interest in no time. But when there is as much on the line as there is with us, it never hurts to be extremely careful." He shifted his cane from one hand to the other. "Therefore, I am removing all restrictions from you two at Cragbridge Hall. I expect you to act like adults, so I will give you all the same privileges as adults. You can leave your room and your dorms at any time of day or night, especially if you suspect someone is coming after you. You also have to be available to go to the basement at any time. I would urge you, however, to live life normally until the situation calls for it. Do not make exceptions unless and until you find an exception necessary."

No restrictions. Abby was being treated like an adult.

The twins both nodded and thanked their grandfather. Mom was about to object, but Grandpa gestured to let him continue.

"I have also cloaked your rings' tracking system. I don't want teachers—or anyone else who may hack the system— being able find you two. If by chance anyone has bad intentions, as Mr. Hendricks did last semester, having your rings cloaked will prevent them from finding you. If they somehow find you anyway, and you are kidnapped or lost, I will remove the cloak and find you myself. I will do the same for Rafa and Carol. You can fill them in about the attacks, but not about those on the Council of the Keys—understood?"

Abby and Derick both nodded again.

• • •

Derick's mind whirled. Why did Muns even have to exist? Without him, Derick would be able to focus on school and friends and not have to worry about people sneaking into history to change it, messing up the balance of time, and destroying the world. That was a lot for any seventh grader to worry about. He wondered if he was safe walking around school. After what happened last night, he wasn't sure. But he did try to take Grandpa's message to heart.

The only thing he knew to do was to try to find the answer to the question Abby had asked. But his sphere was still empty. He had just tried again, hoping that somehow it would be different this time. He was about start in on some homework—another round of Portuguese vocab—when a message came from Rafa:

> Derick, the guys said that it's a possibility for you to come avatar with our club, but they want to meet you first before anything becomes official, kind of like a tryout. We are meeting in fifteen minutes. Can you make it?

Avatar club. Oh, he wished he had time to focus on that. He wished Muns hadn't struck, that he didn't have to find the answer to Abby's question, that he didn't have to figure out what to do with a newly blank sphere—it all felt more important than him getting into a club . . . even the avatar club.

Then again, if he suddenly changed what he was likely to do before, someone might notice. They might realize that he was siding against Muns and that might bring more trouble. Besides, he might get a little help with his Portuguese vocab hanging around Rafa.

He walked down the hall toward the avatar labs. He had made it through his shortened classes for the day. Zoology had been a little strange. Dr. Mackleprank taught as usual, but Derick thought that it seemed he had a lot on his mind. If he hadn't known, though, Derick never would have guessed that Dr. Mackleprank had been drugged and burglarized the night before.

The avatar club would be good, give him something other than Muns to think about.

Rafa met him at the door to the avatar lab. "Glad you could make it." Derick wanted to update him on everything that had happened, but that would have to wait. "Nervous?"

"Um . . . no," he lied. "Well, sorta."

"No worries. Just give it your best shot." Rafa led the way down the hall and into one of the small labs. "We decided it would be easier if we all met together as avatars and not in person. They know I recommended you, but they don't know who you are. If we only meet as avatars and things don't work out, no one feels awkward." Rafa handed him a set of sensors.

"Makes sense." Derick threaded on his black straps with sensors attached. "Should I grab a particular animal?" *Please don't say giraffe. Please don't say giraffe.* Derick had practiced in the lanky animal for a short time again that day and, though he'd improved a little, he knew he wasn't going to impress anyone.

"A gorilla."

*Yes!*

"And bring it to the field, room 1—the biggest one. We need the space. I'll turn on the audio system so everyone can hear each other."

"All right," Derick said, excited to step into anything but a giraffe. "Let's do it." He usually felt rather confident about his abilities, but he had to admit he was a little nervous. Being invited to hang out with the elite group of avatar controllers in an elite school could be a little intimidating. He heard the door click as Rafa left.

Derick selected his avatar, knowing the computer system would bring it to the room. "Here we go, Kong. Let's see if we got what it takes." After a brief wave of nausea, he stared out at the largest of the practice rooms. A gorilla, two squirrel monkeys, and a lion ran, swung, stretched, and pounced.

Derick just watched for a moment, taking in the scene, noticing their agility. They were good—really good. The lion crouched low to the ground and pounced, landing near the gorilla, who was in the middle of a backflip. He wouldn't have expected any less, but to see it made him nervous and excited all over again.

"Hey, back off. I'm still warming up," a boy's voice said. Though he wasn't in the same room, Derick could hear the boy's voice over the audio system just as Rafa said. "You enjoy your time as the so-called king of the jungle, because that is the *only* time you are going to rule anything tonight." The boy had a Southern drawl.

"You're wrong," a girl with a Latin accent responded. She had to be the lion. "I'll be queen."

A squirrel monkey leapt off a tree branch, flung itself into a backflip, and landed on a branch in the neighboring tree. It swung one-handed down two more branches, and then stuck a landing on the ground. It waved at Derick. "Hey, Tryout." It was another girl's voice. "So you call your gorilla Kong, huh? Not very original, but I guess it'll do."

"Yeah," a third girl's voice kicked in—probably the other monkey. "Sounds like Rafa hooked up the mic system quicker than you thought."

Derick could feel his face reddening. He was grateful that didn't come across on the avatar. "Yep. Busted. I'll try to keep the talking to myself to a minimum."

"Probably a good idea," the first monkey added. At least he thought it was the first monkey.

"Okay, but I do have some really interesting conversations with myself," Derick responded.

"I'm sure you do," the Latina lion said.

"Good to hear you've got some spunk and confidence," the gorilla with a Southern drawl added.

"I try," Derick said.

"Well, we'll see if your trying is good enough." That had come from one of the monkeys, but Derick wasn't sure he even wanted to try to keep track of who was saying what anymore.

Something about hearing their voices and the challenge

ahead excited Derick. He didn't feel as nervous. Plus, he had faced men with guns while he was in an avatar. He could do this.

"All right, everyone." Derick heard Rafa's voice—he was glad to hear a voice he knew for sure. He saw Rafa enter as a gorilla. "Good to see you've met our possible new guy. As we discussed, we'll do something we haven't done as avatars before so we don't have an unfair advantage. I figured since we have six people, we'd split into two teams."

"That would be fantastic if this guy made it," one of the girls said. "We could play a lot more sports if we had three on three."

"Don't get ahead of the game, now," the Southern drawl said.

Sports? Playing sports as animal avatars. Awesome!

Rafa lifted a ball. It was about the size of a volleyball, but red. "Handball."

"Never played it," the Latina responded.

"Is that even a real sport?" the Southern drawl asked.

"Yes, it is a real sport. It has been an event in the Olympics for over a hundred years," Rafa explained. "And of course I chose something you hadn't played before. That's the idea—something new to make it a little more even." Rafa's gorilla tossed the ball from one hand to the other. "Here are the rules. You can only take three steps with the ball and then you have to either dribble or pass. Once you pick up your dribble you can't dribble again until someone else has had the ball. You can use your body to block and defend, but you must be between the other player and the goal; you can't pull from behind or push from the side. And finally, you have to throw at the goal from outside a curved line around the goal—about nineteen feet out." Rafa motioned with his arm about how far out the arc would be. "You can jump from outside the line but you have to throw the ball before you touch the ground."

Okay, it sounded like a mix of soccer and basketball. Cool.

"I'll draw the lines and set up some makeshift goals while you switch avatars." Rafa thumped his hairy chest. "Let's go gorillas for this."

"I was hopin' for rhinos," the Southern drawl said.

"It would be tough to play handball in a beast that has no hands," a girl's voice countered.

"Just go change," Rafa said.

Derick couldn't believe it. He was about to play an Olympic sport with a bunch of robot gorillas!

From the moment they started, it was a crazed blur. At one point a gorilla passed the ball to his teammate, who flipped on her hands, caught it with her feet, and then shot it into the goal. Such acrobatics made it very hard to defend. Some gorilla bodies banged against each other harder than Derick thought they should. They were using very expensive equipment.

"So, I don't mean to be a stickler here," Derick said, "but don't we need to be careful with the avatars?"

"They are actually extremely durable," Rafa explained after he stole the ball from the opposing team. He paused in his explanation long enough to pass the ball to Derick, who whipped it around to the girl on their team. He didn't want to hold it too long. He knew the others were better than him. "They have to be. In order to interact with real gorillas, you have to be ready to bump bodies a little bit."

Hearing the explanation, Derick bumped a gorilla out of the way to make himself open. Oh, that felt good. He could get used to being a beast.

"Oh, I like *this* kid," the Southern boy said, coming back to bump into Derick.

Derick faked a shot, then passed the ball to the girl on his team. She leapt off the ground and flung the ball into the goal. Not bad. Derick felt the rush of having done something right.

"Maybe I *don't* like this kid," the Southern boy corrected.

After the game, Derick took his sensors off slowly, knowing that the others were probably discussing if they should let him in. Thanks to a nimble steal and shot by Rafa, Derick's team came out on top, but it was him that was on trial, not his team. Please. He wanted this. He really wanted this. The girl on his team had even put her gorilla arm around him, and said, "Not bad, Tryout. I've seen better, but not bad." He hadn't known if he was being complimented or not, but either way he was pretty sure Carol would be jealous—even if this girl was a gorilla at the time.

Rafa entered the room. "Hey, *rapaz*, you did all right out there."

"Thanks," Derick said, "but you guys are a league above me."

"Maybe a little, but we're also older."

"So did you decide?"

Rafa paused before answering. Pauses aren't good. "Not yet. We'll talk it over some more and let you know."

It took a lot of restraint not to groan. They had taken long enough; what had they been talking about? Maybe he hadn't been perfect out there, but he had done all right. He wanted an answer. Then he remembered everything with Muns. "Oh, and I need to catch you up on a few things. Do you have a few minutes?"

Rafa did. Derick made sure no one was within earshot and confirmed that Rafa had turned off the audio system. He didn't want this ringing throughout the avatar lab if anyone was still practicing. He told Rafa about the attacks and the Council, but this time it was Derick's turn not to use names. He told him that their restrictions were lifted so they could keep an eye out for anything strange and to protect themselves.

"Wait," Rafa said. "Two were attacked? Was one of them Dr. Mackleprank?"

Derick didn't answer. He just stood there trying not to react—not to give anything away.

"I've got to go," Rafa said, and rushed out the door.

# ASSASSINATION

The Gettysburg Address was short—much shorter than Abby realized. Like under five minutes short. Maybe even half that. The other speaker was quite the windbag, going on for hours it seemed, but Abraham Lincoln, the president of the United States, got straight to the point.

Abby had watched the tall, gangly man working on his speech almost nonstop. He even made corrections and changes on the train as he went to give the speech. Maybe that was part of what made it great—he just kept making changes until he got it right.

She didn't mind learning about the president. She couldn't remember all the dates and names, but she liked him. She had seen his humble beginnings—the one-room cabin in Kentucky with a dirt floor. She saw him reading whenever he could, even at times when he was supposed to be working. She saw him as a lawyer in the courtroom during the day and telling story after story with his friends at night. She saw him failing in his first attempt at public office, then trying to get into Congress, attempting to get a position at the Land Office, and running for Senate. And she noticed that he had other entries showing other failures. He had maybe more than his share.

Finally, he was nominated to run for president. A rival called him "a two-face," and Lincoln reacted by saying, "If I *had* two faces, do you think I would wear this one?" Abby loved it.

She saw Lincoln working on the campaign trail and eventually being elected president. He surrounded himself with cabinet members who thought differently than he did. He wasn't a polished type of person like other politicians Abby had seen. He was just him. He stayed up through the night agonizing over the Civil War. He lobbied and pushed to free the slaves.

Abby typed a few notes with her rings. She had a history assignment on the sixteenth president due tomorrow, and she had to keep her grades up. She had a list of other events she had to watch. She scanned down the list of available events until she saw the assassination. She knew he had been shot at a theater. The event had an asterisk by it, which meant that if students felt the event was too violent, they didn't have to watch it. Abby wasn't sure.

She selected it, knowing she could stop the playback if it got too intense. She watched the president and his wife step into a theater booth about twelve feet above and off to the side of the stage. She was still surprised at how tall he was. He had to be well over six feet tall, towering over his wife. The play was already underway, but it soon paused, and the entire audience arose as the orchestra played "Hail to the Chief." There had to be more than one thousand people, maybe closer to two thousand, packed into that small theater.

Abby fast-forwarded, watching Mrs. Lincoln and her husband holding hands. Cute.

The Bridge perspective switched and Abby saw a man—younger, maybe in his late twenties with a mustache and a slightly receding hairline—approaching the president's box from the hallway behind. He handed a card to an usher there who let him pass.

Abby scanned her notes again—John Wilkes Booth. He was a well-known actor and had performed at the theater several times. No wonder the usher had let him pass.

Booth stepped through the first door and then barricaded it behind him with a stick. He looked through some sort of hole in the next door between him and the president. Abby wondered how the peephole got there.

Booth waited. Why?

Abby heard the raised voice of an actor on the stage. "You sockdologizing old man-trap!" The audience burst into laughter. Booth opened the second door and pointed a small revolver at the back of the president's head.

Abby stopped the scene; she didn't want to see it. Booth had waited for a funny line so the sound of laughter would cover up a gunshot, a shot that would kill the same man who had fought to keep the United States of America united, who had worked and pressed to free the slaves—a man who had fought for what he believed in.

She opened her notes and scanned page after page. It was amazing that historians years ago had been able to figure out the details of this terrible event without the Bridge. They couldn't see it happen as Abby could, but they had pieced it together from accounts, evidence, and logic. They were like the Sherlocks of history. Booth had made the small peephole in the second doorway to the president's box earlier that day. Again, he was no stranger to that theater. Historians had learned exactly how he did it—and even why.

Abby stopped. Ms. Entrese. She had been shot. She wasn't dead, but someone else had shot her for standing up for what she felt was right. If Abby knew exactly how that strange man shot her with a tranquilizer, would it help anything? Would it help them find the man and capture him?

Abby closed her eyes for a moment, then opened them. She had to finish this assignment. She moved her fingers to select the next event in history.

She couldn't do it.

They caught Booth, the man who had assassinated Lincoln. Whoever had tranquilized Ms. Entrese was still out there somewhere. Grandpa said that the camera had malfunctioned somehow and didn't record the actual attack. Could she figure out what had happened?

Abby stepped out of the Bridge booth and walked down to the art rooms. They were about the only place she knew she could find paper. She took several sheets back to her room. The assignment on Abraham Lincoln would have to wait.

Once inside her dorm room, she tried to imagine it was her English class. Her bed could be Ms. Entrese's desk. Abby propped up a pillow to represent Ms. Entrese. Carol's half of the room would be the desks. She tore off several pieces of paper and rolled them into balls. They would be her darts. She had seen this in an old movie once. She then rolled a sheet of paper into a thin tube. It would be her straw. She would try to recreate what had happened.

She had seen the footage from the hallway of the man entering through the door. It probably hadn't been locked. Abby stood by the door to help her imagine. The easiest and quickest way would have been to shoot Ms. Entrese with a dart immediately. Abby loaded her paper straw and shot a wad of paper. It didn't even come close to her bed, let alone the pillow representing Ms. Entrese. Abby would make a terrible assassin. She tried again and again, gradually becoming better.

Wait. Abby tried hard to remember. She closed her eyes and tried to picture the scene as she had happened upon it. She was surprised at how vividly she could remember. Maybe because it had been so traumatic. Or maybe it was because of all her practice for English class on the Chair trying to flesh out the setting for book presentations. She could picture the desks. Some of them had been moved out of place, including the one where Abby sat. She could picture Ms. Entrese collapsed behind her desk, her chair behind her. Then Abby really wanted to make sure she remembered correctly. Yes. She could picture the small dart stuck in the right side of her neck.

She thought it through again, just to be sure. But the right-hand side of her neck would have been away from the door. Maybe that just meant that she had heard the intruder coming in and turned to see who it was.

Abby walked to the mirror but faced off to the side of it. She then turned to see how much of her neck was exposed. Not much. It was highly unlikely that Ms. Entrese had merely turned as the man entered and was shot in the right side of the neck.

Abby closed her eyes again, trying to remember. What other clues were there? What would Sherlock Holmes or Joseph Bell have noticed? The chair. Not the famous invention, but the chair Ms. Entrese sat on behind her desk. It was a foot or so behind the desk and upright.

Abby grabbed the chair from her dorm room desk, sat down, and then tumbled out the side, pretending to have been hit by a dart. She got up and inspected the chair. It hadn't moved.

Abby sat again. She stood up, hearing the chair rub against the ground as the back of her knees pushed it back. It was just like the position Ms. Entrese's chair had been in.

So perhaps when the man entered, Ms. Entrese had stood. But she didn't move far, because she had collapsed behind the desk.

But even if she had stood, he couldn't have shot her on the right side of the neck from the doorway, unless she had completely turned. But if she had turned, it was likely she would have fallen and hit or moved the chair. No. Maybe the man had circled around to be right in front of her. And that was probably when she stood to face him. That would account for the desks that had moved. Ms. Entrese had shown her bravery even when facing one of Muns's men.

Why had he waited to shoot her? He probably said something to her. Maybe he told her how Muns's revenge fit her fighting against him. Maybe she knew the answer, just before she had been hit with a dart and fell unconscious.

# RESTRICTIONS

Really?" Carol said. "I get *all* my restrictions lifted? You have to be the best friend *ever*! I can't believe that no one wanted to be your roommate. Don't get me wrong, there might be a possibility you could outdo even this, but it would be hard. I guess you could somehow get me a download of all of Bros Nixon's movies, free passes to Disney Universe for the rest of my life, and a date with your brother; that would seal your place in the Best Friend Hall of Fame. But what should we do first? Maybe go visit the boys' dorms?"

"It doesn't mean we can just do anything that we want," Abby said, blowing another spitwad against a target she had set up just above the trash can. It hit just above the target and slid down into the can. She was getting better. "It's past curfew and if we get busted out there without a good reason we could very well have everything taken back." She shot again. This time it hit the outer left ring of the target.

"Did your grandpa say that?"

"Well, no, but I'm sure that's how it works." She rolled another ball.

"How do you know if he didn't say it? Besides, if something happens we can just claim that we were looking for that creepy guy. In fact, I bet we could find him. I'm a smart cookie. That's what my mother calls me. I'm not really sure why being smart should be compared to a cookie. It doesn't really make sense. Cookies don't even have brains. Plus they aren't very good for you, so eating a lot of them isn't very smart. Unless you were about to have a diabetic seizure, and a cookie would save the day, then one is very smart. Plus they can have chocolate in them, and chocolate is always smart."

"You are so strange," Abby said, shooting again. She hit the second circle.

"You're getting pretty good," Carol admitted, "but let's go."

"We don't really know what we are looking for, and I've got a ton of homework."

"What? You aren't going to let homework get in the way, are you? Remember how last semester we totally saved the day? What if homework had stopped us then?" Carol paused, waiting for an answer.

Abby didn't know what to say. Carol didn't usually stop talking. "No. I think we should just stay."

"Fine. You shoot your paper and work on your

homework. I'm at least going to stand guard at the window and see if anything strange is going on down there."

Abby sighed and climbed onto her bed and turned on her rings.

"I'm a sentry at my post. I'm like those guards in England that just stand completely still. They don't twitch. They don't talk. They don't even blink."

"You don't talk?"

"Hey, I hadn't started yet."

"Now?"

"Almost. If I do see something should I tell you, or should I go all Wonder Woman and try to take care of everything on my own?" Carol mimicked a few twirls and kicks.

"You aren't very good at the silent guard thing," Abby pointed out.

"Just answer my question."

"Okay—tell me. If something is actually happening, I need to try to help out."

"Got it. Going into guard mode." Carol made a few strange noises imitating a robot turning on.

Then, for one of the first times Abby could remember, there was silence in their room. It was such a change that Abby felt uncomfortable. She was so used to listening to Carol talking about her latest conversation with some boy, retelling a memory about acting in some webseries (which usually focused around an actor boy), or sharing her memories of home . . . involving crushes on some of the neighborhood boys. Now it was silent.

For about a minute. It wasn't much, but it was a record nonetheless.

"I'm really feeling the guard thing," Carol said. "I think my vision is sharper than ever. This could be my calling."

Abby sighed.

"I'm holding so still, I didn't even move to say that. Seriously," Carol added. Abby could tell she had tried to say it with her mouth closed.

"Guards don't have to speak with their mouths closed." Abby looked at Carol over her bed railing. "That's a ventriloquist."

"Oh, well, that's awesome too. I'm mastering all sorts of careers tonight."

"Yes, you are." Abby surrendered, closing her eyes. As Carol began talking about writing a puppet show about guards and who she would cast as the other guard puppets, Abby zoned out. She thought about Muns. What was he planning to do next? Who was this guy who had tranquilized Entrese and Mackleprank? Her thoughts began to come faster, one leading to another. Without realizing it, Abby started to drift off to sleep.

•  •  •

A hand covered Abby's mouth.

She jerked awake and tried to scream. Her arms flailed at her attacker.

Wait. She recognized her. It was only Carol, who

quickly pressed a finger to her lips, signaling for Abby to quiet down.

Abby looked around their room. She didn't see anything. No one with a hood. None of Muns's men. Just her and Carol. "Why did you wake me up that way?" Abby whispered. "You terrified me."

"*Shhhhhh!*" Carol shushed, then pointed out the window. "Someone's outside on the grounds. In fact, I think it's two someones."

"Really?" Abby said, moving toward the window. She gazed out at the darkness below. She could see the silhouettes of hedges carved to look like Saturn and the Mayflower, and behind them the other buildings—the Hall, the science building, and so forth. It was all blanketed in darkness except for the dim moonlight that cast darker shadows in one direction. A slim robot passed in front of the door to the Hall and continued down the path. There were more robots on patrol these days, and the human guards were working longer hours too. Abby didn't see anyone or anything out of the ordinary.

"Wait a minute," Abby said. "If the reason for waking me was someone sneaking around outside, did you *have* to cover my mouth and shush me?"

"Oh, it just seemed like the right guard-type thing to do. I guess I was just caught up in the moment. Anyway, whoever it was went along the teacher's apartments, then walked in the shadow of the hedges going toward the main hall. I think they're in the bushes on the pathway just there, waiting for the robot to get out of the way." She pointed.

Following Carol's finger, Abby watched closely. A few seconds later, two shadows moved from behind a hedge shaped like George Washington and approached the door to the main hall. Whoever it was raised a hand and the door opened. They had clearance.

"Let's go," Abby said, grabbing a sweatshirt. "Should we send a message to my grandpa?"

"I'd wait until we know more. But you may want to message the boys." Carol raised her eyebrows. "Just in case."

No surprises there.

In a few moments they were out of the dorm and on the grounds beneath. Their unlimited access had worked. They had to find out who had snuck into the main hall in the middle of the night.

. . .

Derick read the words one more time.

> The guys want to meet one more time before they decide if you can join.

One more time? Couldn't he do anything right? What happened to the Derick that always succeeded? He was terrible at the giraffe avatar. He couldn't figure out what to do with his sphere. And now he still hadn't made his way into the avatar club. At least he still had a chance. Perhaps he hadn't succeeded already, but maybe he could.

He read on.

> Oh, and I apologize for running off so fast. I had noticed that Dr. Mackleprank hadn't completely been himself lately. When I learned he might have been attacked in the night, it made some sense. But I had to check up on him. We are very good friends and I try to be there for him the best that I can. I think he is doing extremely well, especially considering what he has been through.

It was nice to know that everything was okay with Mackleprank and that Rafa and he were such good friends, but something about it didn't completely sync up. Rafa had run out of the lab with such urgency. It hadn't been a casual stroll to check up on a friend. Then again, it wasn't every day a friend got attacked in the middle of the night at the most secure school in the world. He'd have to think about that some more.

He couldn't help but read the words again.

> One more time before we decide.

Ugh.

His rings vibrated again.

> Someone is sneaking into the Hall. Carol and I are going in.

Derick stepped into his shoes and sent Rafa a message at the same time.

• • •

Abby and Carol sprinted across the grounds. Abby almost screamed when she looked over to see a bush sculpture of a bear.

A robot whirled out in front of them and a thin hand extended. Again a near scream.

"Whoa there, Bolts," Carol said. "We're okay. We're un-re-stric-ted." She said every syllable with pride.

"Just stick out your hand, Carol," Abby instructed, holding out her own. After a quick scan, the robot reversed out of their way.

"Well, it worked," Abby said.

"So awesome. If there wasn't someone creeping around in the dark, I'd suggest we use our all-access pass to find the kitchen and see if there are any leftover eclairs—ooh, or those brownies from yesterday. But I secretly think the lunch crew eats the leftovers."

"Carol, focus." Abby let the door scan her and opened it wide.

"Like you haven't noticed that no one in the cafeteria is a beanpole."

In a few moments they were in the dark schoolhouse, hoping to figure out who else was sneaking in in the middle of the night.

"This feels like an awesome spy movie," Carol whispered. "But so rarely is it two girls, and if it is, usually they're wearing dresses that are too tight and don't have enough material. Yeah, like you could do much spying in high heels and a formal dress. But it's just . . ."

Abby shushed again. Two moments of silence in one night was apparently just too much to ask.

They crept along the wall, making it to the next intersection of halls just in time to see someone turn the corner. "There." Abby pointed down the hall.

"This is so incredible," Carol whispered. "I bet this is where we confront them. I may even have to use a little karate." She mimicked a few movements. "I don't really know karate officially, but I played a girl who did taekwondo in a commercial. Some people said that I looked like a natural. Well, my mom said that, but I'm sure other people were thinking it."

Whoever it was they were following was going down to the engineering hall. Were they checking on Mrs. Trinhouse? Did they know she had a key? Was she in her room, working late? Should Abby send her a warning? No. She would wait and make sure.

Abby felt a hand on her shoulder. This time the scream nearly burst from her lips.

"Derick?" Carol said much louder than a whisper. "Rafa?"

"We heard there was some excitement," Derick said quietly.

"Yep," Carol answered. "And with you two here it just got a lot more exciting."

Rafa laughed.

"I hope you weren't trying to sneak up on whoever it is just yet," Derick said. "Because I could hear Carol all the way down the hall."

Abby looked at Carol, who shrugged.

"Maybe it was just your heart sensing that I was getting close," Carol suggested.

"I'm not sure about Derick's heart," Rafa said, "but my ears heard you talking about taekwondo."

Carol waved him off.

"This way." Abby gestured down the hall.

The four students quietly scrambled in the direction Abby pointed until they turned a corner and saw two silhouettes in the dim light. Then the taller of the two turned down one hall, and the shorter down another.

"Let's split into two groups and follow them," Carol whispered, and grabbed Derick's arm.

"Good idea." Derick didn't flinch. "Rafa and I will take the taller one. Message us if you run into any trouble." He slipped out of Carol's arm and he and Rafa scampered forward.

Abby swallowed her laugh. It was a nice change of pace from holding in her screams.

"That's *not* what I meant," Carol whispered, disappointed.

Abby shushed her, and the two girls ran along the hallway close to the lockers.

So much for calling in the boys as backup. The girls were on their own. Abby couldn't help but wonder if she should be doing this. Was she walking into a trap? Abby drafted a quick message to her grandpa. Though she didn't send it, she wanted to have something ready. Her heart beat faster. She couldn't help but think about the images of the figure who had broken into Dr. Mackleprank's place—and Ms. Entrese on the floor. Abby and Carol passed through the commons, watching the mysterious figure walking along the side of the wall in front of them. He quickly leaned as far up against a wall as he could. Carol and Abby did the same, not knowing if he would look back at them. A second later, a robot passed in the adjoining hall.

After a few moments, the figure moved quietly again, but with a purpose. He climbed a staircase to the second floor. He waited at the top; Abby and Carol were frozen at the bottom of the stairs. After hearing footsteps and then hearing them fade—probably from a human security guard—the figure moved again. Abby and Carol followed him several more yards before the silhouette jogged up another staircase—the stairs up to the Watchman, the tower at the center of the main building on campus.

Both Abby and Carol knew those stairs were sealed off at the top. Though there may have been access to the inside of the tower years ago, there wasn't anymore.

Gazing up around the steps, Abby could see the figure reach up and press something. A few short seconds later, he disappeared into the ceiling. There had to be some sort of trapdoor, but there hadn't been one before.

Why was someone sneaking into the Watchman? It would be a fantastic lookout. You could see most of the campus from there. But it was the middle of the night. What would they be able to see in the dark?

"Should we follow him up there?" Carol asked.

181

"No. If he has blowdarts, he'll get us for sure. Let's wait here."

They waited for a long time. It felt like a short eternity before feet appeared again and the figure dropped down into view. He was shaking his head, but he was coming back their way.

Abby looked at Carol, wondering what they should do. Should they run? No. If the figure had blowdarts he could simply shoot them as they ran. Their only hope was to slink as far into the shadows as they could and pray they weren't noticed. Abby hoped Carol followed her example. The only movement she dared was to double-check to make sure her message to Grandpa was at the ready.

The closer the figure got, the faster Abby's heart beat. But also, the closer he got, the more Abby could discover about the person. He was definitely an adult or an older student. Since he was out and about after curfew, he was most likely an adult. And not a he—definitely a *she*. It had been too dark to notice before.

*Please don't see me. Please don't see me. Please, Carol, don't say anything.*

That short hair. That walk. That silhouette. All at once it came together—Abby recognized her. But what was *she* doing crawling into the Watchman in the middle of the night?

# INTERROGATION

Derick and Rafa followed quickly and quietly. The figure was on the move. There were so many twists and turns, Derick decided whoever he and Rafa were tailing was taking the long way in case anyone was following. Eventually he ducked into a classroom, only closing the door partially behind him. He probably didn't want to risk the sound of the door latching shut.

Derick and Rafa crept closer. Rafa went first, but Derick was only a step behind. They were inches away from the door when it flew open. The figure grabbed Rafa and threw him inside. A second later, Derick felt himself lifted off the floor and then flying toward a row of desks. Umphhh! He slammed down hard on top of one of them.

Derick caught his breath and turned to find himself looking down the barrel of a gun. It had slid out from underneath the figure's sleeve and was aligned with his pointer finger. In fact, there was a matching barrel on his other hand pointed at Rafa.

Derick's breath felt thick, like it was in no hurry to escape his throat, for it might be his last.

"Oh, it's you two," a deep voice said. Derick looked up into Mr. Trinhouse's face. "And here I thought I might be stopping that awful sneak."

Derick tried to get a few more breaths. Rafa began, "We saw you moving through the halls at night and thought you were up to something."

He smiled. "Well, you need to be careful. I have decent reflexes. I'm glad I didn't shoot you both." The smile faded away. "Unless I should. You aren't behind this all somehow, are you?" He pressed the gun barrel further in Derick's face. "You aren't rebelling against your own grandfather, are you?"

Derick shook his head wildly.

"And you aren't in on it?" He stepped toward Rafa.

Rafa shook his head as well, though Derick thought he looked a lot cooler under pressure than Derick had just been. Rafa had beat him again.

But what if it was Mr. Trinhouse that was up to something? He seemed convincing, very convincing, but wouldn't that be the way a traitor would play it?

Mr. Trinhouse eyed them both carefully. He opened his mouth and then closed it again. "All right, you're coming with me." Mr. Trinhouse kept both guns on each of them, but then let his eyes dart to a spot on the wall quick enough for him to tap it. A section of tile in the floor rose, revealing a way into the basement below, another entrance down to the original Bridge. The question was why Mr. Trinhouse was going there. "In," he said, motioning toward Rafa. "Stop once you hit ground." Rafa looked at Derick then did as he was told. Derick followed.

They wandered until they arrived at a turn Derick thought looked familiar, but didn't completely recognize. Two other figures waited in the dimly lit corridor. Derick hoped they weren't accomplices.

"Sorry I'm late," Mr. Trinhouse said. "I had a couple of kids following me."

"Derick? Rafa?" Grandpa's voice called out loud and clear. He looked at Mr. Trinhouse. "Put your guns away."

"I won't apologize for it. They were following me and I don't know who we can trust," Mr. Trinhouse said.

Grandpa and Coach Horne stood together. Derick exhaled with relief and quickly told his and Rafa's part of the story.

"I know Rafa's not a part of the Council," Mr. Trinhouse said, "but I also knew I couldn't explain what I was about to do, nor could I simply walk away. He would suspect me of crimes I was *not* committing."

"It was probably wise to bring him," Grandpa said. "Well, Derick and Rafa, because of your vigilance, you get to be in on our interrogation this evening."

Interrogation?

"I asked these two men to assist me. We are bringing the prisoners up to the English class so they can sit in the Chair and we can find out what they know. We couldn't bring them up during the day, so this is our appointed hour."

"And Mr. Trinhouse and his wife are going to sit in the Chair too," Coach Horne added.

Mr. Trinhouse nodded. "She will meet us there."

Soon, they had hauled the prisoners up through the secret passageways, blindfolded so they couldn't memorize the route they'd been brought by. Grandpa approached the two robot guards standing sentry outside the English classroom. After the sentries scanned the prisoners, they opened the door and Coach Horne put the first man in the Chair. Grandpa asked Mr. Trinhouse to wait for his wife to arrive outside the room with the two guards. Grandpa then messaged Coach Horne, Derick, and Rafa and invited them to sync to a certain audio line. Derick didn't know why, but he synced anyway.

"You know Charles Muns," Grandpa began, addressing the first man in the Chair. Immediately the image of Muns formed on the screen behind him. "Why did you go back in time?"

"I won't tell you," the man said, but the image of Muns on the screen changed, his clothes slightly different, obviously a different day. He spoke, though Derick only heard it through the audio line he had synced up to. Genius. If the man was blindfolded and the audio from the Chair was patching in somewhere else, he wouldn't know the significance of where he was sitting.

The memory of Muns on the screen spoke. "If you do this for me, I will take you back in time to the championship."

In a flash, Muns disappeared and Derick saw a younger

version of the man playing football. He took a snap from the center and stepped back, scanning the field for an open receiver. His blockers started to give way, and the man raced to one side to avoid the attacking defense. Derick could only imagine what being tackled by one of those giants would feel like. His bones hurt just thinking about it. The quarterback dodged to one side, causing a defender to miss, and then danced away from another. He was good. Then his arm reeled back and launched the football in an arcing spiral.

It flew through the air fast and directly toward a wide receiver only feet from the end zone. But a defender leapt in front of him, reaching up with one arm. His fingers tipped the ball, knocking it off course. It tumbled high in the air. Both the receiver and defender dove, but the defender caught it. Interception. Derick watched as the quarterback took off his helmet and threw it to the ground, the clock running out of time behind him.

Another image appeared, the same man telling his mother that he hadn't gotten the scholarship he'd hoped for. Then refusing to go to college. Then working odd jobs. Then drinking.

It ruined him. One mistake ruined him.

No. That wasn't right. So he didn't get the scholarships—he could have still gone on to college. Even if he didn't have the money, he could have applied for loans. Maybe he could have tried out for the college team. He didn't have to shortchange his dream. He *chose* to. Unfortunately Muns had convinced him that his one mistake meant everything.

Grandpa let the man sit in silence until his memories faded. Grandpa didn't let on what he knew. The door opened and the Trinhouses quietly slid into the room. "Did you know you were going to get caught?" Grandpa resumed his interrogation.

"That's absurd. Why would I ever go in if I knew I was going to come here?"

But the image told a different story. Muns appeared, giving instructions. "Someone will release you, and then your one job is to find keys like this." Muns held up the one key he had. It was the same kind of key Derick had just earned by surviving a Civil War battle.

"Did someone manage to release you from your cell last night?" Grandpa asked.

A crooked smile slowly crept across the man's face. "Oh, you've got a rogue on your hands, because it wasn't us. We slept all night on our fine accommodations." The man spit his last words. He pictured a simple mattress in a dark room. He told the truth.

Someone was supposed to release them, but it wasn't last night. This was very bad.

"That is better than you deserve," Grandpa's voice rose. "Do you know that you could have changed history? And that change could have set in motion other changes that then might have altered our own reality so much than neither of us would even exist. In fact, that change could have led to greater tragedies, perhaps wars. Perhaps your change may have led the earth and the human race into destruction."

The man cowered back. Images of the man imagining wars and a ruined world filled the screen behind him.

Grandpa continued, his voice growing almost to a shout. Derick wondered if he was trying get the man emotionally off-balance so he would give something else away. Grandpa stepped closer to the man. "Did you ever stop to think that it was too much to risk to go back and play a *football game?*"

The man's brow furrowed. "I didn't . . . wait. How did you know that?" If he hadn't been on edge emotionally before, he was now.

Grandpa grabbed him by the collar. "The side you are fighting for may kill us all. Now tell me, who at Cragbridge Hall is on Muns's side?" Derick held his breath waiting to see who the traitor was. Would he see the Trinhouses?

No images appeared.

"I don't know," the man said.

"I don't believe you," Grandpa said.

"I'm telling the truth. I don't know."

After several more tries, the man still didn't give any more useful information. The other man gave much the same results.

To make matter worse, no new information came from asking the Trinhouses questions. Either they could imagine lies as if they were real memories or they had been telling the truth. They had left the briefcase in a locked room and it had been opened the next morning. No images flashed of anyone who had come into their apartment or of any secret plan.

This was very, very bad.

# THE IMPOSSIBLE AND MURDER

Mrs. Trinhouse wore fashionable enough clothes, so she was up with the times. Her hair was well done, her makeup simple but pretty. Callouses. She had callouses on her fingers. Maybe she played guitar. She yawned again. Mrs. Trinhouse had begun her lecture, and though tired, she was just as peppy as ever. But Abby wasn't listening very well. She was trying to be like Joseph Bell or Sherlock Holmes. She wanted any clue that might help her understand why Mrs. Trinhouse had been at the Watchman last night.

Abby logged onto her rings, selected the Cragbridge Hall homesite, and found Mrs. Trinhouse's information page. She smiled big in her photo. No surprise there. She was from Ohio. She studied at Princeton. There was a massive list of engineering and math awards. She was married and had taught at Cragbridge Hall for seven years. In her spare time, she loved to play guitar, hike, sing and dance.

Abby had been right about the guitar. Maybe she *could* be observant. But there was nothing else there that gave Abby any clues.

"Though we normally use our virtual booths in math and engineering," Mrs. Trinhouse said, "today I'm going to begin by using the Bridge in our classroom to show you an episode from history. Watch it closely." She flicked her fingers and showed a three-dimensional image of someone from the past. A young man, maybe in his late twenties, walked into class. It was probably a college somewhere, and since the teacher was already lecturing, the student was late. Abby watched as he sat down and copied two problems off the blackboard.

A guy writing down math problems? Not the most interesting of stories.

The next scene showed the same young man in an apartment that wasn't very clean. He was working on the problems from the board. He showed all the signs that it wasn't easy—rubbing his temples, writing, then erasing, writing and erasing again. How boring was *this*? Watching someone else do homework. Doing her own was boring enough.

Abby thought about her homework. She probably looked the same way as she struggled to find the right answer. It didn't come quickly for her either. Was that why Mrs. Trinhouse was showing the story? Was it for her?

Finally, the man started writing faster and moved his

head closer to the paper. Abby saw a smile cross his face. He had done it.

The image fast-forwarded to the young man entering the same classroom as before and setting his homework on top of a large stack of papers. The professor wouldn't get through all that for a while.

The image faded. "Now," Mrs. Trinhouse narrated, "this is a Sunday morning about six weeks later."

The young man lay sleeping in a simple twin bed. Someone pounded on the door. He didn't move. Abby could relate. She had felt the same way this morning.

More pounding.

Eventually the young man stumbled out of bed and made his way toward the door. He didn't look happy. It was probably one of the few days he could sleep in. He clumsily twisted the knob, opened the door, and stared at his professor.

"George! George!" the professor shouted, "You solved them!"

George looked down, blinked a few times, and then realized the professor was holding the pages he'd turned in. "Wasn't I supposed to?" he asked, trying to suppress a yawn. Just watching him made Abby yawn too.

The professor looked his student in the eye. "Those weren't homework problems, George. I put them on the board as examples of problems that leading mathematicians haven't been able to solve." George's eyes grew wide. "And in only a few days you solved them both!" The professor's arms raised into the air.

He had solved the unsolvable? He wasn't that old. And he was still a student.

The image fast-forwarded. George was grown, no longer a student, but giving a lecture. "This is the same student later as a professor at Stanford," Mrs. Trinhouse explained.

George spoke. "If someone had told me that they were two famous unsolved problems, I probably wouldn't have even tried to solve them. This is an example of the power of positive thinking." The image faded into nothing.

Cool story. Mrs. Trinhouse was obviously teaching the entire class, but was she especially trying to encourage Abby? And if so, was it sincere? Or to get on Abby's good side, so she didn't suspect her? That had happened last semester with her history teacher. Abby wouldn't let it happen again.

"One of your advantages as students," Mrs. Trinhouse said, "is that you don't know what should be impossible. And I'm surely not going to tell you. So today I want you to start on a project that will continue through the whole semester. But you will each need one of these." Mrs. Trinhouse walked to her desk and then returned with a flat container. She opened it to reveal a series of little spheres.

Immediately Abby thought of the sphere her grandfather had given her. The deleted one. The empty one. The one she didn't know what to do with.

Mrs. Trinhouse walked up and down the rows, letting each student grab a sphere. Great, now Abby would have two she didn't know what to do with.

"I want you to begin to make something all your

own—your own house, your own amusement park, your own car, your own world. It doesn't matter. Pick something. Go big. Go for the impossible. I have programmed each of your spheres with our world's laws of physics, but otherwise, you have free rein to create whatever you like. These spheres are a blank canvas. A blank canvas is one of the most beautiful things—it has endless potential. You can create anything. Your sphere is just waiting for you to decide what is possible."

"C'mon," Mrs. Trinhouse said, and clapped her hands. "Let's push some limits. Try something ambitious. Let's follow George Dantzig's example and do something others think is impossible. Be sure to either ask me or search our class site if you need any help with your math equations or engineering questions. All the building materials we have on file will be available to you."

It worked. It was inspiring. But Abby was still thinking about what Mrs. Trinhouse had said about a blank canvas. Was that Grandpa's point? Did he clear off the sphere so Abby could make her own creation on it? That's what a blank canvas is for, right? And he did say to put the sphere back in its place and make the most of what happens.

Abby walked to her booth and put on the suit and sensors. But instead of putting the sphere Mrs. Trinhouse had given her into the console, she put in the one from Grandpa. She had to decide what to build. A house? She had always had ideas about how to put rooms together and decorate. No. She didn't think that would be enough to get a good grade. She would probably have to be more ambitious. A car? No. That would require a whole bunch of engineering Abby didn't understand. What about a castle? Oh yeah.

Her imagination filled with the possibilities. She knew she had to start with a design. She used her rings to search for real castles. She loved the classic look of the Bodiam Castle in East Sussex, England. Its thick towers looked so solid and majestic. It was built by a knight to defend the area against France in the Hundred Years War. But it had no rooms in the middle. All its rooms and covered spaces were on the outside in the walls and towers.

She also loved the Bran Castle in Transylvania with its towers, pitched red roofs, and spires. The info said that it was often referred to as Dracula's castle—a place that inspired the writing of the famous book, though it really had nothing to do with Dracula.

Abby started to get an idea of how large she wanted her castle to be. She drew a plan with squares on it, each small square on the plan equaling about two feet. Based on the models and plans of existing castles, she planned her own. She could use parts from each that she liked. They would blend into something original. She spent the entire class measuring various places from the walls to the towers and the gates and calculating how tall and thick certain places would need to be. She made a decision. She wanted it to be a modern castle: screens and modern furniture, heating and air conditioning—no drafty castle for her. Maybe even a garage. She'd have to park the car somewhere, right?

She also consulted the list of materials, and in the end

decided on granite. She would use various sizes of stones. She learned that just one stone in the Western Wall in Jerusalem was longer, taller, and thicker than a bus. It weighed the equivalent of two hundred elephants. She had no idea how the Jews had moved such a stone over two thousand years ago. In her virtual world, she could move it with a sweep of her hand, but she didn't think she would need any that big.

It was only at the very end of the class period that she began to set the huge stones of the castle's foundation. This was going to look amazing!

Grandpa suddenly appeared. He seemed just as real in the virtual world as he did in real life. Apparently the sphere still had at least enough code left to show Grandpa; it wasn't as completely erased as she'd thought. He leaned against a large block of stone. "Well done. Some might have thought a blank sphere was useless. They might even have discarded it because it was empty. But that is precisely what makes it great. And you decided to make something of it."

Abby felt a blanket of relief fall over her. She was on the right trail, a step closer to getting her answer.

"We could compare building on an empty sphere to life." Abby was used to her grandpa always trying to teach her something. "Each one of us starts off with nothing, but we make decisions, we learn. In a way, it is like building something. Each choice fills our world with something new, something more. I have something else to teach you, but first I need you to build the best you know how." Virtual Grandpa smiled and disappeared.

Awesome. Abby could work on her homework and toward finding an answer at the same time. She stacked a huge granite block on top of two others. She couldn't help but wonder what exactly Grandpa was going to teach and how it would help her with her question—and how would that help her fight against Muns?

• • •

"Okay, I'm going into my cage to work," Dr. Mackleprank said.

"*Sem problema*," Rafa said.

"English . . . English," Derick reminded. He picked out the word for "problem," but what did *sem* mean?

"Rafa just said that it wouldn't be a problem," Dr. Mackleprank explained.

"And Dr. Mackleprank's cage is his office or his lab—kind of both," Rafa said. "I guess we both need interpreters."

The avatar teacher laughed.

"We'll be here a bit longer," Rafa explained. "We have avatar club today."

"Oh, that's right," Dr. Mackleprank said, palming his forehead. "Still trying out?" He looked at Derick.

Derick smiled and nodded. Abby had passed on the news about the spheres, and Derick had started to build something, but had taken a break to come try out again.

"Well, good luck. Maybe they can help you a bit more with the giraffe," Dr. Mackleprank said. He had really pushed Derick today in class. "You have work to do." His weakness had definitely been noticed.

Derick winced, knowing Rafa was listening. He was hoping to keep that a secret. "I'll keep practicing," he said, though that was the last thing he wanted to do.

Dr. Mackleprank waved goodbye and walked through the main lab to a back room and closed a heavy door.

"Giraffes, huh?" Rafa said.

Derick looked down. "Yeah. I—" Derick rubbed his temple. "I pretty much stink. But I'll get better. Let's just not do it in the club for a while, okay?"

Rafa smiled. "You might want to practice. I don't always choose what we do. We rotate. They could choose something with giraffes today." Derick didn't like that possibility.

Derick and Rafa began walking toward their equipment, but Rafa looked back at Dr. Mackleprank, who was now leaving the lab. "He's been spending some long hours in his office these days."

"What does he do?"

"Grade papers, work on avatars. He's always fiddling with something."

"Like his half-put-together robots back there?"

"*Sim*. How did you know?"

"He spoke with me back there the other day after our relay race."

"It must have been pretty important. He doesn't normally bring students there. He has a whole closet of parts and prototypes, but he keeps it locked up tight. He doesn't want anyone messing with his stuff."

"I wouldn't either," Derick said.

"I don't blame him, but he has been acting *estranho*," Rafa said. "He doesn't usually forget when club meets, or speak of others' weaknesses. I asked him if he was feeling okay since the attack. He says he's fine, but I think it really affected him."

Derick remembered Rafa racing out of the room when he found out about Dr. Mackleprank being shot by a blow-dart in the night. "Hey, that would be some scary stuff. Anything I can do to help?"

"Not that I know of."

"So, how did you and the doctor strike up such an amazing bond?" Derick asked.

Rafa smiled, walking toward the large room where they would practice for the club. "When I came to Cragbridge Hall, the avatar lab made me feel at home. Since Dr. Mackleprank has spent some time in Brazil and knows my culture, it was an easy friendship. We could talk soccer and samba and capoeira. When I showed some talent, it gave us an excuse to work together some more."

"Wait. Why did the avatar lab make you feel at home?" Derick asked, walking alongside his Brazilian friend.

Rafa glanced quickly at Derick and then away. "Oh, it's just there are a lot of animals and stuff where I lived in Brazil. You know, I lived close to the zoo. My parents used to take me there a lot." Rafa blinked several times.

"You okay?" Derick asked.

"Yeah," Rafa said. "Sorry, there's a lot of tension around here lately. Makes me *nervoso*." He pulled his hair out of his ponytail, flung it around for a moment, then pulled it back in. "*Oi.* We'd better get you hooked up before the others come."

In a few minutes Derick was hanging from the branch of a large tree with five other squirrel monkeys nearby. "Hey, Tryout," one of them waved. "It's good to have you back." It was the boy with a Southern drawl. "I hope you make it into the Crash."

"The Crash?" Derick asked.

Another monkey came closer. "We wanted to name the club after a group of animals, but 'the herd' or 'the pack' seemed too cliché." Derick recognized her voice. She had been on his team for handball. "So we went with the Crash."

The girl with a Latin accent spoke. "A crash is what you call a group of rhinos."

"For the record," the fourth monkey said, hanging upside down from a branch. "I wanted 'Murder.'"

Derick raised his monkey eyebrows. "What?"

"A murder is the name for a group of crows, but we decided that it would probably get us into trouble for saying stuff like she just did," a girl said.

"Like, 'let's meet for murder,'" the Southern boy said,

"Or 'murder today after school,'" a girl added.

"Or 'I love murder,'" another girl said.

"I get the idea," Derick said. "It was probably wise to steer clear of that one."

The other monkeys agreed. A few added a couple of monkey shouts.

"Pansies." That was the voice of the girl who wanted "Murder" for the group name.

"All right," the monkey with a drawl said. "I wanted a rematch of handball, but someone else chose monkeys."

"I had an idea," one of the girls said. "Let's play some football."

"I thought we had agreed that we would play something new so that no one has an advantage," Rafa said.

"We did. So we'll make it new. Let's play football *in the tree*." She emphasized the last words, her voice rising with excitement.

Derick perched on top of a branch, noticing hundreds of other branches surrounding him. It was a maze of wood and leaves jutting out of a trunk.

"The opposite sides are touchdowns," the girl explained. "You can pass or run for it, you just have to do it on the branches."

"I'm in," the Southern monkey said. The others voiced their approval.

This was going to be crazy.

Soon Derick was jumping from limb to limb, trying to guard a monkey on the opposite team. They dodged, passed, ran, and leapt with the ball. It was tough to tackle a monkey, but sometimes Derick was able to drag it by its tail to slow it down. This time Rafa was on the other team.

Derick ran with the ball along a branch and leapt to another. Then he rolled underneath it and hung upside down. But when he tried to right himself again, he stumbled, almost falling. He pitched the ball to his teammate, but it was a step behind her. She had to grab another branch and fully extend herself to catch it.

Just a few minutes later, Derick tried to stay with Rafa as another monkey launched the ball through the trees toward him. Rafa bobbled the ball, narrowly snagging it before another monkey collided into him. He fell off his branch, but caught another.

What was going on with Rafa? Today he was less than an invincible prodigy. Was he just worried about Mackleprank, or was there something he wasn't telling anyone? Was there any chance he had something to do with Muns?

By the end of the session, Derick still didn't know if he'd made it. They said they would talk it over one more time and message him. How long would it take them to make up their minds?

• • •

Abby was starting in on her last tower. It was thick and strong with a series of rooms stacked on top of one another. It was different from the ancient castles, though. Her tower had a sun roof to be more energy efficient and large flex-paned windows. She intended on making this tower a library. She loved the idea of rooms stacked on top of one another with books everywhere and a spiral staircase going up through them. She had inherited her love for physical books made from actual paper, not just digital ones, from her grandpa. Once she was done here, she would go back to the last tower. She had an idea that she'd put a water-slide around it down into a pool below. She would have to extend the pool from what she had originally planned, which might affect her courtyard and ballroom space, but she thought it would be worth it.

After school, Abby had returned to her virtual booth, placed the sphere from her grandfather in it, and continued her work. Then she returned again after dinner. She had spread the word to Derick and Carol, who were building in the booths next to her. They had all worked a few minutes past curfew. That didn't matter as much anymore.

Grandpa appeared again in Abby's world, walking with his cane. He looked around for a moment. "You've done good work here." Abby wondered if the virtual Grandpa could somehow quantify the quality of her work in order to say that, or if he was preprogrammed to say it no mat-ter what. "You have made fantastic choices. You were given freedom and used it well. However, it is time to add an-other level of understanding to prepare you to find an an-swer to your question. You see." Grandpa took a few steps forward. "In many ways, your life is like a blank canvas, an empty sphere. You can make it whatever you want it to be. However, your canvas, your world, your sphere is never truly isolated. Your life is never isolated."

In a flash, Abby no longer stood alone in her world. Derick and Carol stood with her. She knew that they had also been in booths in the same room, but she didn't expect them in her world.

"Um, how did you guys get in my world?" Carol asked.

"I think you came into mine," Abby said.

"Grandpa's doing it somehow," Derick explained. "My guess is that our spheres are connected." Abby remembered how Mrs. Trinhouse had allowed all of her class into the same world at once. Maybe this was something like that. Derick pointed in front of him. "And looks like he brought our worlds together too."

This was definitely different from Mrs. Trinhouse's class.

Abby's castle was no longer the only creation. To Abby's left was a movie screen ten stories high. Beneath it was an array of couches, fluffy chairs, swimming pools, swings, gardens, and parks. Abby looked over at Carol.

"It's all my favorite places to watch a movie," she said. "Plus with a screen that huge, it would be just an awesome experience. If I can rig it to play all my best webseries, then it'll be perfect."

To Abby's right was a crazy mix of stairs, walls with ropes, dummies standing in fighting positions, sports fields, hoops, mud pits, jungle gyms, and climbing walls. "It's an avatar training space," Derick said. "They've been on my mind a lot lately."

Grandpa stood in front of all three of them. "You have to share space with others. Other people are creating their lives at the same time you are creating yours, even in some of the same spaces." Abby looked again at her brother and her friend. "And as that happens, your choices influence others. Sometimes you may adopt ideas from others." Abby watched as one of her walls gained a huge movie screen, while a couch and fluffy chairs appeared on the ground beneath and the opposite wall turned into stadium seating. A small castle sprouted up on the avatar field, with dummies along the top and a climbing rope dangling down one tower.

"Sometimes you may try to separate yourself from others." Abby watched as Carol's theater grew huge walls around it. Derick's avatar field did the same.

"As you build and make your choices, you may even accidentally hurt others," Grandpa said. One of Abby's castle walls grew taller, but then several large stones fell, crushing part of Carol's wall and smashing into one of her pools, cracking its foundation and splashing water everywhere.

"Pool-party pooper," Carol mumbled.

"But you learn to create, sharing the same space." Grandpa took a few paces. "Let me give you a real-life example. You decide how to act in school." Instantly a classroom appeared. It was as though it simply grew out of the ground. A teacher stood in front, with kids in desks throughout the room. "Your actions affect others in the class. Your effort may inspire others. Your answers may teach others." One student raised his hand. After the teacher pointed to him and the boy started talking, heads turned to listen. "They may actually become better for being in the same room with you."

That made sense. Abby could think of several students she loved having in her classes. They gave answers she wanted to hear. They asked questions she wanted to know the answers to.

"However," Grandpa continued. "There are others who decide not to learn." One of the students put his head on his desk. "Their example will affect the morale of the class." A few others began putting their heads on desks. "They may even choose to be rude or degrading"—one student threw something across the row, hitting another student; that student repeated the action, hitting another—"which can affect others' desires to learn and even their opinions of themselves." A student retaliated with another throw, and his victim bowed her head away from the rest of the class.

"Though we can decide how much we will let others influence us, they will still influence us. We must act deliberately, understanding these principles. But what if," Grandpa continued, "there could be another influence?" The castle shuddered. "Something from outside your world. Something that you didn't have the power to influence, but that could destroy you." The ground quaked. Abby heard cracking. The top stones of her castle began to fall, dropping heavily to the dirt below. Soon the wall with the screen began to wave back and forth. Why? What was causing this? More stones fell. The walls moaned, and then one pitched forward and collided into Derick's avatar training ground with a mighty thud. A tower crashed into the movie screen. The destruction continued until all was a pile of rubble and dust.

Abby wanted to cry. She was tired. She had been working on her castle forever. In a few moments it had all been destroyed. She had planned on turning it in as her project in Mrs. Trinhouse's math and engineering class.

Grandpa appeared in the wreckage. "I'm sorry, but this was the best way to teach this lesson. How does it feel to have the power to choose and to make something beautiful—and then have someone else destroy it?"

He looked solemn as he walked forward. "What if this lesson repeated itself over and over again? What if *every* time you tried to create something, someone else interfered with your choices, your world? I have often spoken about the need to preserve history the way it is—to not allow anyone to meddle with it, to change it. It is for this reason. Freedom is power. Some will use their freedom to create wonderful, beautiful things. Others will use it in other ways, some discouraging and even destructive ways. Both will have natural consequences, but unless someone is being destructive, we have no right to steal their power to choose. We have no right to destroy their work or meddle with their choices if we cannot naturally influence them in person, in the time we live in."

That made sense. But the next words Grandpa said rang in Abby's mind.

"And what if it was more than history we had to protect?"

What did that mean? More than history?

Grandpa raised his virtual cane. "Please bring your spheres to the simulator in the basement for a final test."

# PLAN C

There was no time for the simulator now. Derick raced through the corridors of the basement until he approached the large metal door crossed with gears and bars. Abby and Carol were right behind. They had all been on their way to the simulator when they had received a message about another emergency.

Derick reached into his pocket and used his fingerprint to draw his key from a protective compartment inside. He looked at his key again. He had earned it, and now he would finally use it.

The large door lurched open and Derick moved further beneath the school. There was no gorilla there yet. Because they were already on their way, they must have been much faster than expected. Knowing Rafa would be there soon, they left Carol outside again, and Abby and Derick stepped into the large room with the original Bridge.

Derick saw the familiar frame of his grandfather standing in front of the console, and for just a moment caught a glimpse of what he was looking at on the other half of the room. Derick didn't recognize it and didn't have enough time to take in too many details, but it looked modern, a few people wearing lab coats standing in a room. The image faded, and Derick heard a faint noise, as if maybe someone had dropped a marble. He checked the floor quickly, thinking maybe his sphere had fallen out of his pocket. Grandpa adjusted his Cragbridge Hall blazer for a moment.

Grandpa must have selected another entry, for the scene quickly changed. The other half of the room filled with an old city—not ancient, but old. The streets were lined with wooden houses packed so close there was no room between them. A couple of young beggars stood on the street corner, calling out to the people who passed them. They had thick English accents.

Grandpa stood at the controls of the Bridge and moved its perspective to follow two people as they walked down the street. Grandpa sighed and turned.

"Derick, Abby," he said, surprised. "How long have you been here?" His eyes were wide, and he quickly placed his cane against the ground.

"We just got here," Derick said.

"You were incredibly fast," Grandpa said.

"We were on our way to the simulator, still trying to

find answers to Abby's question." Derick explained. They gave him the update on where they were in the process.

"Good," Grandpa said. "It is becoming more urgent. The more Muns strikes, the more I understand that someone else must know the answer to that question."

"Is that where the problem is?" Abby asked, pointing to the other half of the room.

"Yes," Grandpa said. "Hopefully the others will come quickly."

"And what were you looking at before?" Derick asked.

Grandpa stood completely still for a moment, then rubbed his chin. "I must be careful, but time is of the essence. I cannot answer that now, but only reiterate that you must complete your search for the answer to your questions. You are almost there."

"Is Muns in the past again?" Coach Adonavich asked, trotting into the room, winded from her run to the basement. Coach Horne entered behind her.

"It appears so." Grandpa pointed. "These two are our problems." He followed two people with the perspective of the Bridge—a man and a woman. From their clothes to their hairstyles, they looked like they belonged in old England.

"They used an energy burst in a back alley several streets ago," Grandpa explained. "They could only be here to stop the Great Fire of London." He moved the Bridge a little further into the future, and the majority of the city was a blazing inferno.

"I know we can't allow Muns to change history, but is

it okay that I wish we could save some of this architecture?" Coach Adonavich asked.

"It was tragic," Grandpa said. "So much of London in flames. The museum. Shakespeare's Globe Theater. But though this is tragic, it also served its purpose. This was the time of the Black Plague that killed thousands. The Great Fire killed the rats that were disseminating the disease. It is possible it led to the end of the plague."

"Let's stop them," Coach Horne said.

Grandpa looked around, and paused. "Has anyone seen Dr. Mackleprank?"

No one answered. Grandpa quickly moved his rings, waited for a moment, and then continued. "We will have to move to plan B." He typed on his rings again.

"What's Plan B?" Derick asked.

A gorilla barreled into the room.

"Awesome," Derick said. He imagined a gorilla bounding into history.

"That will make a statement," Horne said.

"Yes," Grandpa said.

"But will Rafa still be able to control the avatar once it is in the past?" Derick asked. He knew Rafa was in the lab upstairs controlling the robot. It worked from far away, but would it work with the robot hundreds of years in the past?

"I believe so," Grandpa said. "As long as we leave the keys open on our side, the past should be an extension of the basement. If we close them, then he will undoubtedly lose his ability to control the avatar."

Derick nodded. He hoped his grandpa was right.

The gorilla let out a huge grunt.

Grandpa looked at Rafa for a moment, then asked for those with keys to use them.

Rafa growled and pounded his chest. He then began moving his fingers as though he had rings on.

"What's wrong, Rafa?" Derick asked.

A message sprang up on Derick's rings. He could see that it went to everyone in the room. It was the only way Rafa could communicate other than grunts and growls.

**Why am I going in? Where is Dr. Mackleprank?**

Grandpa looked at him. "We need to take care of this quickly, Rafa. We can answer as soon as you return."

Rafa folded his long gorilla arms.

Grandpa sighed. "He hasn't responded to my messages." He paused, letting his message sink in. "I have security searching for him as we speak, but right now . . ."

Rafa didn't wait for Grandpa to finish his sentence. His avatar fell limp on the floor. He had disconnected and had gone to look for his teacher.

Derick looked at the limp robot beast. He wanted to run after his friend, but he also knew that someone was about to change history. "What's Plan C?" he asked.

Grandpa looked back at him. "You."

• • •

Derick raced through the hallways of Cragbridge Hall, knowing every second was valuable. His grandpa must have sent word ahead because he walked right in to the avatar lab, though it was guarded by several men and security robots. It was nice to see them there. At least that crazy guy couldn't attack him while he was helping his grandfather.

He slipped into his suit, pulled down the visor, and hooked into the suspension system.

He selected Rafa's gorilla avatar and brought it to life. Though Derick was in the lab, he saw everything through his gorilla eyes in the basement.

Grandpa pointed to the intruders one more time and brought the Bridge perspective behind them.

"And what happens if the Bridge connection doesn't work once he crosses over into the past?" Abby asked.

"Then I'll go in and get Derick," Coach Horne offered. "I mean, the gorilla," he corrected. "And I'll get those two as well. In fact, why don't I just go in right now?"

"Calm down please, Coach Horne," Grandpa said. "You're still recovering from your injuries."

"We're here." Mr. Trinhouse entered the room, his wife behind him.

"Please guard the entrance to the Bridge," Grandpa said. "We will call you in if we need any more help." Grandpa had even thought to replace Rafa's guard position. "Now, Derick, it's your turn."

Derick nodded at his grandfather and stepped closer to old London, stepped closer to two people who didn't belong there. He took a deep breath, and crossed over. He felt a wave of nausea. It was working, wasn't it? Or was he feeling the connection being severed? Was this okay? Should they do experiments first? Was there a chance that it could do some damage to him? To his brain? He felt heat and then a chill.

He blinked. He looked at downtown London in the 1600s.

Yes! His heart beat faster. This was going to fun—he hoped. Maybe even better than handball or monkey tree football.

Just as he approached the two intruders from behind, one of the two looked behind her. Maybe he wasn't all that quiet as a gorilla. Her mouth dropped open. Derick couldn't blame her. There was no way she was expecting a gorilla to appear out of nowhere in seventeenth-century London.

Derick raced to meet them. Within moments, he grabbed the man and lifted him over his head. The man screamed—it sounded kind of sissy. Derick would have laughed if he didn't have a lot more to do. Derick threw the man back in the direction he came from and watched him disappear. Awesome. He must have traveled into the base-ment of Cragbridge Hall, but Derick couldn't see that from this side. This was like some crazy sci-fi dream come true.

When he turned back around the woman was gone. Where could she have gone? Ducked down an alleyway? He began to run in the same direction where she had been.

He heard footsteps walking behind him. It was probably just a pedestrian, but he couldn't be seen. He jumped against the wall. That wasn't going to be good enough. Whoever was behind him would still see a strange gorilla on the streets of London. He looked up, then began to use the windows and brick to climb to the top of the building.

When he arrived on top, he looked down the various alleyways beneath him. Then he hopped across the roofs of several buildings, looking below for the woman who had gotten away. He could do this. He leapt across the roofs, feeling like an action hero in a movie. Okay, so most heroes in movies aren't gorillas, but he still felt great. He looked down the next alleyway and saw the same woman he had confronted before.

He climbed down the side of the building, dropping into the alleyway in front of the woman.

She barely had time to scream before Derick grabbed her and lifted her over his head. But before he could toss her back through time, he realized he didn't know where to throw her. He had moved quite a ways from where he had come in. Had his grandpa followed him with the Bridge? Where could he throw the woman so she would go back to the future where she belonged? A blast sounded behind him, and suddenly, where to throw her was not his most important problem.

Derick whirled around to see three more people burst in to the alley, weapons aimed at his head.

He froze. It was an ambush. Muns's men had used another energy burst to come after him.

All of a sudden, Coach Horne appeared behind the men. With a few mighty swings, one man went down. Derick threw the woman into a second. But the third was the problem. He leapt back in the direction from which

215

Coach Horne had come. He was trying to get into the basement of Cragbridge Hall. If he made it, he would be armed—in the room with all the keys.

Then Derick felt a quick wave of nausea. In London, the gorilla fell lifeless to the ground.

They had closed the connection. They couldn't let an armed soldier in. He could capture them all and take their keys.

Derick stood in the avatar lab, unable to tell what had happened in the basement. He tried to reconnect with the gorilla avatar in seventeenth-century England, but it wasn't working. He tried again—nothing. This was all his fault. If he had been able to get both intruders quickly, this never would have happened. But he had missed the woman.

He tried again. The connection picked up for a second, but failed again. Had they opened the Bridge for just a moment?

Finally, on his fourth try, the connection restored. He rose up, his gorilla body ready to crash into one of the assailants, but he didn't need to. Coach Horne was dragging someone behind him, as was Coach Adonavich. Mr. Trinhouse had another. They had had to call in all the backup. Luckily they had been victorious.

"Grab one of the others before they send in more," Coach Adonavich said, seeing him rise from the ground.

Derick got up and grabbed the remaining three assailants at once and pulled them in the same direction. He loved the strength of a robot gorilla, but he hated thinking that he had not done well enough. Because of him, it had almost turned out horrifically bad.

•   •   •

Abby realized she had been holding her breath. Things had come so close to going terribly wrong. Luckily, Grandpa had thought quickly and moved the perspective of the Bridge over the third man and Coach Adonavich had dropped on top of him.

Now they were dragging the intruders out of the past. More people for the cells.

As Abby turned back toward the Bridge console, she caught a glimpse of a spider moving back into a small crack in the wall. Gross. Every now and then Abby was reminded that she was deep in a basement, several stories under the ground.

She had been trying to piece all the information she had together. Grandpa had said, "What if it was more than history we had to protect?" What could that mean? When they had entered the Bridge room, what was Grandpa looking at that seemed so modern?

Abby took the controls at the console of the Bridge and began to scroll upward, closer to the present in time. The scene the Bridge actually displayed on half of the room wouldn't change unless she selected an entry. With the keys in place, could she scroll to a more recent time than fifty years in the past? She tried to work as subtly as she could, knowing that at any moment, one of the members of the Council could come and remove a key. That might change the options in time that she could choose from. And she might have to do some unwanted explaining. She saw Coach Adonavich drop the intruder she had been carrying and come closer to the console.

Abby scrolled faster, the years streaming by. She was coming close to the 2000s. Could she come all the way to the present? She didn't know if that was possible. Was a machine designed to show the past limited to *only* showing the past?

She saw Coach Adonavich approaching out of the corner of her eye. Abby turned to face her. "Good job," she said to Coach Adonavich, trying to act natural. She could still see the dates rising.

"Thanks," Coach Adonavich said. "Let's get our keys before any of these guys wake up."

Abby reached forward as if to take her key, but watched the scrolling intently. It slowed and then stopped in 2025. Fifty years ago.

Abby was wrong.

# IN THE NIGHT

Abby yawned again. She sat in the virtual booth and looked at the other members of the Council of the Keys. It was thirty minutes before school started and she was in another meeting. She had planned to sleep through breakfast, but a message from Grandpa woke her. If this kept up, her grades would dive even more from falling asleep in class.

Grandpa stood solemnly at the head of the virtual mahogany table. "Things have gotten worse."

Immediately a hallway appeared. Abby had seen it, or something like it, before. "This is the hall outside of Dr. Mackleprank's room," Grandpa explained. The light suddenly flickered out. "Our night sensors were also cut. How someone breached our security, I don't know."

"Another dart?" Abby asked.

"Yes," Grandpa said. It seemed that Grandpa's brow had formed a whole new set of wrinkles. "Dr. Mackleprank is awake now and doing fine. His dart only lasted the night. It appears as though they wanted to ensure that he would not interfere with another attempt at using an energy burst to alter time. Muns saw him through his Bridge during the incident with the *Hindenburg* and knows what a great fighter he is."

"Where is Coach Adonavich?" Coach Horne asked. "I just noticed that we started without her."

Grandpa bowed his head and flicked his finger. An image of Adonavich appeared. She was in a bed in the medical room next to Ms. Entrese.

A hush fell over the group. Abby's throat tightened, her insides clenched. Not again.

Grandpa lowered his head. "She must have been attacked last night, after our incident at the Bridge. The nurse says that like Minerva Entrese, she will likely be out for months."

Abby's lip quivered. She blinked hard and looked around the virtual room. She noticed Horne's fists tighten. He punched the table in front of him.

"Whoever it was left more chess pieces," Grandpa said. "One with Dr. Mackleprank and one with Coach Adonavich. They think they're winning this game." He cleared his throat. "And they succeeded even more last night." Grandpa held up an athletic shoe. "This is Coach Adonavich's shoe, and here—" Grandpa pointed to the sole of the shoe, "—is the compartment I made to keep her key safe. When we found her this morning, it was open."

Mrs. Trinhouse closed her eyes and whispered, "They have another key."

"Yes," Grandpa agreed. "However, it would be extremely difficult to get a key out of Cragbridge Hall without us discovering it. We have more security at each entrance and sensors that will detect a key."

"But our increase in security hasn't helped stop these attacks," Mr. Trinhouse said.

"Good point." Grandpa nodded at Mr. Trinhouse. "But it is still likely that the stolen key could be somewhere here on campus. After all, it appears that our attacker is still here as well. We must prevent them from gaining another key and escaping. If they do, Muns will have the ability to change time without the energy bursts. And then I don't know if we could ever keep up with him."

"How did they know where she kept her key?" Derick asked.

Grandpa shook his head, his wispy white beard swaying. "That is a mystery."

Murmurs ran through the room.

"But that is not the only mystery. Watch the security footage." Grandpa moved his fingers and a view of the hall outside of Coach Adonavich's room appeared. The lights went out.

"Wait," Derick interrupted. "I thought you put like extra security on the doors. Made it so no one else could come in."

"I did," Grandpa confirmed. "That is one point that greatly puzzles me. And you see, there is no sign the doors or their locks have been tampered with or codes cracked."

"Could they get in past security through the window?"

"We would see that from the cameras on the grounds." Mrs. Trinhouse pointed toward the window. It was only a virtual window, but it made her point just the same. "Do they show us more?"

"There is nothing but darkness. More of the same." Grandpa rubbed his scalp. "Any of you can feel free to watch the footage. Security has analyzed it and can find nothing."

Abby thought it through. Those were the only entrances, weren't they? "Wait. What if someone was already hiding in her room when she came back in?"

"Good thinking," Grandpa said. "But we would have footage of them entering at some time, and we cannot find it. We would also have footage of them leaving, or they would still be in the room. We have no such footage and have searched her room completely. There is no one there."

"Can we see the room?" Abby asked.

Grandpa flicked his fingers. "This is what I recorded this morning."

Abby looked closely. This was her time. She could be like Joseph Bell. She checked the doors and windows. They were the only ways in. Unless someone took down an entire wall and put it back up as though it was new, there was no way anyone had entered. So much for her detective skills.

"Was it one of the group we just put in the cell

downstairs?" Coach Horne asked. "Every time we bring someone in, it seems that one of us gets attacked."

"I will interview them, but fear we will get much of the same." Grandpa stood and started to pace.

"But even if it was one of them, they wouldn't know where Adonavich's key was," Mrs. Trinhouse said.

"I knew where her key was," Abby said.

Everyone hushed and looked at her.

"I did," Abby confirmed. "I saw her take it out to use it in the Bridge, and put it back again. And so did all of you."

"Do you think one of us is a traitor?" Derick asked.

Everyone looked at one another.

"It may be a coincidence," Coach Horne said, "but last night was the first time the Trinhouses were at the Bridge with the rest of us. That would have been the first time they saw where Coach Adonavich kept her key."

"It *wasn't us*." Mrs. Trinhouse was out of her seat. "And I'm tired of being accused." Mr. Trinhouse pulled her back down toward her seat, but glared at Coach Horne.

"Well, we're the only ones, right?" Derick asked. "No one else knew, did they?"

"There is a chance someone else may have caught a glimpse somehow, spying on Coach Adonavich as she used her key to pass through the last door to get to the Bridge." Grandpa had started his pacing again. "But there are only a certain few who even know the basement exists."

"We're coming down here more and more often, which increases chances," Derick pointed out.

"And there are others with keys, aren't there?" Abby asked.

"Yes," Grandpa said. "Though I find it unlikely they would have seen. Coach Adonavich is especially vigilant at keeping her key a secret."

"Then could anyone else know where she kept her key?" Abby asked.

"There is one more." Coach Horne raised a finger. "Dr. Mackleprank."

"But he was unconscious from a dart," Derick argued. "He couldn't have done that."

"Is there a chance he could have been pretending, that it was a setup?" Mr. Trinhouse asked.

"I don't believe that. I trust him completely," Grandpa said, pausing to face Mr. Trinhouse.

"He is the only one who was hit with a dart and didn't go into a coma for weeks," Coach Horne said. "That's suspicious."

"I trust him," Grandpa said, more emphatically.

"Perhaps we should all interview each other in the Chair," Coach Horne suggested. "And that includes Mackleprank."

# ANOTHER INVENTOR AND THE SPECKLED BAND

Derick knocked on the door of another apartment in the boy's dorm. A minute later, Rafa opened it.

"*Bom dia*," Derick said, hoping he was saying good morning. "Can I come in?"

Rafa hesitated a moment, then nodded. "Sure."

Derick walked into the apartment, its walls plastered with digital posters. One changed from a soccer player to a jungle cat. A smaller frame rotated through pictures of an olive-skinned woman with a young boy. It had to be Rafa with his mom.

"You alone?" Derick asked.

"Yeah, my roommate is at breakfast. I'm not hungry."

"Me neither," Derick admitted. "Are you okay?" It was an uncomfortable question, but he needed to ask it.

"*Mais ou menos.*"

"More or less," Derick translated. "My Portuguese class is helping already."

The far corner of Rafa's mouth curled up into a smile, but Derick could tell it was insincere.

"I hear Dr. Mackleprank is fine," Derick said.

"For now." Rafa blinked several times. "But he's been attacked twice."

"I know. I know. It's out of control. I think we should move him to a different room."

"Yeah, but that's not the point." Rafa wiped his eye. The room grew heavy instantly. "Someone has it in for him."

Derick didn't know what to say. "Well, we need to figure something out because I need you both okay and well. I nearly blew it last night. Either you or Dr. Mackleprank has to go into the past if Muns strikes again. I'll just mess it up."

"I'm sure you did fine," Rafa said.

"I needed a ton of backup," Derick admitted. "It's not easy for me to say, but you're much better than me. I'd like to think that I can catch you and be just as good as you, but I kind of doubt it."

"You're learning well." Rafa closed his eyes then slowly opened them again.

"Thanks. But I can tell this stuff has really bugged you. Even the last time we played with the avatar club, you weren't at your normal level of awesomeness."

Rafa didn't say anything.

"Look," Derick said. "I think there is more to this than

you're letting on." He rubbed his chin. "I mean, usually you're like invincible, perfect. You drive me crazy."

"Teachers are getting attacked in the night!" Rafa said, his voice rising. "Isn't that enough of a reason to be upset?"

"Yes, of course. But the way you took off when you found out that Mackleprank wasn't answering his messages, you seemed desperate." This was tough to say. Derick didn't want to seem like he was accusing Rafa of anything, but he did want to understand what had happened. "You reminded me of me when my grandpa was kidnapped and my parents were missing."

Rafa opened his mouth then closed it again.

Derick waited a few more moments, making sure Rafa wasn't going to say anything. "I was desperate last semester and I was up against a wall. And you bailed me out." He rubbed his forehead. "There was no way we could have saved my grandpa and my parents without you. And I know you're the guy with all the talent, the one who doesn't fail." Derick paused. "I'm not. But I'd love to return the favor. You probably don't need any help, but if there is anything I can do, let me know."

Rafa looked at Derick for a moment.

Derick nearly patted Rafa on the shoulder, but thought better of it. He got up to leave. He made it to the door before Rafa spoke. "Wait. I owe you more of an answer after the way I have acted. Last semester you shared your secret with me and I know I can trust you." He paused. "You know your grandfather worked on the avatar technology."

Derick nodded.

"He's responsible for the connection between our brains, the sensors, and the robot. I think it may relate to the same technology that's in the Chair. At least there's a mind link there too. But it wasn't your grandpa who developed the actual robotics."

"Mackleprank?" Derick guessed.

"No," Rafa said. "I'll let you look it up."

Derick turned on his rings. There were several theories about who had invented the avatars, but one of them stood out—a woman from Brazil. "It was someone you knew? Someone from home?"

Rafa took his hair out of his ponytail and let it fall over his eyes. He paced quietly around the room. "My mother said that I used to watch some of her experiments. She even bought me some of those robotic remote controlled animal toys when I was growing up. As she got better at the robots, she let me play with the more durable prototypes. My dad was really never in the picture." He flopped his hair to one side of his head. Derick noticed moisture in the corners of his eyes. "I'm talented at the avatars because I've been practicing on them all my life."

"Your mom invented the avatar? Oh, I'm jealous," Derick confessed.

Rafa smiled. "Says the grandson of Oscar Cragbridge."

"Yeah, but he never let us try any of his inventions until we got here."

"Given what my mom learned, it probably is better to keep his inventions under wraps so he can control who sees them and when." Rafa shifted on his bed. "Some people, when they found out what my mom could do, wanted the technology. There was a long list of reasons why, but some of them seemed shady. When she did her research on some potential buyers, she realized her inventions were capable of doing some of the worst things imaginable, and that's what they wanted them for. They could use avatars as spies or even assassins. No one would expect a dog or a monkey to be deadly. And they weren't willing to back away when my mom told them no."

Derick looked away a moment, trying to process all that he was hearing.

"Thankfully, my mom came to your grandpa for help." Rafa looked at Derick, his eyes glazed with tears. "He is not only a genius, but a man with a big heart—*um grande co-ração*. He brought me here and has helped my mom stay hidden."

Derick's jaw dropped as he realized the implications of what Rafa just said. "Your mom is in hiding?"

"*Sim*. Yes. I communicate with her every day, but it's . . . very unusual how it works. As you can imagine, we have to take every precaution to keep her location safe. She has to move every few months just to be sure."

"It's that bad?"

"Have you ever thought what a drug lord or dictator could do with a robotic animal? No one would suspect any-thing. It would be the ultimate weapon."

"Makes sense."

"Because of your grandfather's help, I was willing to give you a chance when you stole the avatar earlier this year."

"Thanks for that. We owe you one."

"No. I had a small chance to pay you back."

Derick wondered what all this had to do with Dr. Mackleprank. "Does Mackleprank know all this?"

"Yes," Rafa said. "He and your grandpa are the only ones. Well, and now you. He's the closest thing I have to a parent here."

"I don't know what to say," Derick admitted. He knew what it felt like to have his parents missing, but not to be away from them for years.

Rafa shrugged. "I don't know what I'd want you to say. But I sent your grandfather a message. I want Dr. Mackleprank under protection all the time."

Derick wanted to say that everything would be fine, but he knew Dr. Mackleprank would be invited to defend his own innocence on the Chair that afternoon after school.

· · ·

Abby stared at Mrs. Trinhouse. She taught with the same zeal as always, bubbly and bouncing. Perhaps she didn't feel affected by all of this. Or maybe she was somehow involved and thrilled that it had gone the way she planned. Or maybe she could just hide it really well.

"Any questions so far?" Mrs. Trinhouse asked.

Abby had questions. She wanted to ask, "Why were you in the Watchman in the middle of the night?" and "Were you the one who attacked Coach Adonavich?" She couldn't, of course. She tried to think of what Sherlock would do. *It's obvious*, she thought to herself, hoping to think like Sherlock or Joseph Bell. *It's obvious that . . . I don't know much of anything.*

In a few hours when school ended, Abby would get to see what Mrs. Trinhouse thought while sitting in the Chair. They hadn't been able to take everyone up to the English classroom just after their meeting because school was starting—the teachers couldn't draw attention to themselves by missing their classes, not to mention it would be tough to use a Chair and ask sensitive questions with a classful of English students in the room.

"We will go ahead and give you time to work on the projects you started last class," Mrs. Trinhouse instructed. "I'm excited to see your work. I'm ready to be astounded by it."

Astounded? Perhaps she would have been if it hadn't all been destroyed to prove Grandpa's point. Abby knew she was behind on her creation. She had to finish it to get a good grade. And she needed that good grade to stay at Cragbridge.

She took a deep breath. If she wasn't careful, fear would sweep over her. Fear of getting kicked out. Fear of someone sneaking in the night and shooting her with a tranquilizer. She exhaled. She had to try to move ahead.

Abby stepped into a booth and put on her visor. She logged onto the class page and stared at the all of the possible building supplies. Should she remake her castle or start something new? She could make anything. Maybe a roller coaster, or a beauty spa, or . . . She couldn't finish her thought. She pictured Ms. Entrese and Coach Adonavich. She took another deep breath. Nothing she could build would help that.

Or would it?

What if she could get a good look at the room where the intruder had entered and attacked Coach Adonavich? Maybe there were blueprints. She changed her rings to search for the plans of the teachers' apartments at Cragbridge Hall. She thought she remembered that building blueprints were on public record. Yet she found nothing but an article stating that Cragbridge Hall, because of the avatars, the Bridge, the Chair and other Cragbridge inventions, not to mention its surveillance needs, did not have blueprints available to the public. And Abby also knew that her grandpa had a time machine in the basement. All of the secret passageways leading to it probably shouldn't be there for everyone to see.

She had seen the room once in the video when they found Coach Adonavich. That would have to be good enough. Abby closed her eyes and tried to remember. The room she saw was a rectangle. She estimated the size, not bothering to make it part of a greater whole, just a freestanding room. She built the sides with wood framing and paneled over it. She added a doorway to the bathroom, as well as another to the kitchen and living room.

She tried to remember more. There was a floating bed against the wall. Abby selected repulsor magnets, the tech that caused the real beds to float. She selected other materials, putting the room together the best she could. Trophies stood in a case built into one wall, a mirror covered another wall, and a window looked out toward the Watchman. She thought she could remember a duct on the floor for heating.

Abby stood in the middle of the virtual room she had made, inspecting it closely.

There was a window. But there was no footage of anyone entering or leaving. There was the bathroom. It might have a window, possibly a fan leading outside, but those would be too small to enter through, especially for the man they had seen.

She looked at the bed. Wait. She had something. She could remember the dart in Coach Adonavich's neck. It hadn't gone in straight—it leaned. And it didn't lean toward the door. That meant no one would have shot her from that angle. It came from the side of the window. Yes, the window would work. Perhaps someone had poked their head in and blew the dart. That was possible, but not without being caught on camera. Could they have been on the roof somewhere and shot through an open window? Yes, but the window wasn't open. They might have shot through the closed window, but there was no hole. And after the coach was comatose, they still would have had to come in to get the key.

Abby's mind filled with questions.

Why would he walk over to the window before shooting? Wouldn't that have been foolish? Someone might have seen his silhouette. No. The lights were out.

"Do you mind if I see what you are working on?" Mrs. Trinhouse asked.

"Uh," Abby stammered. "It isn't done yet." She lifted her visor.

"Oh. I don't mind if you don't. I love to see a work in progress."

"I'd rather show it to you later," Abby said, hoping Mrs. Trinhouse would go for it.

"I don't want you to feel pressure." Mrs. Trinhouse put her hand on Abby's shoulder. "And I know there is a lot going on, but you *are* a little behind in your work. We need to make sure you keep up on it, because we definitely need you around."

Nice words. Abby wondered if Mrs. Trinhouse meant them. She was able to act excited when she gave her lecture. She could probably act sincere and concerned right now.

"But Abby," she said, lowering her voice. "I wonder if you should back out of that group we both belong to. Your brother too." She was obviously referring to the Council of the Keys. "I'm not sure anyone your age should have to deal with the pressure or the danger. Let us adults handle it."

She sounded like Muns.

"I just don't want anything to happen to either of you."

Abby looked back at her teacher. She gave a half-smile.

"Think about it," Mrs. Trinhouse said. "And let me know if I can help with your project."

Abby put her visor on. She would look again. She would not back down. She would figure this out.

• • •

Abby tried to walk to the cafeteria, but she couldn't. She walked to the med center instead. She had tried all class period, but she still had no idea how the intruder got in. Soon she was sitting in a hard chair between Coach Adonavich and Ms. Entrese. She held her head in her hands. Her shoulders lurched as she cried.

"I'm so sorry. You two were both brave enough to stand up to Muns, and I can't figure out how he did this. It doesn't make any sense." She looked over at Coach Adonavich. She remembered running to the mountain top in her gym class and playing one of the most competitive games of basket-ball ever. The coach had drive and determination. Grandpa trusted her, and she had been one of the two others who had turned the keys to help Abby save her parents.

The fear came back like a storm, clouding over Abby. If Muns could get someone as smart and quick and athletic as Adonavich, then what chance did *she* have? Abby had made it clear that she was opposed to Muns. Was she going to end up like Adonavich? One night she would get a dart in her neck and the next thing she knew, she'd wake up to a new reality. Muns would have won. Everything would be different. Unless he changed the past too much, then maybe he would alter history enough that she would never exist at all. She might never wake up, having never existed.

She cried some more. She hated the feeling. She hated how it filled her, crowded all her other thoughts out. She didn't want to be afraid, but she couldn't help it.

She looked at Ms. Entrese again. Memories flooded back through her. Ms. Entrese had put her in the Chair at the beginning of the year. Though their relationship had started out rocky, she had taught Abby well. Abby thought of the Sherlock Holmes story she had planned to show Ms. Entrese in the Chair as her first assignment of the new semester—"The Speckled Band."

It was a murder mystery. A woman had died in the night; her last words were "the speckled band." Her sister suspected their stepfather, who lived in the next room over, but there was no evidence. Thankfully Ms. Entrese hadn't been murdered.

Abby turned on her rings and opened the story—perhaps trying to distract herself, or perhaps just to wish she were more like Holmes. She began to read. Holmes sat in one of the wicker chairs and gazed at the room the woman had been murdered in. He took in each detail. He paused on a tight new bell rope, used to call a servant, that hung down from the ceiling, its tassels resting on the bed's pillow. After examining it closer and giving it a pull, he discovered it was no bell rope at all. It did not call anyone. "Very strange," he muttered.

Abby read on and Sherlock pointed out what else he thought was strange—the ventilator shaft that went to the room next door and not to the outside for fresh air.

All three characters moved to the room the ventilator shaft connected to—the stepfather's room next door. Abby imagined an especially large bed for what the book detailed was a large man who could bend an iron rod into a curl. Holmes walked around the room, taking in the books on the bookshelves, a wooden chair, a round table, and an iron safe. Sherlock carefully looked at it all.

Abby read quickly now.

"What's in here?" Sherlock asked, tapping the safe.

"My stepfather's business papers."

"Oh! You have seen inside, then?"

"Only once, some years ago. I remember that it was full of papers."

"There isn't a cat in it, for example?"

"No. What a strange idea!"

"Well, look at this!" He took up a small saucer of milk which stood on the top of it.

"No; we don't keep a cat. But there is a cheetah and a baboon." Abby loved that part. The stepfather had be-friended gypsies and was intrigued by the wild animals they had. He had adopted a few. This guy was weird.

"Ah, yes, of course! Well, a cheetah is just a big cat, and yet a saucer of milk does not go very far in satisfying its wants, I daresay. There is one point which I should wish to determine." He squatted down in front of the wooden chair and examined the seat of it with the greatest attention.

"Thank you. That is quite settled," Sherlock said. And that was it. He had solved the case. Of course he didn't tell Watson until it was all over, but he had solved it. Abby knew what the solution was, but only after she had read the whole story. It was obvious her second time through, but impossible to detect on the first.

She would love it if that could happen to her—if she could solve this problem while it was happening. She couldn't be content to understand it only in retrospect—then it would be too late. But her problem had nothing to do with this mystery.

Wait.

The ducts. Sherlock Holmes had figured out that it had to do with the ducts.

Abby looked at her watch. She only had ten more minutes of lunch. She messaged Derick and Rafa. She had an idea.

"The Speckled Band," she mumbled to herself and ran out of the room.

# FRIENDS IN CAGES

Abby blew into the tube. A paper ball shot across the hall, hit the wall, and fell to the ground. It had hit just two bricks below where she was aiming. Someone else inside of Cragbridge Hall was better than she was, but she was still hoping that practicing would give her more insight as to who they were. She had upgraded her tube, finding that the school-supplied hangers in her closet were made from long hollow pieces of plastic. She had cut the bottom off one and found it worked much better than a rolled-up piece of paper.

She shot again, this time just a brick to the left of where she had aimed.

"Hey, Sis." Derick stood in front of her. "Has the brick wall been acting up again? Good thing you're here to put it back in its place."

Abby turned and blew again.

"Gross!" Derick jumped and then wiped the spitball off his ear.

"I was going for between your eyes. I'm not perfect, but I'm getting better."

"It's still gross." Derick picked up the paper ball his sister had shot at him and threw it back at her. "Does this have something to do with your theory?"

Abby put the tube back into her backpack. "Not really. I'll tell you about it when Rafa gets here."

"*Estou aqui.*" Rafa approached the brother and sister team.

"Good. Thanks." Abby waved. "Can we talk in the lab?" She nodded toward the large locked doors in front of her.

Rafa nodded and opened them up. Once inside the larger lab area, with several stations for students to hook up their equipment, Abby began, "I have a theory. The thief didn't come through the front door, or through the window. Usually the simplest answer is the best place to start. What about the vents?" She looked around the room for a moment, then pointed to a vent in the floor.

Rafa looked where she had pointed. "No one could fit through that vent."

"Yes, but that was the same problem as in the story. But in the story it turned out to be a snake, through the vent."

"What story?" Derick asked.

"'The Speckled Band.' It's Sherlock Holmes," Abby answered.

"You're suggesting . . ." Derick said as he pointed at his

sister ". . . a snake came through one of the vents and attacked people with blowdarts? A snake can't even *hold* a blowdart."

"No." Abby shook her head. "But what if it was a small animal? Not a real one, but an avatar?"

"An avatar?" Rafa asked. "But an avatar can't leave the lab."

"Not unless it was stolen." Abby nodded toward her brother. "You did that once last semester."

"But even if they steal it," Derick said, "could an avatar blow through one of those tubes to attack with blowdarts?"

Abby raised her tube. "That was my next question."

"Technically, yes," Rafa answered. "They have to be able to breathe out air in order to mimic animal sounds. It's part of the robot equipment."

"But if that guy in the hoodie used an avatar to attack, his name should be on the registry," Derick said. "They keep a log of everyone and what animal they use and for how long. It's all recorded. That's how Rafa threatened to expel me from the school. So if we can check the registry, that will narrow down if we have any suspects."

"Right. That's why I asked you two to meet me here." Abby turned to Rafa. "I was wondering if you could show me the registry."

Rafa nodded. "We can check the logs."

"Can you show us last night?" Abby asked.

Rafa quickly logged onto his rings and began moving his fingers. "Let me show you this onscreen so you can see it for yourself." With another flick of his finger, the registry was on the large screen in front of them. "This list is the normal classes logged on." He scrolled through name after name of students. "But this was all during the day; you can see the time here."

He continued, "But when it comes to last night, you can see I was in a fish from about eight to nine P.M. Sometimes I like to go for a swim at night."

Abby glanced at Derick. She could see jealousy on his face.

"After that, I'm on the registry again." Rafa pointed. "This is when I was in the basement. Then I logged off to check on Dr. Mackleprank. And here is when Derick took over. No one else logged on for the rest of the night. Doesn't look like your theory holds."

Abby looked at it closely. "And then there's nothing else until this morning when students came back in?"

"Nope." Rafa scrolled to show her a long list of more students' names.

"Can anyone alter the logs?" Abby asked.

"No," Rafa said. "When anyone uses any of the avatars here at Cragbridge, it's on the log. There is too much on the line not to keep track."

Abby saw Derick and Rafa exchange a look. She noticed her watch. She only had a few minutes until class started.

"Can you search by person?" Derick asked.

"Yes," Rafa answered.

"Can you show me mine?"

In a moment, Derick looked at a string of his name and dates.

"You've been practicing that giraffe a lot," Rafa said, pointing out a few sessions.

"Yeah," Derick admitted. "What about you—can you show me your logs?"

"Sure," Rafa said. Another string of numbers and dates appeared. It was a long list and only covered a few dates.

"You sure do this a lot," Abby said.

"*Com certeza*," Rafa answered. "Several times a day, every day. I'm really trying to perfect it."

"What about Dr. Mackleprank?" Abby asked. She wasn't sure she wanted to know. Would she see his name there somehow? "Can you show me his logs?"

Rafa looked at both of them. "It was not Dr. Mackleprank," he said, a firmness in his tone. "But I will show you all the same." He scrolled again and there was another list of dates and times.

It wasn't him. Abby was wrong.

•  •  •

Everyone seemed to be eyeing each other suspiciously. Abby looked at each of them: Derick, Grandpa, Coach Horne, and Mr. and Mrs. Trinhouse. Could any of them be a traitor? Definitely not Grandpa or Derick.

Abby hoped no one suspected her. She tried not to look nervous, but knew she was probably failing. Nervous and guilty can often be confused.

Coach Horne sat in the Chair and described what happened the night before. It was rather a dull story aside from helping Derick stop the intruders. Before Grandpa called him, he was fast asleep. And after all the action, he went back to his apartment, didn't even bother changing out of his clothes, and crashed on his bed again.

One by one, each member of the Council took the Chair and told about where they were before and after the incident pulling intruders out of the London fire. But it was Mrs. Trinhouse that Abby watched extra closely as she related her evening.

Mrs. Trinhouse had stayed up late researching on her rings. Nothing about meeting anyone. No sinister plot. Then she got the call and came to the basement with her husband. After, she stayed up on her rings some more and then finally went to bed.

"Can I ask a question?" Abby interrupted. Grandpa nodded. "Why did you go to the Watchman a few nights ago?"

Immediately the image of Mrs. Trinhouse crawling up into the belly of the school's tower appeared on the screen behind her. Mrs. Trinhouse gasped. She closed her eyes for a moment then looked up at Grandpa.

He placed his hand on his chin and looked back at her. "Yes, go ahead."

Mrs. Trinhouse began, "My husband and I worked with Oscar to develop a sensor array that can detect Muns's large energy bursts. We hid it in the tower. Being up high only strengthens its ability to sense the bursts." Images of Mrs. Trinhouse, Mr. Trinhouse, and Grandpa together appeared on the screen. They were looking at a machine about the size of a desk. Then the view shifted to the three of them putting the mechanism in the tower. "Mr. Trinhouse had to remove part of the floor and install a trapdoor all in one night. It was a lot of work."

"But that doesn't explain why you went there," Abby said.

"I was doing a routine check," Mrs. Trinhouse responded. An image appeared of her quickly looking at the machine, but that gave way to scenes of her thoroughly inspecting it.

"I believe there was more to it than that," Coach Horne said.

"There was," Mr. Trinhouse said. "While I went to help bring the prisoners to the Chair she was inspecting the machine for any alterations."

"Alterations? Why?" Abby asked.

"The machine could measure energy bursts, but nothing else," Mrs. Trinhouse said, glancing at Grandpa. "I was looking for clues as to how Oscar knows not only that Muns used a burst, but where in time he has gone."

Grandpa rubbed his head and gave a tired smile. "And I have given her the tools to find the answer to that question."

Members of the Council exchanged glances. Who else was looking for the same information Abby was? It made sense that Grandpa would ensure others were on the trail to find out as well. Perhaps they already knew. But did that mean the Trinhouses were innocent? What about the suitcase that had its insides taken from right under their noses?

Grandpa spoke again. "I think it is time I place guards in

front of and inside of Abby's and Derick's rooms, along with my own, my son's and daughter-in-law's room, and Coach Horne's. We cannot afford any more incidents."

"And not the rest of us?" Mrs. Trinhouse asked.

Grandpa looked back at the math and engineering teacher. "If you wish, I will do so, but that may give away that you have keys."

"Maybe you could place guards on random doors as well. That would throw them off," Derick suggested.

Grandpa nodded. "It would also give them a list that they could check off. They would weed it down eventually. I think for your safety we must do this." The Trinhouses also opted for guards at their apartment.

"And now," Coach Horne said, "I understand that we didn't have Dr. Mackleprank in for this discussion earlier. He is not a member of the Council, but can we invite him to sit in the Chair and answer our questions?"

• • •

Dr. Mackleprank? Derick was upset. Mackleprank couldn't have done it. He had been shot by tranquilizer darts. And he had not been using an avatar to sneak around.

Grandpa raised his cane. "I have messaged Dr. Mackleprank and he is unable to be here."

Mrs. Trinhouse gestured toward Grandpa with her hand. "But you said he was doing well, that he had recovered."

"I will assure you that I have questioned him and am entirely satisfied that he is innocent," Grandpa testified.

Coach Horne grunted. "You realize that is very suspicious."

"Yes, I do," Grandpa answered. "However, I feel you will have to trust me. You have trusted me thus far and you will have to do it again."

Dr. Mackleprank had been a great teacher. He was a confidant and a friend. If only there was a way to help defend him. Derick stood.

"I have something to say." Everyone looked at him. He felt a little shy and powerful both at the same time. "I'm not sure if I'm supposed to tell you this or not, but I think I should. Dr. Mackleprank had his own locket. He gave it to me. I completed the challenge in the simulator and got a final key. Why would he bother stealing someone else's key if he could have had one himself?"

Everyone seemed lost in thought.

Grandpa looked over at Derick and nodded. Maybe it was the right time to say it. Or maybe he was just impressed with Derick trying to protect his teacher's good name. Derick couldn't tell.

"But why would he give away his key?" Mr. Trinhouse asked.

"That doesn't make any sense," Mrs. Trinhouse said.

"I am well aware of the reason," Grandpa said.

"And you aren't going to share it?" Coach Horne asked.

"I'm sorry," Grandpa apologized. "I'm not at liberty to say. I cannot break confidences. Again, you will have to trust me that Dr. Mackleprank's reasons are valid, and that I trust him."

"We also checked all of the avatar logs to be sure no one was using them to enter in through the ducts," Abby said. "Dr. Mackleprank was not listed. No one was."

"We need to know why he can't come sit in the Chair like the rest of us!" Mr. Trinhouse demanded, standing tall.

"He is otherwise engaged," Grandpa said.

"What could he possibly be doing that is more important than this?" Coach Horne asked, now on his feet as well.

Grandpa just shook his head.

Coach Horne threw his arms in the air. "We are never going to figure any of this out with all of these secrets." It felt like Coach Horne was right. "If he will not come to the Chair, there has to be another way to prove if he is guilty or innocent."

"There is," Mrs. Trinhouse said. Everyone turned to look at her. She paused and spoke more quietly. "Put him in a cell. If there is another incident while he is locked up, we know that he is innocent. If nothing else happens, we are protected and have our man."

Put him in a cell? That seemed cruel. She was proposing to treat him just like Muns's soldiers who had tried to change time.

Derick and Grandpa both fought against it, but in the end, the majority agreed. It was the best way to test his innocence. As Derick was logging off, he heard his grandpa's voice. "It has come down to locking my friends in cages."

# THE ANSWER

I can't believe they put him in a cell." Derick shook his head. "There is no way he did it."

"I have no idea what to think anymore," Abby admitted.

"I don't even know what you're talking about," Carol said. "I know. I know. It's your secret club stuff."

They climbed down one more ladder headed to the basement where the simulator waited behind a thick door. "Are you sure we should even be down here?" Carol asked. "I mean I know we can be, but whoever it is has been trying to get keys, and wouldn't this be one of the first places he would look?"

Abby didn't answer. Carol had a point.

Derick knew Abby was nervous. She was more than nervous. She was scared. But he also knew that she wouldn't back down. That wasn't Abby. He admired that about her.

"We have to figure this out," Abby finally said. Derick thought he heard a bit of a tremble to her voice.

"Yes, we do," Derick agreed, stepping down the ladder. "Plus, whoever it is only seems to attack at night."

"I hope he doesn't decide to venture out into new territory today," Carol said.

Derick dropped from the bottom rung on the ladder to the floor below and walked toward the simulator door. The silence of the place was eerie. If someone jumped out right now, he would definitely scream and try to attack him. Or run away.

"Did you just get a message from Grandpa?" Abby asked. "He wants us all to be inside in one hour. And he's going to change up the rooms where we sleep just to keep us safe. He'll tell us where soon."

"Got it." Derick didn't stop walking further into the room. "That sounds like a smart idea."

"That means we only have time for one of us to go in," Carol said. "Unless it's like super quick, but knowing your grandpa, this is going to take a while. He doesn't go for those Quicknote versions of lessons."

"I need to do this." Derick approached the lockers. He knew a suit hung inside much like those he used in the avatar labs. And like with the avatars, when he stepped inside the simulator, he could feel whatever the person whose life he was simulating felt.

"No, I can," Abby volunteered. She took a few steps forward and grabbed Derick's arm.

"No." He didn't look back at her. "I failed last time. And I need this."

"But you tried again and you made it. You got a key," Abby tried to encourage him.

"Barely," Derick said. "I need to completely succeed."

Abby and Carol agreed to let him go. He put on his suit and approached the large door with gears and bars that guarded the simulator. When he was less than two feet away, his pocket started to glow. No—it wasn't his pocket, it was the sphere inside.

"Looks like it knows you're here." Abby pointed at his pocket. "Some location technology, no doubt."

An image of Grandpa almost immediately appeared. "It looks as though you truly want to know the answer to your question. You have been determined and hopefully have learned lessons that have prepared you for your answer. But I'm afraid I must put you through one more simulation. Unlike what you have done before in this particular location, it is not a simulation through an event in the distant past. This one is closer to you. I warn you, it is very difficult. It will bring up questions in your mind that will only be answered after the test."

So he wasn't about to step into the past. What was he about to step into? And what kind of questions would this experience raise?

The image of Grandpa reached out a bony finger, his beard shaking with his jowls as he spoke, "Know that I do this with a purpose. Pay attention. It will not be easy. In fact, it may wrench at your very heart. In some ways, it may require you to want your answer more than air."

Derick thought of the young man who learned from Socrates. He began taking heavy deep breaths—just in case.

"What you are about to go through," Grandpa explained, "is very real to someone. It is a piece of their life. If at any moment you cannot take it anymore, simply press the button on the back of your neck. You will return to the simulator and can leave. But if you want the answer to your question and the power and opportunities that come with it, you have to see the experience through to the end."

The words "cannot take it anymore" rang in Derick's ears. He took another deep breath and approached the door. He held his glowing sphere in one hand as he retrieved his key and opened the door with the other. The gears and bars twisted and turned and the heavy slab swiveled open. Derick stepped inside.

When the door closed behind him, it sounded extra hollow, as if it was sealing him in a vault. Derick expected his world to change, to see the situation of his challenge, but nothing happened. He stood alone in the dark with a glowing sphere. In a moment, ripples of light shot through the orb. *It must be processing some sort of code or sending a signal—maybe both.* A light on the wall of the dark room lit just enough to show a mechanical arm reaching out. It was similar to the arms in the virtual booths in the Portuguese and Math and Engineering classrooms. Derick placed his glowing sphere inside.

The darkness changed quickly. Soon Derick stood in a

room that was mostly white, with bright lights above him. He immediately felt terrible. He wheezed and choked. His mind felt slow, like it was pinched, with not enough space to do its work. His body felt weak, drained of everything it had. He collapsed to the ground.

He heard voices and felt hands lifting him up and setting him down on a bed.

"Are you okay?" a man asked. Derick opened his eyes, but the light hurt. He saw a man, not very old, wearing clothes covered with a cartoon goose in several different poses. Weird clothes. The man checked him all over, asking if certain places hurt. Derick answered that most everything hurt. He could hear other voices, but he gave them similar responses.

"You're going to be just fine," the man said. "You've been quite a trouper."

Derick felt a squeeze on his hand. He turned to the other side. This time he managed to open his eyes a little wider. The pain had subsided a little. He saw a woman.

"Don't worry, honey." She placed her hand on the side of his face. "The doctor will be back in to tell us how to help you get better." Was this the mom of the person whose situation he was in?

Another surge of pain. He closed his eyes and let out a groan. Someone had really felt this? Derick wanted it to stop. He could press the button on the back of his neck. No. That wasn't an option. How could anyone feel like this all the time?

Someone moved. A man. The dad? He paced at the

foot of the bed a couple of times, moving his fingers quickly. Wait. He was using rings! This wasn't the past. This was modern. It couldn't be older than a few years. It might even be now.

The man in the cartoon outfit checked his vitals with a small rod that scanned him from head to foot. He must be a nurse.

The mom squeezed his hand, then brought her head down and kissed his forehead. "You're going to be just fine." Her voice shook, and he could feel her hand tremble.

The dad pressed one of his rings, turning them off. He approached Derick. "There are a whole lot of people cheering for you, Son. Aunts and uncles, cousins, neighbors—the works. We'll figure this out." He sounded strong and confident. He knew everything would be fine. And then, for just a flash, the man's eyes filled with tears. He blinked, and they were gone. He was terrified too.

Another wave of pain. Another groan. Derick's eyes watered. He tried to open them again, but had to hold them closed.

He felt a pinch in his arm. And then, slowly, the pain lessened. They had given him some sort of medicine.

He opened his eyes and saw a woman enter. She wore a light blue shirt with a long white coat over it. She also wore a mole—a small black dot on her cheek, so she could talk hands free on her rings, commanding them what to do. She must be the doctor. "I've looked over the scans," she said. "And . . ." the doctor's voice broke. "And it's a new thread of cancer."

Derick watched as the mom burst into tears. The dad turned away, turned back, and then away again.

The doctor bit her lip, waiting for the parents. She touched Derick's arm lightly. "This never gets any easier. But I'm going to have to recommend emergency surgery."

"Wait," the dad said. "What kind of surgery?"

Derick tried to listen as he heard about the cancer. Though a cure for the grand majority of cancers had been discovered years ago, several new threads were becoming more and more common. They hadn't been able to determine why. The doctor recommended they go in and remove a tumor on his brain. She would use small tubes to enter the brain and dissolve the tumor, "but any time we do surgery on or near the brain there are heavy risks." The doctor discussed Derick—strike that, the person whose life he was witnessing—becoming mentally handicapped, losing eyesight, or even dying.

Heavy risks. "But what will happen if we don't?" Mom asked.

The doctor pressed her lips tightly together. "The tumor will grow and then you'll lose him. You might have a few good years. You may only have months."

Derick's dad turned to him and took his hand. "This isn't easy, bud. We're going to need you to be strong." He brushed his arm along his own eyes. "I'm going to need to be strong." The mother grabbed his other hand. "Do you think you can do this? Can you be amazingly brave and go through with the surgery?"

All words were gone. *Kids* had to face this? Shouldn't

they just be worried about homework and friends and the next thing they were going to do for fun? But there he was, looking up at a dad and a mom, both terribly concerned, both waiting for an answer. His answer.

"It'll be all right," the mom reassured.

Derick could see the doctor in the background, waiting. The whole room felt heavy—not how rooms are supposed to feel. This was so different from being in the Civil War and choosing to rush down the mountainside with only a bayonet. It took at least the same courage, maybe more. It was something Derick had never felt before. He still felt pain, and fear, but the idea that the surgery might go wrong and he might die shook him. If this were really him, he wouldn't have enough time to graduate from Cragbridge Hall. He might not even live to start the next year. Suddenly he didn't care so much about avatars or the avatar club. He didn't care about failing every now and then. All he cared about was family and the time he had left. If this were real, he would gather his mom and dad around him, Abby and Grandpa too. He would spend as much time as he could with them while he still could.

"I can do it," Derick managed to say. He wished saying it aloud would have brought some sort of assurance that it would be all right.

Soon Derick was being transported down a hall. A nurse was escorting him with his parents by his side. Then they stopped. "All right, Mom and Dad," the nurse said. "You'll have to wish him luck here, and then leave him to us." The nurse was surprisingly cheery for the situation. He must have to deal with similar circumstances all the time. He explained to Derick that they would be going into a sterilized room for surgery and his parents would have to go to the waiting room.

Too much. They couldn't even be with him? His mom bent down and hugged him. He could feel her tears on his neck. She didn't say anything. She didn't even try. He hugged her back. Soon his father joined, all three of them in one teary embrace. And they stayed that way for a long time. This was different than pain. It felt like blackness covered over Derick. He knew it wasn't real. He knew he was just in a simulator, but it felt real. It felt like something had taken all hope and left him with nothing.

Then he entered the room. There were people in masks and lots of machines and lights. He had never felt so alone. A nurse had him breathe into a mask and he soon felt himself falling asleep. He had no idea whether he would wake up again.

Derick woke up. He was in a bed and his parents were beside him. But he felt week and brittle again. He hated it. He felt useless. He wanted to jump out of there. He wanted his life back. He wanted to press the button on the back of his neck and go back to his life where he could move and breathe without pain. Where he knew he could live a long life. Then again, maybe situations outside and inside the simulator were more similar than he thought. If Muns succeeded, was the time he might have with his family ending? Would Muns ruin everything?

But Grandpa had said this was very real to someone.

Someone else out there didn't have the power to simply back out, to press a button on the back of his neck and feel good again. He had to face this. He didn't have the choice. It felt like hours passing, over and over. Derick tried to get up and walk and succeeded, but it took so much energy. The pain flashed again. Over and over, Derick felt like he passed days in the same way, until he lay in bed, barely able to breathe.

The mom and dad were beside him again. So were several others. There were a lot of smiles, but a lot of tears. They hugged him and told him to hang on. Derick felt a surge of pain and closed his eyes. Then the doctor came in. She said they had performed another test, and she recommended that when he had recovered enough, he have a follow-up surgery.

*Again?* He had to face it *again?* Everything inside him wanted to scream. He felt like crying, but he had no more tears.

Once more his parents knelt at his bed and asked if he could be brave. He didn't want to. He didn't have any more in him. But eventually he closed his eyes and nodded his head.

And Derick was back in the simulator, an image of Grandpa waiting for him. "You have endured," he said, "an experience that someone real has had. In fact, I'll show him to you."

Derick saw images of a boy. He saw the doctor come in. He saw the crying. He saw the boy with his heart-wrenched family. But he also saw something else. He saw the boy in bed, smiling. Having felt what the boy had felt, Derick wondered how he could do that. He saw the boy writing messages to friends and even other patients on his rings. He drew virtual pictures and sent them along as well. There was even a time when the boy visited others in the hospital. He had to ride in a wheelchair, but he visited his friends.

"Every day, every *moment* is a gift," Grandpa said. "And there are some who truly understand that. They live it. And if I'm going to divulge this next secret to you, you must understand it too. You must treat the present with the love that others who understand this do."

Derick felt strange. He had spent so much time worrying about succeeding, about getting into the avatar club, about getting his key, and about finishing this challenge. But now, though he knew it was all important, some of that attitude felt selfish. He didn't have to be the best. He didn't have to succeed all the time. He had time. He could work hard and get better. Not everyone had that same luxury.

"Please take your sphere." Grandpa gestured toward the mechanical arm that returned from the wall. Derick retrieved his sphere, holding it tightly.

"You have now passed a series of challenges, as you did to gain the final key. These challenges were more to teach you. You see, when I discovered the secret to seeing the past, even I didn't realize the power that I had found. We could see the past from any angle. We could come in from on top, from the side, it didn't really matter. And to those who are in the past it is like we are invisible. We can come in and affect anything. They can't see us coming." Derick remembered being in a virtual world where he was invisible. There were some similarities. He hadn't thought of it that way before.

"There are fewer limits to this power than perhaps you suppose," Grandpa said, pointing his cane in Derick's direction. "For with the power to discover the past comes an equally dangerous power. I've decided that the secrets of it can't die with me." Grandpa took a deep breath. "The Bridge also can allow us to see and even enter the present."

Grandpa paused, obviously letting the information soak in. Derick tried to think of all the ramifications this could have.

"This may not sound like much at first, but it is a tremendous responsibility." The image of Grandpa rubbed his temples. "Using the Bridge, you could see anywhere in the present from any angle. It could be a great tool for gathering information." Derick's mind swam in the possibilities. If this meant what he thought it did, through the Bridge they could find out what presidents discussed in high-level meetings. They could spy on drug lords. They could even see bank accounts. It would be the greatest spying tool in existence.

"And," Grandpa said, "what if you could enter anywhere in the present? It can become a portal. We can enter anywhere from any angle." Derick could go to Hawaii in an instant. He could see the Second Eiffel tower. He could go anywhere.

The image of Grandpa banged his cane against the ground. "But I need to stress again that this power should not be used unless completely necessary. Just because we *can* does not mean that we *should*."

Grandpa cleared his throat. "Obviously, you now know that the Bridge can show the past sooner than fifty years ago." All of a sudden it made sense. Once Grandpa knew that Muns had used an energy burst, he could use the Bridge to search the place where the energy burst had been generated. He might need to go into the past a few minutes, but he could see the time they had entered and then bring up the Bridge to that time. He could probably even read the code from their machine to make sure he had it exact.

"However," Grandpa continued, "I placed a barrier at fifty years in the past because I noticed something: the closer we use the Bridge to the present, the more difficult it is on the invention. Even merely looking at the present for longer periods of time can cause the Bridge to begin to tremble. I do not know why, but approaching closer to the present makes it more unstable. If you enter the present, it intensifies. So you must only use this ability under the direst of circumstances, and you must not stay long." The image of Grandpa took a few steps. "If you accept responsibility over the present as well as the past, then please place your sphere here." One brick slid out of its place, leaving a half circle opening in it. Derick paused for a moment—thinking about the power offered to him. He eventually set his sphere in the holder. It glowed again, streams of light dancing inside it.

"You will find," Grandpa said, "that if you approach the Bridge and set your sphere just above one of the keys, an arm will rise from the console and take it. If one person has a sphere and a key, he or she can view the present. Knowing that gathering information would be essential if anyone ever discovered my secret, I made this simple. Remember not to look long. Also, there must be three keys and three spheres in order to *enter* the present."

If Grandpa knew all this, he had obviously viewed the present before. He had his own key and his own sphere, so that was possible. But had he entered the present? Maybe. And if he had, perhaps Derick's parents had spheres as well to help him. That made sense. "You," Grandpa explained, "must realize that this is a truly great power, and for some it may be a truly great temptation. When someone finds they might be able to manipulate the now, they may understand its power and crave it. So please protect this secret."

Derick had not thought of it that way.

"Remember the warning," Grandpa said. "Use this only when absolutely necessary. If you view the present for too long, you may damage the Bridge. And if you enter the present, you do not have long at all."

# NOT WHAT
# YOU THINK

Abby tried to soak it all in. Derick had let them in from the other side of the simulator and told them what he had learned and experienced.

"We need to use it," Abby said. "Let's go to the Bridge." She started walking further down the hall.

"What?" Carol asked. "Did you not hear the part about only using this when the world is going to end or something?"

"Yeah, I heard it." Abby kept walking. "But this might just be that situation. Muns already has another key and he may be set to gain a third. But with this sphere, we can find out who has been attacking and tranquilizing people in the middle of the night. And who has Coach Adonavich's key."

"Do you think we should ask your grandpa to see if this is a good idea?" Carol asked.

Abby stopped. "He's probably already thought of it and done it, but he wants us to act for ourselves. He wants us to learn. And I want that. I want . . ." She paused. "I *need* to see for myself."

Carol and Derick looked at each other. "I think I do too," Derick said. "Someone I really respect has been accused and is locked up. If we notice something Grandpa didn't, we may be able to prove he is innocent."

Carol eventually nodded. They continued on to the room with the large metal tree-looking Bridge and approached the console.

Derick placed his key. "Let's find the right time first and then we'll put in the sphere."

"But we can't," Abby responded. "We can't even search within the last fifty years until the sphere is in."

"Good point," Derick said. "When should I search?" They spoke together and decided to start at the beginning— when Dr. Mackleprank and Ms. Entrese were first attacked.

Derick moved his sphere just above the keyhole. One key and one sphere, that should do it. Once again, it began to glow. Just as Grandpa had said, an arm emerged from the Bridge and collected the sphere. When it was inside the Bridge, Derick began scrolling through the dates. There were no limitations. He found the entry for a few early mornings before and selected Ms. Entrese's English room.

The other half of the basement became a class Abby had sat in many times. Ms. Entrese entered wearing a black dress and shoes. She hurried to her desk and began to typing on her rings. She must have been getting ready for the day.

The lights went out in the English room and the hallway outside.

Abby heard Ms. Entrese gasp as a man entered.

"You startled me," she said. "Can I help you?"

"Yes," he answered. Abby looked at him closely, trying to make out any features. But his hoodie was over his eyes and it was quite dark. It was only by the residual light from down the hall that Abby could see anything at all. "Muns sent me." Abby didn't recognize the voice.

Ms. Entrese stood from her chair, pressing it back like Abby had imagined. The man circled around. "I have a message."

"Well I have a message for you," Ms. Entrese said, her voice sharp. "You can tell him that what he is doing is dangerous and wrong. And I will tell you that you are a fool for following him. You will one day regret all this. I'm glad I chose to fight against him. It was right. And no matter what happens here, I still stand behind my decision."

Chills ran through Abby. How could she be so brave and bold in such a terrifying situation?

The man hesitated for a moment. Why? Was he doubting? Then he stood up straighter. "Your words will do nothing for you."

"They aren't just words," Ms. Entrese said, unflinching.

The man pulled a straw out from his jacket and loaded the other end. A dart. "Muns sends the message that this is a very fitting way to take you out of the picture. You would understand if you only knew more about me."

And in the next instant, the man blew and Ms. Entrese fell to the floor.

"What did that mean?" Abby asked. "If only she knew more about him?"

"No time," Derick said. "We have to see Dr. Mackleprank before we start putting too much pressure on the Bridge."

He selected earlier in the night.

The other half of the basement turned to a teacher's apartment. After the lights had been out for a while, the intruder appeared and latched his device to the door. Within a few seconds he unlatched it then stepped inside and closed the door behind him. Once in Mackleprank's room, the man quickly blew a dart. Mackleprank lay in bed, and didn't flinch as the dart hit his skin. There was no talk. No struggle. No fight. It was hard to believe when Dr. Mackleprank could kick like a ninja.

Then the man turned on the lights and searched the entire room, throwing objects across the ground. He was fast, and then he left the room and ran up the hall.

The Bridge started to tremble.

"Stop it," Abby said. "Pull your sphere."

"Almost. I need to see if there are any other clues. He's innocent." Derick fast-forwarded.

They saw him get up in the morning and touch his neck. He looked at it in the mirror. He called Grandpa on his rings and spoke with him. They watched as he went to his first class.

"Derick," Abby said. "Now."

The Bridge trembled again.

Derick was just about to stop it when he saw Dr. Mackleprank put on the sensors and enter a lab booth to control an avatar. He was going to demonstrate for the class.

"I can see his movement in the lab itself with this," Derick said to himself. Because the labs had no windows, no one could watch the person inside. Derick couldn't resist the chance to see the master at work.

The Bridge trembled again.

"Now."

"Yeah, Derick," Carol agreed. "The most important invention in history is starting to freak out a little. I think we should try to take care of it." Derick didn't respond. Dr. Mackleprank locked the door and then leaned against the side. And then he fell asleep.

What?

Derick changed the perspective to where the avatar was in the adjoining room, just as Abby pulled out the key. The image of time stopped and the Bridge calmed.

"Don't ever do that again," Abby said. "Grandpa trusts you."

"Did you see that?" Derick asked, his eyes still wide.

"Yeah," Carol said. "He's a terrible teacher. He just went into the lab to sleep."

"But the avatar moved." Derick pointed where the image had been. "If Dr. Mackleprank was sleeping, who was controlling it?"

· · ·

"I'm sorry, Abby," Grandpa said. "I cannot meet right now. I am extremely busy."

"Just a couple of quick questions, Grandpa," Abby pleaded.

"Okay, but make them quick."

Abby looked at her grandpa through her rings. "First, I found the answer to my question. Well, Derick actually finished it and Carol helped out."

Grandpa gave a tired smile. "You are amazing young people."

"Thanks," Abby said. "We used the sphere to search the attacks."

Grandpa's face suddenly changed, then softened again. "I suppose if ever there was a time, it was this. I have also searched them."

"We thought you might have, but I just had to look," Abby admitted. "We only saw the first two attacks."

Grandpa rubbed his chin. "The others are even more perplexing. No one approaches the door. With no lights and some sort of heat distractors messing up our night vision, we cannot make out a thing. And there's a low hum that keeps us from hearing anything."

"Are the Trinhouses and Mackleprank innocent?" Abby asked.

Grandpa nodded. "Yes, they are. At least there is no evidence against them."

"But we stumbled onto something about Dr. Mackleprank," Abby said. "When he went into a lab he didn't hook up. He fell asleep and somehow the avatar still worked. Who was controlling it?"

Grandpa looked at her, his eyes unblinking. "Another great question, Abby."

"And do I have to go through another series before finding out who it is?" Abby asked.

"No. Well, at least I won't ask you to. If you want an answer to that question, you will need to ask Rafa."

• • •

Abby, Carol, and Derick met up with Rafa in the avatar lab. The Brazilian looked up at his friends. "It's good to see you, but we only have a few minutes before we have to get to our rooms."

"Yeah," Derick said. "And I think the two of us are rooming together now." He scratched his neck. It wasn't going to be easy to bring this up.

Carol looked at Rafa. "This might get really uncomfortable," Carol said. "Well, I've heard I make people uncomfortable a lot, like I'm too expressive, too forward, and too hyper, but that's not what I'm talking about. We've got to ask you a difficult question—like crazy mysterious difficult."

Rafa looked at Derick. "I didn't tell them anything," Derick responded.

"Oh, you two have manly secrets," Carol teased, eyeing Derick, then Rafa. "Well, Abby and I have a bunch of secrets too. Like—"

Abby interrupted. "Why does Dr. Mackleprank look like he's sleeping when he's controlling an avatar?"

Rafa's mouth fell open.

Silence.

"How did you know that?" Rafa finally asked. "There's no security camera in the booth he uses."

"Why isn't there?" Abby asked.

Rafa closed his eyes and then opened them. "I don't know if I should tell you."

"Our grandpa said we would have to ask you," Abby said. "You are the only one who can tell us."

Rafa moved back and forth. He ran his fingers through his hair several times. "I just—this—" Rafa breathed out and back in. He looked at each of the three students intensely. "Do you promise to tell no one? *No one? Ever?*"

They all agreed.

"I trust you, and I trust your grandfather, but I don't know that I trust anyone else." He paused. "And this means the world to me."

No one said a thing.

Rafa spoke again. "Dr. Mackleprank is not who you think he is."

"What do you mean?" Derick asked.

Rafa rubbed his eyebrows then looked up again. "Do you remember when I said that your grandfather once did a great kindness for me and my family?" He looked at Derick, then proceeded to tell the girls what he had told Derick earlier. "You see, my mother is the principal inventor of the avatars."

"That explains why you're so good at them," Carol said.

Rafa nodded. "I've been able to experiment with them all of my life. Your grandfather came in at a certain time and really helped my mother with major breakthroughs in the process. Without him, you would not feel what the avatar felt, nor would they be as quick to react. In short, they would only be very lifelike robots."

"And that is how Grandpa helped you?"

"That is only part of it. You see, there is a great potential in avatars. They could be used to learn, as they are here, or they could be used for very destructive purposes. They could be spies. You could substitute someone real for a simple avatar. The possibilities are endless."

"Yes."

"Well, even before the avatars were announced, some . . . *groups* found out about them. They wanted the avatars for their own purposes. At first, it was all friendly, but it soon became very dangerous." Rafa exhaled and gripped his hands together. "And from there, your grandfather helped my mother go into hiding. She has been safe and sound ever since."

Pride swelled within Derick. Grandpa had truly helped her greatly. But then he had a question. "I don't get it. What does the story about your mother have to do with Dr. Mackleprank?"

Rafa just looked at them. "Think about it."

"Okay? I'm not coming up with anything," Abby said.

"Of all the places in the world," Rafa stretched out his

arms, "the one where my mother would like to be is here, with me."

"But she can't because she's in hiding," Derick added.

"Unless she happened to be a great inventor," Rafa said. "Of avatars."

"No!" Abby said in disbelief.

Derick gasped. "Dr. Mackleprank is an avatar! There are human avatars! And he's really your mother?"

# WAITING

N o way no way no way," Carol said, jumping up and down. "That is the craziest thing I've ever heard! Crazier than watching all of the *Little Elvis in Space* series all in one day, or crazier than giving up ice cream, and crazier than eating one of those, like, octopus appetizers. Oh, they are so slimy and gross. This is like 700,000 times crazier than that."

"Wait," Derick said. "So that is why Dr. Mackleprank looked like he was sleeping in the avatar room, because your mother had to leave him as an avatar and go into the other avatar."

"And she controls all of them from somewhere in hiding," Carol added. "Still so crazy."

Rafa nodded. "Yes, avatar signals can go around the world."

"But Dr. Mackleprank has been tranquilized twice. How do you tranquilize an avatar?" Abby asked.

"You can't," Derick answered.

"Obviously the dart wouldn't make her pass out," Rafa said. "My mother had to fake it. Once someone tranquilized her, she could hardly just keep moving like nothing had happened. Someone would find out her secret. Plus, both times she was attacked, she was out of the Mackleprank avatar at the time. The first time, she didn't even realize she had been attacked until she reentered the avatar and felt a pain in her neck. The second time, she didn't realize until she got the message from your grandpa," Rafa pointed at the twins, "telling her to go to the basement. When she came back into Dr. Mackleprank, she felt the dart."

"But wouldn't whoever the bad guy was know something was up when Ms. Entrese was out for weeks and Mackleprank was up the next day?" Abby asked.

"That was your grandfather's decision," Rafa said. "He quickly analyzed the darts and based on how much of the tranquilizer each one held, it actually looked as though the dart that hit Mackleprank was only intended for the night. It was the first time my mom had done anything against Muns. It was probably a warning more than anything. And the second time was to keep her out of the way."

"But wait," Derick blurted out. "When you were in the gorilla in the basement, why were you in such a hurry when you heard that Mackleprank had been attacked? Your mom was fine, right?"

"Everything was happening very fast and I hadn't heard

from my mother yet. I went to make sure she was fine and that her secret was safe." A corner of Rafa's mouth curled up. "You can't just leave one of the world's most sophisticated robots lying around, pretending to be tranquilized. Your grandfather said everything was okay, but I didn't want to take any chances. Plus, the person most likely to figure out her secret was whoever it was who shot her. It was time to be extra careful."

"It explains why Dr. Mackleprank couldn't sit in the Chair," Abby added. "Because he's not human. A robot can't have its mind read."

"*Exactamente.*"

"And that is why Dr. Mackleprank gave me his locket," Derick said. "Because he couldn't go into a simulator as a robot either."

Rafa nodded.

"So, super crazy," Carol said. "I really can't even think of the right way to express this. Take the craziest thing you know of, dip it in crazy batter, fry it in crazy oil, dip it in crazy sauce, chew it all up, and that would not be as crazy as this." She paused, tapping her finger on her chin. "No. That didn't quite do it. But it did make me a little hungry. Doesn't crazy batter and crazy sauce sound mouthwatering together?"

"Wait," Derick said. "Why would your mother have a key in the first place?"

"I believe your grandfather hoped that one day she would live at Cragbridge Hall in person. But when Cragbridge received the avatars for educational purposes, it would be the first place anyone would check for my mom. So she hasn't lived here yet, at least in person. My mother couldn't have known she wouldn't be able to finish the challenges as an avatar."

"Wow," Abby said. "It is going to take me a while to get used to this."

. . .

"Holy cow!" Carol whispered to Abby in the bed across from her. "We have an armed guard outside our room. And one inside." She gestured at the woman standing at attention, a gun drawn over her forearm, against the far wall.

There was also a guard at the door. Abby had seen him as she and Carol moved to an apartment in the teacher's quarters. Grandpa had left their room empty and found this open space. It was unpredictable, and in this case, unpredictable was very good. Grandpa assured them that he had picked only the most trusted of those on the security staff. In a way, they were hiding—with guards. It made Abby feel safer, but not completely. She would rather have spent the night with her parents and Derick and Grandpa. She wanted them all as close as possible. But if they were all together, that might make it too easy for the attacker. He could get a bunch of keys in one stop.

"Maybe 'holy cow' wasn't the right expression," Carol whispered. "I don't even know what it means. Is it like a cow with wings and a halo? So weird."

"I have no idea," Abby whispered back.

"Super toad!" Carol said.

"What?"

"I was trying out another expression. Instead of 'holy cow,' maybe you can just pick any adjective and any animal and it would work."

"No, I don't think so."

"Dancing piglet!" Carol whispered a little louder. "Oh, it totally works. Bloated antelope! Ugly barn owl! Hippie hedgehog! I'm going to have to write these down."

"Shhhh," Abby shushed, but she was secretly glad that Carol could lighten the mood.

Then the lights went out.

Abby heart leapt to her throat. Over the pounding in her ears she could hear the guard shuffle her feet. Was she pointing her gun at the enemy right now?

Something hit the door. It wasn't a knock, and more of a thud than a scrape.

"Are you okay out there?" the security guard asked. A moment later, she repeated, "Are you okay?"

Abby quickly turned on her rings and messaged her parents and Grandpa:

> Something's happening. We may have just lost the
> guard outside our room.

Her fingers shook as she typed.

Then a hum began in the room. It was just like Grandpa had described. Grandpa sent a message back.

**Someone is on the way.**

"Something's messing with my night vision," the guard muttered. And then they heard her drop to the floor.

"It's him," Abby whispered. "He's here." A surge of terror coursed through her. She couldn't be shot with a tranquilizer; she had to solve this. She had to finish out this semester.

Abby looked at the window, then her door. Whoever it was, he was able to come in without a trace. She didn't even know what direction to face. She couldn't see anything. And with that hum, she couldn't hear anything either. She wanted to grab something to hit him with, but she didn't have a bat or a bar in her room. There was nothing. Wait. Abby grabbed her blanket and pulled it around her neck. She wasn't going to give him a target.

Abby felt something next to her. She screamed. Was she about to get shot? Would she wake up to some alternate reality? Or would she even wake up at all? Suddenly Ms. Entrese popped into her head. She was so bold, so brave. "You coward," Abby said into the darkness. "You come sneaking into people's rooms in the middle of the night. You shoot them with tranquilizers and steal what's theirs. And now you hunt seventh-grade girls. You're just a coward!"

"Whoa," Carol muttered.

The doorknob wiggled.

Carol screamed.

"Leave us alone!" Abby shouted.

"Yeah, you creepy ugly crazy freakish man. Get out of here!" Carol added.

The door rattled again. "Abby! Abby!"

Two voices blended together. It was her parents.

Abby stumbled off her bed and to the door. She entered the code and pulled it open quickly. In moments, she was in her parents' arms. Carol joined her, hugging them both. The two guards who had flanked Abby's parents now continued on into the room.

"You're okay," Dad said, moving them both down the hall away from the room.

"He was here, Dad." Abby broke down into tears. "He was here. He took out the guards."

"But you're okay, right?" Mom asked, looking them over.

"It was terrifying." Carol opened her mouth to say something else, but instead just mumbled "terrifying" a few more times.

"I was so scared," Abby confessed. "So scared."

"You're okay now," Dad comforted.

The lights flickered back on. Abby could no longer hear the hum in the room.

The two girls related everything that had happened. The guards checked on their two counterparts and called for more people to take them down to the med unit. "That's four tonight," one said.

*Four?* Had the man struck somewhere else?

One of the guards approached the two girls. "Is this yours?" He handed Abby a thin screen. It wasn't, but it hadn't been in the room before. When Abby touched it, a simple drawing appeared—a simple drawing of Abby's belt, with an arrow next to the latch. Abby closed her eyes and groaned. He knew where she kept her key.

"Oh, and this." The other guard handed Abby a small black object. As she took it in her hands, she noticed its notches and curves—another chess piece.

• • •

This time they sat face to face. There was no need to do a virtual meeting. Grandpa looked older and tired. "I invited my son and daughter-in-law," Grandpa said. Abby loved seeing her parents there. "They were not in this council, but we know Muns knows them and we need more help. Last night, our attacker hit all the doors we guarded. He took out all the guards. And—" Grandpa flicked his fingers and showed the footage of finding Coach Horne. There were several darts in his neck. Perhaps it took more for such a large man. "He took his key," Grandpa explained.

"He knew where mine was," Abby said.

"And mine," Derick added.

"Yes, it is perplexing why he gave up and only left screens for you two. He wanted you to know that he knows where they are."

"He left no such screen for us," Mr. Trinhouse said. "In fact, he left us alone. I believe he is trying to get you to suspect us."

If that was the intention, it might be working.

"I know you are innocent," Grandpa said.

Abby hadn't done her own research. She couldn't say that for sure, but she did trust her grandpa.

"Now he has three keys," Derick said slowly. "He can change the past."

Grandpa wagged a finger. "I don't believe he can yet. Whoever it is would not have a way of taking the keys from campus. If we can find out who it is, we may still be able to stop him and keep the upper hand."

"I guess we know that it isn't Mackleprank," Mrs. Trinhouse said.

"Correct," Grandpa answered, showing footage of an unchanging door to a cage. He also showed the perfectly still, sleeping form of Dr. Mackleprank.

Of course it wasn't him. That him was a her—Rafa's mother. And she was as loyal to Grandpa as they could get.

Grandpa looked at the remaining members of the Council. "With your permission, I will release him after this meeting. We may need him more than ever."

Everyone nodded.

"What about the others with keys?" Abby asked. "Isn't there another council, another group of people with keys? Has anything happened to any of them?"

"No," Grandpa said. "He doesn't know about any other council as far as I'm able to tell. This is the only group he knows about."

Derick scratched his head. "How is he attacking?"

"I don't know," Grandpa said.

All of Abby's theories had been blown to pieces. She had nothing. Whoever this was had completed his job as a terrorist. She was completely terrified. "Whoever it is knows about our keys," Abby said. "Muns already has three, but if I had to guess, he will want them all. That would give him all the power over time. And he will be coming after our keys when he wants to. That seems to be his message."

Grandpa pounded his cane on the floor. "No!" he yelled. "Do not give in to fear. Do not give up. If I am not mistaken, I can see it in your eyes, and I need you to fight it. We will not lie down. We will not give in. We will fight this and we will win, but you must stand with me."

Abby felt a surge inside her. Could they possibly find a way out of this?

Grandpa stood. "For centuries, people have tried to make their enemies afraid, for if they are afraid they do not fight back as they should. They do not stand as strong. If Genghis Khan's men approached their victims by day, Khan had them drag branches behind their horses. It would kick up extra dust and make their enemies think he had more men than he did. It would make them afraid. If they approached by night, his men would carry extra torches for the same reason."

Grandpa paced back and forth. "Blackbeard the pirate wore all black and put fuses in his hair and beard. It surrounded him with smoke and made him look like a demon. Why? To make his enemies afraid." Grandpa paused to look at each member of the Council. "And why has Muns done what he did? Not only to get revenge, but to make us afraid. To make us wish we had not stood up to him. And I agree with Abby that he must be going for all the keys he knows about. But we *cannot give in. We cannot be afraid.*" He said each word of the last sentences slowly and emphatically.

Abby sat in awe. Her grandpa had courage like those in history he wanted her to learn from. He stood for what he thought was right even under the most difficult of circumstances. She thought of Ms. Entrese again. She had that kind of courage too. Abby took a deep breath. Maybe she could be like them.

Her rings vibrated. She had a message.

Muns.

Her heart dropped. She looked up at her grandfather. "I just got a message from Muns."

Grandpa did not gasp or groan. He gazed back at her, his intensity still high from his speech. "Do you mind if we all see it?"

"It may give us some sort of a clue," Mr. Trinhouse said.

Abby synced to the others and pushed play. Soon Muns's confident face was speaking to them. "Abby and Derick. I'm sorry that you didn't decide to take my first warning. You should have stood clear. But I am a forgiving man, and I don't think children should get mixed up in all of this. I will give you this one chance. You can step away now or things will escalate in ways that will change everything. Simply send me a message back saying that you have decided to give your keys to your grandfather or to your parents and that you have walked away from it all. Then I will leave you alone. But if not, I will treat you both as I do all the others. You have two minutes."

Two minutes?

Abby looked over at Derick. He just wagged his head silently.

"Perhaps he's right," Abby's mother said. "He surely can tell when you've seen his message. Give us your keys and step away. You are too young to have to worry about this now."

"Do as your mother says," their dad instructed. "We want you safe. No matter what."

Abby closed her eyes. She wanted to give them her key. She wanted to walk away. It felt so clean, so safe. Her hand rested on her buckle.

"I can't," she said. "I really want to, but I can't. And I know I'm not an adult, but I still might be able to help. I have to try."

"I think Abby's right," Derick agreed.

"I thank you," Grandpa said. He looked at both of them. "I'm so proud of you. We will get through this. We have to."

"Are you sure?" Abby's mother said. "You still have thirty seconds."

Abby nodded. Derick as well.

They waited, knowing that Muns was waiting too.

# SOMEONE ELSE?

G randpa flicked on his rings and began moving quickly. "He's done it. Two energy bursts at once. I don't know what he has planned, but I don't like it."

Two at once? Abby didn't know what to think.

"Do we need to call in members of the other council?" Dad asked.

"We must have them at the ready," Grandpa said. "Alert them that we may need them, and then have that message ready so that at a flick of your finger we can have backup. But let's not bring them into the basement unless we truly need them. For when we bring them in, Muns may learn who else has keys. Derick and Rafa can guard the entrance. One of them or both could also go in to solve whatever problem Muns has planned. However, I feel it may be best to also bring Dr. Mackleprank and send him into the past."

Abby nodded. She knew who Dr. Mackleprank really was, and would love to have his—her—fighting skills if necessary. She was pretty sure they would be necessary.

"What about our responsibility to watch all the entrances?" Dad asked.

"We need you with us," Grandpa directed. "Again, have the other council ready." That soothed Abby's fears slightly. There was an entirely different group with keys who could help if the situation called for it.

Abby soon walked with two gorillas through the dark corridors beneath the school, but she still felt terrified. She glanced at one and then the other. She couldn't tell which one was Derick and which was Rafa. She couldn't recognize her own twin brother.

Carol had joined her after waiting for the meeting to end. She knew enough and Grandpa felt she might be safer with them than alone.

The members of the group had traveled their different ways to the basement, except Derick and Rafa, who were in the avatar lab controlling the gorillas that walked with Abby and Carol. Mom and Dad would retrieve Mackleprank and meet them in the basement while Grandpa would assess the situation. She knew he needed time to use his key and his sphere to spy on Muns and figure out where he had gone in time.

The gorillas left Abby and Carol at the entrance, each standing guard. Abby loved the fact that they couldn't be defeated by a dart. Darts do not tranquilize robots.

The two girls walked into the large room with the

massive tree-looking Bridge. Soon everyone else was there, but Abby couldn't help but watch Dr. Mackleprank. Knowing that he really wasn't a person at all, but a complex machine was completely astounding. And he was really a woman in Brazil.

Grandpa addressed the group, his fingers moving along the control panel. "There were two energy bursts. One is quite strange. It is in the 1300s in the Sahara Desert—no man's land." The other half of the room filled with a vast desert, its waves of sand looking almost endless. At the bottom of one dune sat a group of men, fully armed. They wore gray combat suits, body armor, and guns along their arms and backs. They didn't look like anyone from the 1300s. They were ready to walk into a modern battle. Abby counted them; there were ten. "Nothing significant in history happened here."

"They are just waiting?" Abby's mom asked. "They aren't trying to change anything?"

"No," Grandpa admitted. "We can only assume they are waiting for the criminal within Cragbridge Hall to use his keys in the Bridge and open the way for them to come into this school—to our time." Grandpa turned to Abby's dad and had him warn Derick and Rafa of the situation. The attacker may try to force his way in.

"I propose we worry about the more urgent of the two energy bursts." Grandpa moved his fingers again along the Bridge controls. "The second burst was back on the *Hindenburg*. This time while it was in flight." The giant metal blimp appeared on the other side of the basement in

Cragbridge Hall. It floated calmly over the ocean, a coast in sight. It looked majestic, gliding through the air with its well-dressed crew and high-class passengers walking along the deck. "It will try to land in less than a half an hour. That is when it will burst into flames."

This wasn't good. The *Titanic* of the sky. It felt intricately planned by Muns; it felt like revenge.

"There are two more intruders," Grandpa explained, "both in a storage area in the dirigible." He showed two people, simply sitting on crates of supplies. They also wore body armor and guns. Muns was going to try to affect history by force this time. They whispered to one another, checked their watches, and made their way toward the door. "They are about to make their move!"

Grandpa whirled around and barked orders for Abby's mom and Abby to join him with their keys. Abby rushed to his side, her pulse quickening. It was wrong. She knew it was a setup.

"Dr. Mackleprank, will you go into the past again and bring back those two men?" Grandpa asked.

"I will do my best," Dr. Mackleprank said, rushing to the middle of the room where the past and present met. At Grandpa's orders, Abby's father and both Trinhouses stood behind him as backup in case he failed.

Abby remembered the first time she watched Mackleprank walk into the past. It all made much more sense now. He had asked Grandpa if he should and once he passed over, he had looked at his hands and feet in surprise.

It was really Rafa's mom making sure she could still use an avatar in the past.

"But they're armed," Mr. Trinhouse said, and sent his gun up out of his sleeve. "Don't you think I should join him?" Mrs. Trinhouse and Abby's father also triggered guns out of their sleeves. Abby had no idea her father even owned a gun. This was serious.

"No," Grandpa said. "Dr. Mackleprank is the best qualified to go in." Of course, it was because he was a robot. He would feel bullets, but not like a human. If the intruders shot enough, they could probably destroy the avatar, but Mackleprank should have enough time to get the job done.

Abby placed her key in the console, standing next to her grandpa and her mother. She looked again at Dr. Mackleprank ready to enter into the past. The machine looked completely human. Abby never would have guessed. Those druglords and governments who wanted to use an animal avatar for their secret assassins should have really thought about using a human avatar. No one would suspect it. And anyone could control the avatar and no one would know who it was. It was a good thing Rafa's mother was on the right side. If she wasn't, she could probably log out and use any other avatars at the school. She could spy on or even attack them. And her name obviously couldn't show up on any of the logs here—they had to protect her identity. No one would know who it was.

It wasn't Mackleprank, right? Rafa's mom couldn't be the bad guy. No. She and Grandpa had too strong of a bond. He had helped her too much. She wouldn't betray him. But what if Muns found out who she was and where she was hiding and . . .

Abby immediately felt sick. Did that add up? She turned on her rings and typed a message to Rafa. It was only a question, but was it right? The more she thought out it, the more it terrified her.

"On my count," Grandpa said, asking Abby and her mother to be ready to twist their keys. "One. Two."

Abby was about to click send when Mackleprank spun around in a whirl. Abby heard something whizzing through the air, and then Abby's dad, Mr. Trinhouse, and Mrs. Trinhouse all crumpled to the ground. Dr. Mackleprank stood with a thin straw in his mouth.

"How—" Grandpa began to say, but after another two darts, he and Abby's mother also fell.

"Don't move," Dr. Mackleprank said, glaring at Abby. "Don't twitch a finger. Or you won't wake up for months." He had the straw pointed at Abby and then at Carol, who waited steps behind her.

Both girls froze. Not this. Abby had been right.

"Good," Mackleprank said. "Now remove your rings and set them on the floor."

Abby could feel his eyes on her, watching intently, but she had to try. She slipped all her rings from her fingers and dropped them onto the ground with a series of pings. But the last one she twitched slightly, hoping the slight movement would be enough to send the message.

Mackleprank stared at Abby. She knew they were just robot eyes, but someone was behind them—someone willing to terrify and tranquilize. Had they seen? It felt like those robot eyes watched her forever. Then Mackleprank glared at Carol.

The avatar of the zoology teacher walked across the room and kicked the rings, scattering them across the floor. It glanced at Grandpa, Mom, Dad, and the Trinhouses. "I thank you for your keys," it said, "and I have something special waiting for you, Abby." She didn't like the sound of that.

Abby doubted her dad had had time to get off a message to the other council. She hoped Rafa had received her message.

• • •

"*Não pode ser.*"

"What?" Derick asked. The two friends spoke, hearing each other in the avatar lab, but it was their gorillas who faced each other.

"She may be right," Rafa said. "It could make sense."

"You aren't making any sense," Derick said.

Rafa shook his head. "Your sister just sent me this." His fingers moved as he forwarded the message to Derick.

> Is there any chance someone has kidnapped your mother and someone else is in the Mackleprank avatar?

It took a moment for Derick to follow the logic. If someone had found where Rafa's mother was and captured her, they could have replaced her with someone else. As long as that person was a convincing actor, no one else would know.

"But they couldn't fool you, could they?" Derick asked.

"She has been acting a little different," Rafa said. "She distanced herself from me a bit. I thought it was because she had been attacked and was afraid that someone would discover her secret."

"But how would someone know how to teach and know all the students' names and everything?" Derick asked.

"Katarina," Rafa said, his voice growing angry. "She has been my mother's assistant for years. She is quite good in the avatars and she knows enough."

Derick placed his hand on his head, his gorilla doing the same. Dr. Mackleprank could have been a complete imposter for days. Derick's jaw dropped. "They are inside the Bridge room with Mackleprank right now."

"Yes," Rafa agreed, "and the door is locked."

Derick bounded forward, his gorilla fists raised.

"Wait," Rafa said. "If Abby is right, my mother needs help, and that is the best way to help them."

"What do you mean?" Derick asked.

"Even if we could break down that door—which I doubt—whoever is impersonating Dr. Mackleprank will escape and could come back as another avatar. But if we could stop their real body in Brazil then we can stop the whole threat."

"I really don't understand."

"Talk to me in person at the lab," Rafa said, then his gorilla fell limp to the floor.

Derick pressed the button on the back of his neck, knowing his avatar would follow suit. In a moment, he stared at his friend back in the avatar lab. "So what are we going to do?"

"My mother has always controlled the avatar from a location in Brazil. The signal is strong enough to go halfway around the world and is uninterrupted." Rafa started moving his fingers, searching something on his rings. "But where she is, there are also other avatars—robots she works on."

That made sense. She would always be working on avatars. She could have some in Brazil just like she had some here. Derick immediately thought about Dr. Mackleprank fixing avatars and realized what that meant—Rafa's mom built avatars with an avatar. Wow. "But how is the fact that your mom was working on avatars going to help us?"

Rafa looked back at Derick, then to whatever he was searching on his rings. "If she left me access to those avatars—and she promised to leave me access to everything—then they will be very helpful."

Derick smiled, realizing what his friend had planned. "You could use the avatars she has been working on in Brazil to fight against whoever captured her. You could fight them from here—halfway around the world."

"*Exactamente.*"

"Can you get me in as well?"

"We are going to find out."

# A FITTING REVENGE

D r. Mackleprank looked at Abby. "Muns gave you a chance. He was willing to let you back out, but you wanted to play with the big boys. Well, now, we'll see how much you like the game."

She backpedaled, coming closer to Carol.

"Muns thinks it is important for you to know how we outwitted you, how you lost what he called an Immortal Game—this one vastly more important than the famous chess match. This one will become immortal. The first attack on the *Hindenburg* was only a gambit. We were simply trying to distract your grandfather and all who side with him so Muns's men could attack several trailers in the jungles of Brazil, where this avatar is controlled." He pointed to himself, identifying himself as an avatar, and waited. He was probably hoping for a look of surprise. Abby didn't give it to him. "Perhaps you cannot understand."

"Yes, I can," Abby said. "Dr. Mackleprank is an avatar that is usually controlled by Rafa's mother, but you took it over." Mackleprank slowed down his movements, probably surprised at what Abby knew. She spoke louder. "You are probably someone close to her, who knows how to act like her, even knows the names of the students she has. I imagine she needed someone's help every day. Someone to protect her as she was focused here at Cragbridge Hall. You're a complete traitor." Mackleprank stood up straighter. Abby was right.

"You tell him, Abby," Carol said. "Tell that freaky robot-stealing weirdo what's up."

Mackleprank spoke loudly, cutting off Abby and Carol. "Rafa's mother was exhausted from fighting those who had tried to enter the *Hindenburg* that night. She didn't see it coming." Mackleprank turned for a moment, looking at the faded image of the *Hindenburg* floating in the other half of the basement. "That was the *Hindenburg's* only purpose then. Well, that and to bring in my equipment and my reinforcements."

Equipment? Oh, the suitcase. Whoever had been controlling Mackleprank must have used another avatar to go through the vents, use the code to get the equipment from the suitcase and leave again through the vents. And because of Rafa's mother's access, none of it would show up on the avatar log.

But Mackleprank had also said "reinforcements." Abby thought of the men in the cell, only down the hall.

Mackleprank continued, "The second blast before the Fire of London did the same, with the added benefit of telling me where you all kept your keys. I snuck in as a spider avatar you probably didn't know existed. Rafa's mother, the real Mackleprank, had been working on it for quite some time. It is stored in the safe at the end of his office. That, and another human avatar I used." He smiled. "The real criminal was right here, next to you."

Mackleprank turned back toward the girls. "And today . . ." Mackleprank moved the controls on the Bridge. The scene of ten armed men in the desert returned. ". . . I need to invite a few more friends to the party."

Abby imagined what would happen if Mackleprank had a small army at his command. Were they going to try to break out of Cragbridge Hall with all the keys? This couldn't be good.

"All right, Carol," Dr. Mackleprank said. "I need you to turn one of the keys with me."

"What kind of idiot do you think I am?" Carol asked. "Yeah, sure. I'll happily help Mr. Crazy Robot guy bring in his army of mindless cretins whom are dumb enough to follow Muns just because he asked me to." She shook a finger. "No, wait. I don't think I will."

"Twist the key or I use my 'crazy robot' arms to crush your friend." Dr. Mackleprank stepped toward Abby.

Carol looked over at Abby, who shook her head.

"Threatening teenage girls," Carol said, tsking in disgust. "What kind of a wimpy freakshow are you?"

"Just turn the key!" Mackleprank bounded toward Abby, slamming his fist into the floor feet in front of her. Abby could feel tremors through the room and saw that the fist had made a small crater in the stone.

"Don't, Carol! He can't do this without one of us," Abby cried out, but she knew it didn't sound very convincing. She didn't want to be on the receiving end of such a blow.

"Okay. Okay," Carol said. "Just don't hurt her."

"No, Carol," Abby cried out. "We can't help him."

Carol bowed her head. "I don't have any other options here, Abby." She did not sound playful anymore.

Dr. Mackleprank returned to the console with Carol, gave the signal, and they turned all three keys. The faded image of desert grew clearer, vivid. A gust of dry air off the hot sand swirled through the basement. Stray grains of sand slid onto the hard floor. The soldiers could now come into the basement of Cragbridge Hall.

Abby expected them to come marching in. But they didn't. Then she remembered they could not see the basement from their side. Mackleprank would need to signal to them. He stepped toward the Sahara.

This was their chance. At first Abby thought she and Carol should try to take the keys and run, but Mackleprank could get them back. He was an avatar. It wouldn't take him much effort to find and capture two girls.

Abby had another idea. She slowly crept to her feet and stepped light-footed behind Mackleprank. If she could push him into the past and then Carol could pull the keys—he would be trapped.

Abby pointed at Carol and then at the keys. She hoped Carol got the idea.

He was only steps away from the opening.

Abby rushed forward and heaved Dr. Mackleprank from behind. "Now, Carol!" she shouted. "Twist the keys!"

But Dr. Mackleprank recovered too quickly. Though he lurched forward a foot, he twirled around and with one fluid motion placed a straw in his mouth and loaded a dart. He was going to send Abby into a long slumber.

Abby swung at the zoology teacher, flinging her arm with as much power and speed as she could. She hit the straw just as a dart shot out and heard it clink against the wall. The straw flew several feet and hit the floor.

"Not bad." Dr. Mackleprank stepped closer. "Good reaction, but very naughty." Abby backpedaled away from him. "Now what are you going to do? Fight to keep the keys? Fight your way out? You punch, you hit coated metal. I kick you, and it feels like you got hit by a tree. There really is no way out of this."

Abby looked at Carol, who had the keys in her hand. "Run, Carol!" Abby called out. It was a long shot. If Abby could slow Mackleprank down, if Carol could use one key to open the door and get out of there, there might be a chance. Abby leapt at Mackleprank's feet, hoping to trip him up, hoping to latch on and not let go until her friend had escaped.

Carol took off with the keys.

• • •

"I can only imagine," Rafa said, lowering his visor again, "that whoever has kidnapped my mom had to be prepared to fight avatars in order to do it. They probably have enough of a team and weapons to take on a small army. If I can gain access, we might be up for a fight trying to rescue her."

Derick gulped. He had a thought he didn't want to say. "What if, um, I mean, do you think there's a chance that they . . ." he couldn't finish his sentence.

"Killed my mother?" Rafa finished.

"Yes," Derick said.

Rafa shook his head. "She is too valuable. She knows how to make the avatars."

Rafa moved his fingers over and over again. Then he scrolled and selected something. "Come on," he whispered. "She would always leave me access. That was our deal." His fingers moved some more and Derick watched in suspense. They were trying to log onto avatars on the other side of the world. The whole idea was fantastic. Derick could move his arm here and something else, thousands of miles away, would move. It almost seemed like magic.

"I—I think I'm almost there," Rafa said. "*Por favor*," he pleaded. "*Por favor*." Then after a celebratory fist punch in the air, Derick knew Rafa had access. "I'm in," he said. "And there are several avatars on the registry." He paused, obviously looking them over. "The problem is," he continued, "that my mom gave them names, but not an animal description. She always did that last. So we can get in, but we won't know what kind of avatar we're stepping into."

Great. Derick was probably about to go against a team of guys with weapons and he had no idea what kind of avatar he was about to enter. It could be anything from a rhino to a monkey. In fact, it could be a fish or a bird, neither of which Derick knew how to work.

"We also don't know where the avatars are kept," Rafa explained. "Well, we don't really know the layout at all. But they are likely locked up. Hopefully I'll be able to override the codes to get our avatars out. I'll check into it."

Derick waited for what felt like forever. Derick wondered what avatar he might get, how many enemies they might face, and how they were ever going to save Rafa's mom. He wondered what was happening with his parents, grandpa, and sister in the basement. He even wondered if Carol was okay.

"*Muito bem*," Rafa said. "You ready to come with me?"

How could he possibly be ready? He had no idea what situation and which form he was about to enter. But of course Derick said yes anyway and lowered his visor. He was ready to log in.

"Do you see the registry?" Rafa asked.

"Yeah."

"Just pick something and let's go." Rafa breathed several times fast then selected something with his finger. A moment later, he swiveled his head from side to side. He must have been checking out the situation.

"Okay, I'm in. It's pretty dark, no one around."

Derick selected the avatar named *Jorginho*, hoping for a lion or something fierce. He felt the usual wave of nausea, and then he looked through different eyes. He blinked several times and looked down at his body. He needed to know what he was and if he would have any chance against armed soldiers.

• • •

Abby stared at Dr. Mackleprank approaching the console of the Bridge. It had only taken him moments to throttle her to the ground and overtake Carol. Now Abby was tied up on the floor. Mackleprank had used Abby's father's belt to harness her. After he made Carol put the keys back and twist them again, Carol joined her.

Mackleprank stepped across the middle of the room into the Sahara Desert hundreds of years ago. Several of the soldiers gasped and even shouted, triggering their guns. Abby couldn't blame them. It must very strange to suddenly see someone step into your reality out of nowhere. After a gesture from Mackleprank indicating where they could enter, the men crossed from the desert in the past and flooded into the basement of Cragbridge Hall. Muns had an army right where he wanted them.

"I need two of you to stay here," Mackleprank commanded, selecting two of the soldiers. "The rest of you have several more soldiers to rescue in cells in the basement. I have sent you the coordinates. Use whatever means necessary to free them. Arm them and give them more instructions. I've also sent you information about teachers I suspect have keys for you to capture and bring back. I believe most of them keep them on their person. I've sent you each files showing you who they are and where their quarters are."

No! He knew about members of the other council. With an ability to use various avatars to spy, there was no telling how many he had discovered.

"Bring the teachers back here as soon as you can," Mackleprank said.

"But we had a different rendezvous point," one of the soldiers objected.

"Yes, we did," Mackleprank said. "But I have discovered something. We will no longer have to fight our way out of here. I will explain later."

What had he discovered? What was their way out?

"But your first worry is that outside this door are two avatar gorillas," Mackleprank explained. "Be ready for them. You will take them by surprise, but after that, they will be a force to reckon with. Though it is always a shame to damage such brilliant inventions, you may need to destroy them. They will likely be the only force you face. Any security above will be something you can easily handle with your extensive training."

Mackleprank used one of the keys to open the massive door. Covering one another, eight soldiers ran out of the room. Abby prayed that somehow Derick and Rafa could defeat them, but with the soldiers' weapons, it didn't seem likely. Abby waited to hear guns firing and gorilla grunts, but she never did.

"The gorillas are here, but no one is in them," a soldier called back.

Abby felt dizzy. That was their only chance to stop the men—the soldiers who were going to hunt down the other teachers. Where were Derick and Rafa? Had they received her message?

Mackleprank thought for a moment. "It looks like they decided to run. Smart boys." He called to the soldiers in the hallway. "Act quickly in case they have raised the alarm with anyone."

He turned to the last two soldiers. "As for you two, we need to deliver the keys we already have to Muns. That is our first priority." Mackleprank reached his hand into his pocket and after a few seconds of jingling pulled it out again. Abby counted in her head, figuring out how many keys Mackleprank had: Grandpa's, Mom's and Dad's, the two coaches', the Trinhouses', and hers—eight. Not only would that give Muns more than enough to start changing history without having to store up energy bursts, but if they grabbed more keys from the other teachers, then it was over. The only other key she knew about was Derick's—and one key could not operate the Bridge. As far as Abby knew, there would be no more ways to stop Muns. He would have them trapped—checkmate.

# CAPYBARA

Derick looked down at his avatar—definitely not what he expected. Stubby legs and a thick middle. He caught his reflection in a sheet of metal leaning up against the wall. He looked like a giant chunky squirrel with no tail.

He heard a quiet laugh. Not in the room somewhere in Brazil, but in the avatar lab at Cragbridge Hall.

"A capybara," Rafa said. "Looks like my mom has spent some time making the largest rodent in the world."

They needed to go face a group of elite warriors and Derick was a rodent. He was probably just under four feet long and two feet tall, but he was still a rodent. How come Rafa's mother couldn't have been working on a mountain lion or an elephant? Heck, he would even have taken a giraffe.

Derick looked up at Rafa. He was in some sort of human avatar, but it wasn't finished. It didn't have a shirt, and metal plating and even a databoard were exposed on portions of its face and chest. They stood in a dimly lit room. It was long and rounded on the corner—maybe a trailer. A few rows of avatars stood in the room. At a glance Derick saw a tiger, a frog, two birds, a large beetle, and a crocodile.

Derick moved over toward a door, his large paws scuffling over the hard floor.

"Shhhhh," Rafa whispered. "I think we're in some sort of trailer. But there could be soldiers anywhere around here. I'd guard it right outside."

"What do we do?" Derick asked.

"We'll have to check it out."

"Can I change into something better first?" Derick asked, moving again to see what other avatars were in the room.

"We both might want to," Rafa said. "Look around. With the codes I passed on to you, we should be able to access any of it. It just may take a few tries to figure out which is which. "

That was what Derick wanted to hear. He looked over at the crocodile. He could control that, right?

The lock on the door twisted. That was not what Derick wanted to hear. He whirled around to see someone crack open the door. The enemy had heard them.

• • •

Mackleprank turned back to the two soldiers in the room. "I have discovered that there is a way to use the Bridge to travel through the present."

Oh no.

"Through a little spying," Mackleprank said as he approached Grandpa. He pressed Grandpa's thumb at the bottom of the Cragbridge Hall insignia on Grandpa's blazer. The insignia shifted forward, showing a secret compartment behind. Mackleprank pulled out a small sphere. No wonder Grandpa wore his blazer all the time; it kept his sphere. "I discovered that with this disc one can see the recent past or even the present. I watched as Oscar Cragbridge used it to find out where Muns had sent his men in the *Hindenburg*." He then plucked two more spheres from Abby's parents.

Mackleprank put three keys in the console and then selected the three arms to collect the spheres. A soldier helped him twist the keys.

"This is bad. So bad. So very, very, very bad," Carol mumbled.

Mackleprank moved quickly to select his place. The other half of the room changed. It became a study with screens covering the walls, a few desks, and a variety of gadgets on top of the desks. There was a chess set on the corner of the largest desk, and Charles Muns sat behind it. Two guards flanked him. Abby hated the sight of him. He had masterminded this whole thing and was going to win—he was going to be able to play with history as he saw fit. This could be the moment that changed the world's future from its potential to its destruction.

Mackleprank instructed a soldier to watch the keys and then approached the threshold from the basement to Muns's study. Abby held her breath. This was it. There was little hope left. Unless someone could come crashing in right now, Muns probably would win this war; he would get everything he wanted.

No one came crashing in.

Mackleprank stepped into Muns's study.

The two men beside Muns quickly engaged their guns, which slid out of their sleeves and lined up with their index fingers. They were fast on the draw. It took less than a second.

"Stand down," Muns commanded his guards, a huge grin passing over his face. He looked at Mackleprank. "You have done well, so marvelously well. I knew you could discover who had the keys and where they kept them. And you confirmed my suspicions that the Bridge can also be used in the present. Splendid."

The Bridge started to shake under the pressure of entering into somewhere else in the present. It hadn't taken long at all.

Mackleprank reached out and dropped the keys into Muns's palm.

The Bridge rattled stronger.

"You will have all that I promised," Muns said. "And more."

The Bridge shook violently, as if a mini-earthquake had hit just the one spot in the basement of Cragbridge Hall. She expected it to blow apart at any moment.

Mackleprank simply nodded and stepped back into the basement, quickly signaling for the soldier to twist the keys back.

It took several seconds for the Bridge to stop its quaking.

As she watched it settle, Abby realized that three keys still rested in the console. Mackleprank had to leave three keys in this Bridge, using them to cross over to Muns's office. Maybe Abby could somehow get those keys back—maybe there was hope.

"I'm glad the Bridge could take the stress," Dr. Mackleprank said. "We still need to transfer one more group of keys and the rest of you. After that I can stay behind in this avatar to make sure the Bridge rattles itself into oblivion and then destroy the three remaining keys."

• • •

As soon as the man in the jungle camouflage saw him, Derick did the only thing he knew how to do; he raced forward. Of course, in a large rodent it didn't quite feel as much like racing as he would have hoped.

"What the—?" the man cried out. Another soldier was soon by his side. Guns rose out of their sleeves and aligned with their pointer fingers. They fired at Derick, who quickly decided to try to weave through the trailer to avoid getting shot. Because the men were distracted by Derick's capybara, it took them a moment to see the unfinished human avatar sprinting toward them. A moment was all Rafa needed. He grabbed one man and threw him against the wall. With a follow-up strike, the man was soon unconscious on the floor.

While Rafa attacked, Derick rounded toward the enemy. He got there in time to crash into the other soldier's legs and let out a strange squeal. Rafa whirled over and kicked the man to the ground. He was out cold.

Yells echoed in another trailer.

"We need to find my mom, but there are more men coming," Rafa said. He looked down at the men on the ground. "And these ones might not stay down long. We are outnumbered and outgunned."

They couldn't hide, and they couldn't waste any time. At any moment one of these soldiers could alert Macklerank they were coming. They were desperate. They needed something now. "Bayonets," Derick said, remembering his desperate charge on the enemy in the Civil War.

"What?" Rafa asked.

"Remind me to tell you the story sometime," Derick said, back in the lab at Cragbridge Hall. "But we charge them. I really wish I had time to change avatars, but we need to go now—take them by surprise." He barked and started running through the jungle floor toward the nearest trailer. Rafa came right behind him.

Half a dozen men filed out of a trailer in time for Derick to jump and ram one right in the torso, sending him sprawling into another. They were definitely surprised. Rafa was on another two.

One man kicked Derick, sending him rolling several feet. That was sure to hurt. Nothing like kicking a mound of metal. Derick rolled over and rushed back to meet the soldiers. He scurried and dove the best he could, trying to knock them to the ground, trip them, or at least bite their toes. But—aagh! He felt a bullet enter into his back thigh.

Then another in a shoulder, and another. His pathetic squeals were louder and uncontrolled now. A large rodent versus armed men didn't have much of a chance. He tried to find cover, but he was too far away from the trees. Each bullet stung, feeling like a hot iron ramming into his flesh.

Derick bit another soldier on the shin, bringing a shout from his victim. Then he felt a huge pain between his shoulders and he was suddenly back in the avatar lab. The capybara must be completely out of order. The rodent had been exterminated.

Derick had failed—again.

•  •  •

Could this get any more hopeless? Abby's heart raced, fear pounding it faster and faster. She couldn't think of anything they could do.

"And now, Abby," Mackleprank said. "It is time to pay you some attention."

"I don't think she wants any," Carol said.

Mackleprank only sneered. He removed the spheres and put them in his pocket. Then he had a guard help him twist the keys again to show a massive blimp gliding through the sky. A sky that was now the other half of the basement of Cragbridge Hall. If someone slipped at the edge of the divide in time, they could fall to their doom.

Mackleprank brought the perspective of the Bridge to a space just outside the baggage area, where the two imposters inside the *Hindenburg* waited.

"I thought they were going to try to change history," Abby said.

"No," Mackleprank said. "That isn't their job today." He stepped into the past and invited the intruders into the basement. Now there was Mackleprank and four soldiers. His army was increasing.

"You see," Mackleprank explained, "Muns wanted to change this event and other tragedies in history, but your grandfather would not allow it. Muns would like him to learn a lesson." The avatar of the zoology teacher shifted the perspective of the Bridge ahead slightly, into the baggage storeroom. He then crossed the basement, lifted Grandpa over his shoulder, and approached the divide in time.

"No!" Abby cried out. He was going to put Grandpa on the blimp that burst into flames and fell over thirty stories.

"You had your chance, Abby. Your grandfather didn't change this history, now he gets to experience it. Fitting, isn't it?" He crossed time and set Grandpa on top of a steamer trunk.

Fitting. The word echoed in Abby's mind as she stared at the terrible scene.

"Muns has enough keys and no longer needs your grandfather." Then Mackleprank, with his strong robot arms, picked up Abby's father with one arm and Abby's mother with the other.

Abby screamed.

"And your parents failed to produce the result Muns wanted when they were last back in time."

Mackleprank took several steps toward the past then

turned. "You can probably guess the drill, Abby. You are now in the same situation your grandpa was at the beginning of the semester. Again, it is very fitting. And you can either change the past or watch them die."

He continued, "I will allow you to use the keys only to stop the entire dirigible from sinking," Mackleprank said. "You can warn the crew. You can urge them to not circle around before docking, allowing the passengers to get off. There may even be some ways of stopping the explosion itself. But you must change it. If at any moment you try to simply remove your grandpa and parents, we will turn the keys from this side and leave you stranded in the past on a blimp that will go up in flames."

Abby couldn't breathe. She had to fix this.

# RELAY

Dumb giant squirrel thing. Dumb guards who invaded and took over this avatar station. Dumb Muns. Derick pounded the ground of the avatar lab.

Wait. A smile crept over Derick's face as a realization flashed in his mind—this could be like the avatar relay. He could keep going back in other avatars. He searched through the names and couldn't do anything more than pick another one at random.

He opened his eyes and looked down. Please be something more ferocious than a rodent.

Spots. Oh, he loved spots.

Derick stood up on all fours and raced out of the avatar storage trailer. He found Rafa fighting with several men, gunshots ricocheting off him in every direction. He fell back several steps and almost fell over.

Derick growled in his jaguar and raced the distance between the trailer and the soldiers. He felt so fast, so light. He might not run very smoothly, but he could sprint forward. Men began firing. He felt several more stings, one in his chest, another in his shoulder. He leapt in the air and came down hard on one of the men. He used his hard metal snout to slam into his enemy's forehead—a jaguar avatar headbutt. The man cried out in pain.

Out of the corner of his eye, he saw Rafa knock another man to the ground. Then he whirled to attack another.

Derick bit a soldier's leg, and careened into another.

More bullets.

Derick bit his lip, trying not to scream. He would never get used to this.

He got up and pounced toward another soldier, but could feel his avatar waning. It was almost out of commission.

Derick pressed the button on the back of his neck and selected another avatar. He soon raced out of the trailer as some sort of boar. He bounded forward, snorting and biting.

"Hey Rafa," Derick said.

"This avatar is almost done, Derick," Rafa responded, panting.

"Bring out another and after you attack, bring out another," Derick said. "We can keep switching, like the relay race. They won't know which avatars we are and which ones we aren't."

"You're a genius," Rafa said. Derick saw him punch a soldier and then fall limp.

Derick managed to plow into one of his enemies with the boar, and then he switched again. He attacked in a tiger, then moved back to the boar, and once again back to the tiger. Rafa came out as a large bird, swooping down at the men, then an orangutan, and then found there was a little more power in the human.

"How many of them are there?" A soldier cried out.

When the boar was out of commission, Derick selected another avatar. He tried to look down but couldn't. He had a large snout on the front of his face. Yes! Derick shuffled as best and as fast as he could through the opening of the trailer and toward the men, his crocodile jaws opened wide.

• • •

Abby couldn't look away. She couldn't bear the thought of losing them. Almost seeing her parents go down on the *Titanic* had etched that thought and feeling on her heart. And her grandpa—she loved him too. He had so much trust in her. "Stop this," Abby cried out.

"You are terrible, terrible, terrible," Carol spat out at Mackleprank. "You bring in guns and threaten middle school girls? Can you go any lower? I mean, do you push down elementary kids at recess? Steal second graders' chocolate milk on Fridays? Trip babies when they're trying to learn to walk? It's not like you can brag about this to all your other villain friends." She acted out a pretend conversation with other criminals. "Oh, you fight off guards and steal rare assets from highly defended bank vaults? Not me, I point guns at seventh-grade girls."

"Quiet!" Mackleprank screamed, and ran to Carol. He pulled back his hand, like he would slap her. Carol closed her eyes and turned, bracing herself for the blow. But Mackleprank never swatted. "Quiet," he reiterated, calmer now. "You have no idea why I have to do this."

Abby *did* have an idea, but she didn't have time to think about that.

Mackleprank had started to walk away and then stopped. The way he stopped and twitched his fingers, Abby thought perhaps he had received a message on his rings. That boggled Abby's mind that a robot could use rings. But it made sense; in the avatars you could see what the robot saw. "Gentlemen," Mackleprank said to the guards with him, "we have a quick change of plans. You," he selected one of the men, "guard these girls." He pointed at Abby and Carol. The guard turned, guns aimed in their direction. "Keep them under wraps unless they are willing to change the past. And you," Mackleprank spoke to the other three soldiers. "You are coming with me to the avatar lab. We have a bit of a pest control problem."

And then they were gone.

To the avatar lab? What was so pressing that he would leave this situation that was obviously so planned, so thought out, to go to the lab? Abby allowed one side of her mouth to curl up in a half smile. Maybe Rafa and Derick were fighting back. Suddenly there was a shard of hope. Abby didn't know exactly what her brother and Rafa were up to, but if they were doing anything with the avatars and Mackleprank came into the lab, they would be sitting ducks. They would be so involved in whatever their avatars were doing, they wouldn't know someone else had found them until they were already caught.

But what could she do? Abby glanced around the room. She saw Carol, several feet away wrapped up in another belt. She saw the *Hindenburg* gliding through the air, now over a big city with a crowd underneath cheering and gawking. Then Abby saw a straw on the ground. Mackleprank hadn't picked it up. She scanned some more and noticed a few darts, one only a few feet away. She glanced away, knowing that the guard may be watching her. She had to distract him if she was going to stand a chance. She looked over at Carol. "Maybe we should just go back in time and change it all, Carol."

"What?" Carol said. "Is your thinker okay? You know we can't mess with time. Your grandpa says it could destroy everything. "

"You might want to listen to your friend," the guard said to Carol.

"She might not have the courage to do it," Abby said, trying to sound upset. "She doesn't have the courage to do anything daring. I heard last time there was trouble down here, she totally freaked out. She broke down." The guard looked at Carol, and Abby had a moment to wink. She hoped Carol would catch on and try to distract the guard.

"What?" Carol said. "You think I just crack under pressure?" Abby thought she could see a dramatic increase in

Carol. She got it. "Well, it was a lot of pressure," Carol blurted, her voice rising. "Like super pressure. Pressure like the heaviest thing in the world on top of me, plus three hundred elephants, two hundred walruses, and several of those super fat cats whose owners don't stop feeding them—that kind of pressure. And they all ate extra donuts for breakfast."

"I don't think that even made sense," Abby yelled back.

"I don't either," Carol shouted. "I'm under that much pressure right now, no thanks to you."

"It doesn't mean you have to freak out," Abby taunted. "We have a lot on the line."

"Freak out? Freak out?" Carol said. "That's not freaking out. *This* is freaking out!" She started rolling on the floor and screaming—most of it was gibberish. She did throw in a movie line about never going to be taken alive, then she started choking, then she seemed to be acting out some sort of death scene. It was really weird, but definitely distracting. The guard kept his distance, but pointed his gun at Carol.

"Stop it," he said. "Or I'll throw you on the blimp."

"Yeah, stop it," Abby yelled. She tried to shuffle her body up to her feet, so she could approach Carol.

"Don't move," the guard said, now pointing his gun at Abby.

Abby screamed and fell back to the ground, rolling slightly when she landed. Her arm throbbed, and she had knocked her shoulder and thigh pretty hard, but she had stopped moving about where she had needed to. She grasped with her fingers for a dart. She had to be careful;

she didn't want to find the sharp end of it and send herself into a coma. Finally, she touched it, and wiggled it into her hand.

The guard was on her immediately. "You get back up." He pointed his gun at her forehead.

"I will," Abby said, trying to shift back to her position on the ground. While the guard wasn't looking at Carol, she made eye contact with Abby, asking with her eyes if she needed to continue. "Just stop it, Carol," Abby said. "No more freaking out."

Carol calmed, though she had a very confused expression on her face.

Abby looked at the *Hindenburg*, then back to the guard. "But I'm serious. I'll go back in time." Sweat now trickled down her brow. "I'll stop the *Hindenburg*. We don't need her," Abby gestured with her head toward Carol. "We can turn the keys. And I can go in."

A gust of wind blew the large blimp and it had to change its course toward the landing. She didn't have long until it burst into flames.

"I don't have much time," Abby shouted.

The guard moved to Abby's side and began to untie her. The two approached the console of the Bridge. "Let's turn the keys on three," Abby said. "One, two . . ." and she stabbed the guard in the hand with the dart.

In one movement, the guard pushed Abby down and pointed his gun. Abby rolled just as he fired, the bullet barely missing her and ricocheting through the basement.

Abby looked up to see the barrel of the gun pointed at her chest.

And then the soldier fell over.

Abby panted for only a second before running to untie Carol. "Help me turn the keys, then find your rings. Tell Derick they're coming. I need to save my family."

# CRASH AND BURN

Derick snapped his mighty jaws, barely missing a soldier's leg. He loved this crocodile. Not only was it powerful, but its realistic hard scales added an extra layer of protection against the bullets. He quickly switched to the tiger and caught a man from behind, knocking him to the jungle floor. In his peripheral vision, he could see Rafa whirling and kicking in the unfinished human avatar. He grunted and panted as he fought. "Where's my mom?" he screamed. The avatar prodigy was one of the best in the world. He was also hopelessly outnumbered, but he was fighting with passion.

Back in the lab, Derick's rings vibrated. He couldn't check messages now.

Still a tiger, he leapt from the ground at another man,

who swung his gun and caught Derick in the gut. He could feel the air rush out of him.

He rolled, trying to recover his breath. Then he caught a glimpse of another trailer, further in the jungle with two more men standing guard.

"I think your mom is in a trailer, about a hundred yards in front of you," Derick yelled to Rafa. "The men who are guarding it aren't coming to help."

"Thanks," Rafa said, panting. "This avatar is almost out. Stall them just long enough for me to get another."

"Feel free to use my croc," Derick said. "He's already the closest."

"No," Rafa said. "I think it's time to go sneaky."

Derick leapt out from behind the trees and raced his tiger toward the guarded trailer. He hoped this would get their attention.

Shots rang out. He tried to gain more speed. He felt bullets sear through him. He leapt in the air toward the guards.

He shrieked in pain, and then he was back in the lab.

"Thanks, Derick," Rafa said. "I'm out of the trailer and sneaking around them."

Derick exhaled. "Don't mention it. No, wait. Actually do. Mention it to everyone, especially the Crash. I want in." He took in one more breath of air, feeling his sweat dripping from his face and running into his mouth. "All right, croc. I'm coming back." He looked through his lenses for his crocodile's name—*Maxilas*—but saw a message waiting. His instincts were not to open it, but when he saw it was from Carol, he quickly clicked.

Mackleprank was coming. And he had full access to the lab. The locks and security measures would not stop him. If Mackleprank and his goons came while both he and Rafa were in the avatars, they were easy prey.

"We have company coming after us in the lab, Rafa," Derick explained. "And more are going after teachers with keys." Rafa continued to creep. "I'm going to try to go in," he said. "I've got to save her." The determination in Rafa's voice was unmistakable. "Just give me some time."

"I will," Derick promised, hoping he could. But even if he could stop Mackleprank, how was he going to stop the other soldiers from getting members of the other Council if they hadn't already? He couldn't be everywhere at once, not even with the avatars. He needed more people.

Oh, yeah.

"Wait, Rafa," Derick said. "Before you go in, could you send a message?"

"To who?" Rafa asked.

"The Crash," Derick answered. "We're going to need backup."

•  •  •

Abby jumped from the basement onto a large blimp in the 1930s. She grabbed her unconscious mother under the arms and pulled, dragging her a few inches. She pulled again—a few more inches.

"That felt so trippy," Carol said, entering behind her. "I've never crossed into the past before—awesome!" She ran to Abby's side and grabbed Abby's mother's feet. "Let me help." With the two of them working together, they succeeded in pulling her back into the basement of Cragbridge Hall. As they gently set her down, Abby heard a loud boom.

"Oh, no," Abby said.

"Flaming explosion time."

They both jumped back into the past and grabbed hold of Abby's father. The blimp lurched downward. Fire crept up the wall to their side. A package beside them ignited.

"Look out," Carol yelled, but Abby's pant leg caught the flames.

"Keep going," Abby shouted. She could feel the fire creeping up her.

The two lunged back into the basement of Cragbridge Hall, pulling Abby's dad with them.

Abby rolled across the hard ground several times before the flames were out. She glanced back at the baggage hold of the *Hindenburg*. Fire engulfed it.

Grandpa was still in there.

• • •

Derick waited behind the door to the avatar lab. He hoped he was in the right avatar for the situation. From Carol's message, Mackleprank and several men were coming all at once. And they would probably all arrive before the Crash. He had to defend the lab by himself.

He heard movement and the beeps and clicks of someone entering. At any moment Mackleprank and armed soldiers would burst in, ready to capture them. Or worse, maybe they were ready to kill. Derick tried to slow his breathing. He tried to remember the rushing Civil War army. Their greatest weapons were their courage, their determination, and surprise. He would need all three if he was going to beat whoever had been impersonating the avatar teacher.

Derick tried to time it just right. He heard the large doors sliding open. Four men raced in.

Now!

Derick took one awkward step and swung his head like a wrecking ball with his long neck. His hundreds of pounds of force collided with all four men before they could get off a shot. All four flew into the wall.

The momentum nearly sent Derick's giraffe to the ground, but he managed to prop himself back up against the wall. "Thanks for making me practice," Derick said, looking down at Dr. Mackleprank. He knew the teacher couldn't hear him—the giraffe itself couldn't speak—but he had to say it anyway.

Mackleprank rolled and lunged at Derick. The others were out, but Mackleprank was a robot.

"I think I've got it now." Derick flung his giraffe neck, catching Mackleprank midair and throttling him to the ground. He didn't get up as quickly this time. Derick heard metal bending and snapping. "That's for Entrese." Derick slammed his giraffe head into Mackleprank again. "And Adonavich." Again. "And Horne." The robot lay with one arm broken off, its chest open, exposing torn metal and broken electronics.

For the very first time, Derick loved giraffes. He had done it. He had used a giraffe to conquer Mackleprank himself. Well, kind of Mackleprank. He felt adrenaline coursing through him.

Then he heard it—movement from inside the avatar lab, deeper than where his body was hooked up to sensors and a suspension system. The sound came from the back of Dr. Mackleprank's office.

Derick realized suddenly that Mackleprank had access to it all. He was coming back in another avatar.

•  •  •

Abby leapt into the flaming room, her arm over her face. The heat pressed against her skin and smoke curled up into her nostrils. She choked several times, but moved to her grandfather's side. The fire had caught about half of the cases and bags, but Grandpa was still okay. At least for now. She remembered seeing how quickly the flames engulfed the entire zeppelin.

Abby hacked again and grabbed hold of her grandfather. She pulled, heaving him further than she had been able to pull either of her parents. Either he was lighter, or adrenaline had made her stronger.

Carol had his feet in moments. She had jumped in too. Abby would have started to cry at her friend's courage if she didn't have flames and all three of their lives to worry about.

They pulled him again, but Grandpa's leg caught against a case. Carol quickly worked it free, then her eyes went wide.

Abby looked over her shoulder. A wall of flame stood between them and their passage back into their time. Her grandfather felt so much heavier now. Maybe her strength was waning or the smoke was taking its toll.

"Let's just go through it," Abby yelled. "Now!" She pulled, her body going into the flames. She screamed, the blaze scorching her. She needed to move more—now! She pulled and pulled again. Finally, Abby, Carol, and Grandpa fell onto the basement floor.

The room was filled with thick black smoke.

"Turn the keys," Abby shouted.

Carol rushed to the console as Abby stamped out the fire on her arms and smothered the flames on her grandfather.

Carol didn't turn the keys, but moved the perspective of the Bridge above and far away from the blimp. The smoke filtered out the other side of the room like it was a giant window. Clever.

They did it. Grandpa and her parents were safe. No one changed the past.

Abby looked over at Carol, who had singed hair and a hole burnt in the corner of her shirt. Then she remembered. "The teachers aren't safe." She looked at the guard whom she had pricked with the dart. Something rose within her. She crossed the room and picked up the straw and several darts that had fallen to the floor. Someone had been sneaking around in the night with these things. Someone had struck her with terror. Now it was her turn.

• • •

A large bull careened through the back door of the avatar lab. Mackleprank was back.

Derick didn't have much time. He decided to wait and, at the last second, he swung his long giraffe neck, hitting the bull with his head.

Then his air was gone. It felt like his lungs had completely collapsed. He couldn't breathe. The bull had hit him at full speed. He had to switch. Derick pushed the back of his neck. Then his eyes opened as a gorilla. "Come on, Kong," Derick panted, exhausted. How long could he do this? He took a deep breath and ran out of the back hall just as the bull was charging toward the lab, where Rafa's real body was moving in a flurry; he must be using his avatar to fight again. Derick's real body was right next to Rafa's. It felt so strange to look at himself from the avatar eyes.

If he didn't get over there soon, and the bull hit them, he might not see his real body ever again.

Derick moved quickly over the tables and collided with the bull. It felt like ramming a wall, but it was enough to knock the bull off course.

After passing his targets, the bull regained its footing and veered back toward Rafa's and Derick's bodies. Derick used his gorilla to charge after him. He hoped this worked. At the last second, Derick jumped and grabbed onto the bull's horns. He pulled to one side as hard as he could until the bull veered and crashed into a string of tables and screens.

"What's going on?" A boy with a Southern drawl asked.

Derick whipped his head around to see a tall boy with dark black skin rushing into the room. "I just saw a trashed giraffe, three unconscious guys, and a bashed up robot that looked like Dr. Mackleprank."

"There isn't much time to explain," Derick blurted out. "But right now this bull avatar is trying to kill Rafa and me!" He mounted the bull, who was making his way toward Derick and Rafa.

"Is that you, Tryout?" the boy asked.

"Yeah. Please help me!" Derick pleaded.

"I'm coming," the boy said. "No one messes with the Crash."

The bull bucked, trying to throw Derick off. He still held on tight by the horns, but his gorilla body was soon thrown in front of the bull. He shuffled his feet across the ground, trying to avoid being trampled.

The boy must have rushed to grab more sensors and hook up, because right when Derick thought he was about to pass out and have his real body pummeled by the bull, a rhino bounded out of the lab and slammed into his enemy. The bull tried to get up, but was pounded again and again by the gorilla and rhino team.

A girl screamed. "Quit screaming and suit up," the Southern boy said. "We need to help out Rafa."

Mackleprank came out again as a lion, but this time a gorilla, a rhino, and another lion were there to meet him. Mackleprank's odds were not good.

"Stop," a woman's voice said. She had stepped out of Mackleprank's back closet—she must have been another

avatar. She had a light build and long blond hair. She pointed at the lion. "You traitor. You put everything I love in danger." She pointed at Rafa. "Especially my son." A chill ran down Derick's spine. It was Rafa's mom. She had been freed and now controlled another avatar. Rafa had broken through. He had fought through soldier after soldier until he rescued his mother. "At this moment, my son is standing over your real body in quite a dangerous avatar. If you focus, you can hear him breathing in my lab in Brazil."

The lion froze.

The woman continued. "I decided not to pull you out of my trailer just yet. I thought perhaps we should see how much the student has learned from the teacher." Derick could hardly believe what he was seeing. It was a woman challenging a lion. Of course they were both avatars, but still.

The lion growled and leapt at the lady, who nimbly danced out of the way. Then Derick watched a fight he would never forget. A woman kicking, dodging, and punching. She moved with grace and rhythm. The real Mackleprank was back, and he—she—could still fight like a ninja. Several minutes later, the lion lay on the floor, its electronic insides exposed and crackling.

The woman avatar stood. Rafa took off his visor and approached her, tears streaming down his face. "I'm sorry it took me so long, *Mãe*." He hugged her.

"Don't worry, *Filho*." She hugged him back and kissed his cheeks. "I knew you would figure it out and rescue me."

Rafa pulled back and put his visor back down. "*Vamos.* Let's get you out of here. Let's get you safe."

# TIRED OF BEING
# AFRAID

Abby and Carol raced out of the basement and out of the small hallway in time to see a series of soldiers with teachers in their custody. Several security guards were unconscious on the floor.

Abby looked down at the straw and blowdarts. There was no way she was going to be able to stop them all. But she had to try.

Abby moved around to the side of the hall and hid around the corner.

"Hey, you uglies," Carol shouted at the men down the hall. Well, Abby wouldn't have to worry about distracting them. "It could just be me, but I don't think it is very nice to pull teachers out of their rooms and drag them down the hall. In fact, I would say that it is just plain rude. Like super rude. Like ruder than licking someone else's candy, or calling them buffalo face. Not that any of that has ever happened to me."

One of the soldiers released the teacher's arm and stepped forward, pointing the gun barrel directly at Carol. "Just run away, young lady." It was the voice of a woman. "I don't want to hurt you, but I will."

"Really?" Carol said. "A woman? Don't get me wrong. I know that women can be fantastic warriors, shoot guns and arrows and stuff. I mean we rock and there is nothing else to say about it. But I really thought no woman would follow Muns. I thought only boys were dumb enough for that."

The woman raised her arm, and then fell to the ground.

Abby was surprised she had hit her. Maybe all her practice had paid off.

The other soldiers quickly moved into some sort of defense formation. The teachers fell to the floor and Carol dove to the other side of the hallway, away from Abby.

This wasn't good. Now Abby had all of their attention.

Abby turned to run away down the hall when she heard growling. Lots of growling. Then there was a lot of yelling and gunshots.

Abby peered around the corner to see the soldiers shouting in desperation as a rhino charged them, a gorilla swung down from the stairway above, and two more lions joined the fray. A second gorilla had managed to sneak behind them and conk two of their heads together. Within moments, all of the soldiers were either unconscious or had surrendered. The teachers were free.

Abby still had no idea what had gone on until Derick

came rushing down the hall. He had been in one of the avatars that neutralized the soldiers. Once the action was over, he came back to explain about the avatar club and how they had come to the rescue.

Each of the teachers shared their thanks for saving them. Abby didn't recognize any of them, though she thought she had probably seen a few of them in the halls. Whether they all had keys or not, she couldn't tell for sure, but she knew whoever had taken over for Mackleprank believed they had.

"Thank you again," an Asian man with slightly long dark hair said. "I must admit, I never expected someone so young to be involved in this."

"Yeah, maybe we didn't expect it either," Abby admitted.

"But we rocked it!" Carol said, with a fist jab in the air. "Oh, yeah. Uh huh. We deserve so much chocolate. "

Derick smiled. He glanced at the soldiers sprawled on the ground. "What are we going to do with them?"

The man thought for a moment. "I think we should have security take them to the police and press charges for breaking and entering, carrying weapons in a school, and several counts of assault. All those charges are true, though we will leave out other details. We won't have to worry about them anymore."

"Shouldn't Oscar be advised?" asked a woman who was short and plump with bushy red hair. "And we should speak as a council before we make any decisions."

She had said "council." Apparently both of them were

part of the other Council of the Keys. Abby could trust them, but she still hesitated to answer. Finally, she spoke. "My grandpa is unconscious in the basement and has several burns. They may be serious. He needs medical attention. My parents and the Trinhouses are also unconscious. They were tranquilized. And I have no idea how long they'll be out. It could be weeks."

Several of the teachers rushed down to the basement.

•  •  •

The reality of it sunk in, and Abby hated it. Though they had stopped Muns's plans, he still had keys. He could be planning how to use them right now. He could be *using* them right now. He could be destroying everything. Grandpa was unconscious. And her parents. And the Trinhouses. And the coaches. And Ms. Entrese. But Muns wasn't. Who was going to stop him?

After all she had been through, she still felt terrified. She still didn't know what Muns was going to do. If only he had been . . .

Abby's eyes widened. She had an idea.

She raced up to the avatar lab and found Dr. Mackleprank's beaten robot body. She searched its pockets. There were still two spheres that looked like they would work. The third was unrecognizable. She quickly tucked them away. Even among those who had keys, there was no telling who knew about the Bridge's ability to interact with the present and the recent past.

Derick was in the avatar lab, cleaning up as best he could with the help of several students Abby didn't know. He said they were the Crash, and they had a lot of questions. They would have to decide how much to tell them later.

"Derick," Abby whispered. "Can you come with me back to the basement?"

"Can I finish this first?" he asked.

"No," she said. "I need some help now."

"I'm coming," Carol said.

"What's up?" Derick asked.

Abby looked at them both. "I'm tired of being afraid."

Soon they all stood in the Bridge room again. Everyone who had been tranquilized had been cleared out and was getting any medical attention they needed.

Abby approached the Bridge. She pulled out the three keys she had taken from the Bridge before she and Carol could unlock the Bridge room and try to help save the teachers. Abby placed all three keys in their slots.

"Derick, can I use your sphere?" she asked.

"What do you want to see?"

"Please," Abby pleaded, "before I change my mind."

Derick hesitated and then handed his sphere to his sister. She placed it above a key, then placed the other two. Metal arms came out of the console to retrieve them.

"You're going into the present," Derick said. "To do what? Wait. We could go get Rafa's mom and bring her straight here."

"That's a great idea," Abby said, "but I have to do this first. Will you please turn the keys with me?"

"You're sure about whatever you're going to do?" Derick asked.

"Yes."

They twisted the keys. Abby knew she had a very limited time before the Bridge started to tremble. She searched the Bridge's history and found the entry she wanted and selected it. A large desk in a finely decorated room appeared on the other half of the basement. Two guards stood at its sides, and Charles Muns sat behind the desk.

"We will move immediately," Muns said.

"Abby, what are you going to do?" Derick asked.

Abby didn't answer. She only watched for a moment until she saw Muns with the keys in his hands. She approached the divide in time, and pulled out a straw and some darts. She could do this. She counted to three and stepped into Muns's study. She immediately blew a dart, hitting the large guard to the left. The guard to the right triggered his gun, but Abby hit him in the chest. Not what she was aiming for, but she was nervous and it would work. She dove behind the desk. One guard circled around after her, while the other called for reinforcement. Within seconds, both fell to the floor.

Abby stood up, glaring at Charles Muns.

"Abby," he said. He sounded calm, but she knew he was on edge. There was no way he could have seen this coming. "So good to see you. I was just . . ."

But Abby didn't let him finish. She didn't have a lot

of time. The Bridge may already be shaking. "I hate your game," she said and knocked all the pieces off the chessboard that lay on the corner of his desk. "I'm tired of being afraid. Your turn."

Muns's eyes went wide. Abby loved it so much, she almost paused. Almost. She shot him with a dart that stuck in his forehead. He collapsed headfirst onto the table.

Abby heard footsteps outside the room. She reached for Muns's hand and pried out the keys, then dove back into the basement of Cragbridge Hall.

Derick twisted the keys, and the quaking Bridge calmed down. "You're crazy. You could have gotten killed."

"*You* are a rock star," Carol said. "Seriously, I need your autograph."

Abby breathed deep. She wasn't going to be afraid anymore.

# NOT GOING ANYWHERE

I'm excited to have a new zoology teacher," Derick said to
Rafa's mother. They had used the Bridge to bring her
from the jungles of Brazil into the basement of Cragbridge
Hall. They also brought the treacherous assistant and put
her in a cell. They would need to ask her questions later.
After giving the Bridge time to stabilize again, they even
went back to retrieve the avatars and their parts. What they
couldn't take, they had to destroy. Derick stuck out his hand
for a handshake.

She hugged him. "I'm not a new teacher, Derick. I've
been teaching you for a while. It's just now I'm going to
teach you in person." Mr. Sul, the Asian man who had
been rescued by the avatars, was also an assistant admin-
istrator. He had worked feverishly with the other Council
of the Keys members to clean up the mess that night, and

turn Muns's men in to the local authorities. It would bring bad press when the world discovered that Cragbridge Hall had been invaded, that it was not as safe as it claimed to be—especially when several teachers and security officers were recovering in the medical unit. It would bring unwanted attention, but there was no way around it. Mr. Sul also hired Rafa's mom as the new zoology teacher after Dr. Mackleprank "had an emergency he had to take care of"— that was what they were telling the other students, anyway.

"Thank you again," Rafa's mother said. "You truly are an incredible young man. I'm glad Rafa is friends with you."

"Thanks," Derick said. "Are you sure you don't want to play?" He gestured toward the avatar lab behind him. "I've always wanted to compete with you."

"Not today," she said. "Maybe after I recover a bit more. I would like to watch, though."

"So what are we going to do today?" Rafa asked. "As your first official practice as part of the Crash, you get to choose."

Derick smiled. "You may have played this sport before, but not this way."

• • •

"Derick said that if he got to pick, they would play baseball," Abby said, approaching the viewing area of the largest avatar field. Carol had wanted to come watch the avatar club play and Abby thought she could probably use a break from studying and visiting her parents and grandpa in the med unit.

"I never really liked baseball," Carol said as Rafa's mom granted them entrance into the lab. They both told her how glad they were that she was safe. "Don't get me wrong," Carol continued, "the boys look great in their uniforms, but it's kind of boring, and long, and boring."

"You said boring twice," Abby pointed out.

"It's twice as boring as a lot of things. Except what's going on here?" They had arrived at the giant windows that allowed them to see into the avatar practice field.

A gorilla held a ball much larger than a baseball. He reared back and threw it, his long arm thrusting it toward a giraffe. The giraffe waited until just the right moment and then whipped his head around like a bat, smacking the ball. It flew over the gorilla's head, where another gorilla ran toward it.

"This isn't normal baseball," Carol said.

The giraffe didn't run, but a squirrel monkey that was waiting beside the base did—a substitute runner.

"Whoever that was must have switched avatars," Abby said. "He hit it with the giraffe and then ran as a monkey."

An outfielder gorilla that had been totally still suddenly raced toward the bouncing ball. It fielded the ball and threw it to the second baseman. "Wait a second," Carol said. "There are nine players in the outfield. If they split the avatar club in half, that means only three students on a team, so each club member controls three avatars. They have to wait to see where the player hits the ball and then change to that animal." She gazed over the defense of gorillas and monkeys. "So amazingly non-boring."

"This has to be the craziest game of baseball I've ever seen," Abby said, shaking her head.

Carol thought for a moment. "I don't know. I once played it where you run into a kiddie pool for first base, step on a water balloon for second, run to third base where someone squirts you with a hose, and then dive into home on a wet slip-and-slide. That was pretty crazy."

"But there weren't giraffes using their heads for bats, were there?"

"No. You're right. This wins."

Abby watched for several more minutes before turning on her rings and stealing some history study time.

"Are you still afraid of getting kicked out for bad grades?" Carol asked.

Abby thought for a moment. "I'm kind of nervous, but I wouldn't say that I'm afraid. All I can do is try the best I can and then see what happens."

"Well, so far, when you do your best, you stop crazy madmen and their robot henchmen."

Abby smiled. "I had a lot of help." She nudged Carol with her elbow and then pointed to Derick and the Crash. "You all helped," she said as though they could hear her.

"Too bad the only teachers of yours that you saved are unconscious, or maybe they would give you extra credit for your heroics."

"Yeah," Abby agreed. "Too bad. I could really use a grade boost." The nurse still didn't know how long they would be unconscious. Thankfully, Muns was also unconscious. They should be safe for a while.

"Well, fantastic," Carol said. "Now that we don't have to worry about Señor Evilbritches for a while, that gives me more time to work on my dance moves." She got up, spun, and shifted back and forth. "The dance *is* in a couple of weeks."

Abby smiled. Maybe before, she would have even been afraid of the dance, of facing all those boys, of wondering if anyone would dance with her, but not anymore. She was tired of being afraid. She would do her best and just see what happened. She stood up and danced with her friend. There is something about defeating an evil genius that can boost your confidence.

"Oh," Abby said, pausing her dancing. "I forgot something." She turned on her rings, wrote a quick message to her former roommate, attached a file, and hit *send*.

> Jacqueline,
>
> This file shows you pictures of my virtual creation—my castle. I'm pretty confident it should bring me a decent grade. You'll notice there is quite an amazing bridge over the moat. I built it. It can stand up to all kinds of dragons. It will never fall. It's not going anywhere.
>
> And neither am I.
>
> Abby

And then Abby danced some more.

# ACKNOWLEDGMENTS

March 5, 2013. That was the day my first novel, *Cragbridge Hall, Book 1: The Inventor's Secret*, hit shelves. My dream was finally coming true. But instead of touring, I sat in a hospital room—exactly where I should have been. A few weeks before, my nine-year-old daughter was diagnosed with a tumor the size of two-and-a-half golf balls pressing up against her brain and her optic nerves. On March 5, she was recovering from neurosurgery. And I need to say thanks. My publisher, Shadow Mountain, responded with such under-standing. They went to a lot of work to reschedule my tour, sent care packages, and even took pictures of themselves wearing mustaches, because mustaches make my daughter laugh. Thank you.

Knowing that I couldn't promote my book, a slew of amazing people took up the torch and sent out the message through blogs, tweets, Facebook . . . the works. Maybe that was a little thing to them, but it was huge to me. A lot of them have never met me; they are just great people. Even some best-selling authors like Brandon Mull, James Dashner, Shannon Hale, Christopher Paolini, and Ally Condie spread the word. Other authors like J. Scott Savage and Frank Cole filled in on the school assemblies so a bunch of excited kids weren't left high and dry. And hundreds more people heard about my daughter through social media, put on all sorts of mustaches, and sent pictures to cheer her up. Thank you.

After we finally brought my daughter home and she was recovering well, she and my wife practically kicked me out of the house to go after my dream. My sister-in-law Kimmie Loose insisted on helping my wife at our house every day so I wouldn't miss any more school assemblies or signings. And when I finally got out, hundreds of people asked me how my little girl was doing. Kids drew pictures and sent letters. An entire school even wore mustaches when I came to visit.

The world is full of amazing people. Thanks. Sincerely, thank you.

Of course, I missed my deadline for this sequel. It was a bit of a rough time to try to write. But Shadow Mountain was patient and supportive as always, and I think it was worth the wait. Specifically, I owe a lot to Chris Schoebinger and Heidi Taylor for loving the sequel and giving feedback to make it better. Thanks to Derk Koldewyn for his editing awesomeness, and to Karen Zelnick for doing so much to set up my school visits, signings, presentations at ComicCon, etc. Thanks to Richard Erickson and Rachael Ward for the design and typesetting. Plus my agent, Rubin Pfeffer, is supportive, fantastic, and very helpful. And I should say thanks as well to Deborah Warren, also with East/West Literary Agency. Oh, and Brandon Dorman can paint a robot gorilla like nobody else! Seriously, have you ever seen a cooler one? I didn't think so.

As always, I need to thank my friends and family. So many have rallied and been so supportive. Of course, my wife and kids top the list. My wife is my sounding board, my first reader, and quite possibly the best and hottest woman in the world. She gives great feedback and reassures me when I'm pretty convinced everything I write is boring slop. Plus she runs our crazy household and finds ways of letting me write. And my kids are my main motivation for writing. The thought of making them laugh, gasp, or call out a "That's awesome!" or "No way!" brings a whole new level to my story. And when I read to them at night, and the story works, it's a total thrill. I think I'll always remember the night we read the scene when Rafa reveals his secret. When I finished, my kids were bouncing in their beds. I turned off the lights and asked them to sleep, but they stayed up for another hour and a half talking about my crazy story. They even made up a Cragbridge Hall song. Yeah, I recorded it on my phone. That will probably go down in history as one of the coolest author moments of my life.

I'm also grateful for my group of great beta readers: Dan Reed; Brooklyn and Matthew Hatch; Jessica, Jared, and Lauryn Moon; Mindy Waite; Platte Clark; Sarah Scheerger;

Will Mason; and Matthew Crawford. Thanks for all the great feedback. Plus, my mom did a thorough line edit of my galleys and saved me from some pretty embarrassing mistakes.

Thanks to everyone who read *The Inventor's Secret*. Thanks for giving me a chance. I hope you loved it. And thanks for picking up *The Avatar Battle*. If you liked it, please share it with your friends. It means a lot. And look me up on Facebook or Twitter (@chadcmorris), or send me a message through chadmorrisauthor.com. I'd love to hear from you. And check out cragbridgehall.com to watch the book trailer, check for my tour stops, and jump on the mailing list for updates.

For those of you who still ask about my daughter, she's doing very well. As of right now, you'd never guess she's had major surgery. A major point of *The Inventors' Secret* was that it is in the hard times that heroes are made. Well, I happen to know one; she just turned ten a few weeks ago.

# DISCUSSION QUESTIONS

1. In English class, Abby had an assignment to tell how books have inspired people in real life or how real life has affected books. How have books affected your life? Have you ever been inspired by a book? Which books and how?

2. To get his final key, Derick had to prove that he had the same determination and character as those who fought in the Civil War. Who do you know that shows determination and good character? What can you learn from them?

3. Abby spent a lot of time in this story worried about her grades. Have you ever been worried about your schoolwork or grades? How much do you think you should worry? In what ways are grades important? In what ways

# DISCUSSION QUESTIONS

are other aspects of your education more important than grades?

4. Derick felt worried because of one of his previous failures. Have you ever failed at something? Did you try again? How did it go? Why do you feel it is important to keep trying after failure?

5. Rafa is Brazilian and speaks Portuguese. Do you know anyone from another country? What traditions or parts of their culture have you learned about? What can you learn from them?

6. Initially Derick thought giraffes were boring, but as he learned more about them, he discovered that they are pretty interesting. Can you think of something that you didn't like initially but became interested in over time?

7. Socrates taught the importance of really wanting to learn, wanting it more than air. What do you have a strong desire to learn? How might you go about learning it?

8. Abby, Derick, and Carol all had the opportunity to build their own virtual worlds. If you had the chance to build your own virtual world, what would it be like?

9. Abby, Derick, and Carol also learned that when they make a decision it affects the people around them. How do your decisions affect other people? What good decisions have you made that may have influenced others? Are there any decisions you are making that you want to change?

10. The Crash enjoys playing sports with their avatars. They also learned new sports. What are your favorite sports? What sports would you like to learn to play?

11. Derick experienced what it feels like to go through a difficult surgery. What difficulties have you been through? What did you learn from them? Who do you know who has had to have a surgery or other difficult challenges in their life? What do you think you could learn from them?

12. Though Abby felt afraid for much of the book, by the end, she faced her fears. What are you afraid of? What have you done to face your fears? What happened? What could you do to face your fears now?

# RECOMMENDED READING

## For more information about Sir Arthur Conan Doyle and Sherlock Holmes:

Pascal, Janet P. *Arthur Conan Doyle: Beyond Baker Street.* New York: Oxford University Press, 2000.

Doyle, Arthur Conan; illus. Rohrbach, Sophie. *Sherlock Holmes and the Adventure of the Speckled Band.* Minneapolis, MN: Graphic Universe, 2010.

## For more information about the Civil War and the Battle of Gettysburg:

McPherson, James M. *Fields of Fury: The American Civil War.* New York: Atheneum Books for Young Readers, 2002.

Stanchak, John. *DK Eyewitness Books: Civil War.* New York: DK Publishing, 2011.

Vansant, Wayne. *Gettysburg: The Graphic History of America's*

# RECOMMENDED READING

*Most Famous Battle and the Turning Point of the Civil War.*
Minneapolis, MN: Zenith Press, 2013.

Murphy, Jim. *The Long Road to Gettysburg.* New York: HMH
Books for Young Readers, 2000.

## For more information about the *Hindenburg* disaster:

Verstraete, Larry; illus. Geister, David. *Surviving the Hindenburg.*
Ann Arbor, MI: Sleeping Bear Press, 2012.

O'Brien, Patrick. *The Hindenburg.* New York: Henry Holt, 2000.

Benoit, Peter. *The Hindenburg Disaster.* New York, Scholastic,
2011.

## For more information about London and the Great Fire:

Clements, Gillian. *The Great Fire of London.* London: Franklin
Watts Ltd., 2001.

Robson, Pam. *All About the Great Fire of London.* London: Hodder
and Stoughton, 2002.

## For more information about Socrates:

Usher, M. D.; illus. Bramhall, William. *Wise Guy: The Life and
Philosophy of Socrates.* New York: Farrar, Straus and Giroux,
2005.

Dell, Pamela. *Socrates: Ancient Greek in Search of Truth.* Mankato,
MN: Compass Point Books, 2006.

## For more information about giraffes:

Helget, Nicole. *Giraffes.* Mankato, MN: Creative Education,
2008.

Parker, Barbara Keevil. *Giraffes.* Minneapolis, MN: Lerner
Publishing Group, 2004.

## RECOMMENDED READING

**For more information about Abraham Lincoln
and his assassination:**

Stone, Tanya Lee. *Abraham Lincoln (DK Biography)*. New York: DK Publishing, 2005.

Cary, Barbara. *Meet Abraham Lincoln*. New York: Random House, 2011.

Denenberg, Barry; illus. Bing, Christopher. *Lincoln Shot: A President's Life Remembered*. New York: Square Fish, 2011.